PRAISE FOR THE BUCKET LIST MYSTERIES

Murder on the Bucket List

"Do yourself a favor and treat yourself to Elizabeth Perona's charming debut, *Murder on the Bucket List*. This warm and witty caper features delightful characters, hilarious antics, and a celebration of friendship. *Murder on the Bucket List* is this year's must-read for fans of amateur sleuth mysteries. Don't miss it!"

—Julie Hyzy, *New York Times* bestselling author of the White House Chef Mysteries and the Manor House Mystery series

"Elizabeth Perona mixes murder, mystery, and a charming cast of characters to concoct an engaging and fun read. High on ingenuity and imagination, low on gore, *Murder on the Bucket List* keeps the reader guessing. Looking forward to many more stories from this promising new author."

—Mary Jane Clark, *New York Times* bestselling author of the Wedding Cake Mysteries and the KEY News Thrillers

"*Murder on the Bucket List* is the best kind of cozy mystery—inviting, engaging, intelligent, warm, and witty. Elizabeth Perona's ensemble cast of senior sleuths puts out a welcome mat I couldn't refuse, and you shouldn't either. What's on my bucket list? Moving to Brownsburg, Indiana, and joining the members of the Summers Ridge Bridge Club for their next adventure. I can't wait!"

—Molly MacRae, national bestselling author of the Haunted Yarn Shop Mysteries

"*Murder on the Bucket List* is the best combination of female friendships, quirky characters, and an intriguing mystery. Elizabeth Perona has created a wonderfully light read, with a fun combo of race cars, suburban life, adventurous seniors, and a killer I did not see coming. Can't wait for the next adventure of the Summer Ridge Bridge Club!"

—Clare O'Donohue, author of the Someday Quilts Mysteries

Murder
on the
Bucket
List

Elizabeth Perona

Elizabeth Perona

Murder

on the

Bucket List

MIDNIGHT INK
WOODBURY, MINNESOTA

FIRST EDITION
First Printing, 2015

Book design and format by Donna Burch-Brown
Cover design by Lisa Novak
Cover Illustration by Greg Newbold/www.gregnewbold.com
Editing by Nicole Nugent

Midnight Ink, an imprint of Llewellyn Worldwide Ltd.

Library of Congress Cataloging-in-Publication Data
Perona, Elizabeth, 1956–
  Murder on the bucket list / Elizabeth Perona.
     pages cm. — (A bucket list mystery ; 1)
   ISBN 978-0-7387-4509-1
 1. Students—Fiction. 2. Murder—Investigation—Fiction. I. Title.
 PS3616.E74975M88 2015
 813'.6—dc23
                          2015005456

Midnight Ink
Llewellyn Worldwide Ltd.
2143 Wooddale Drive
Woodbury, MN 55125-2989
www.midnightinkbooks.com

Printed in the United States of America

DEDICATIONS

To Debbie, I love our life together!
—Tony

To Lucy, I am so glad God chose me to be your mommy!
—Liz

ACKNOWLEDGMENTS

I once again want to thank God for his continual blessings. Truly he is the God of Second Chances. Next, Debbie, I love you. Thank you for your support. Also, I am grateful and pleased and proud to be working with my elder daughter, Liz, on bringing this project to completion. My thanks to her as well as her husband, Tim, and to my younger daughter, Katy, and her husband, Taylor, who have also been a part of my support system.

I also want to thank a number of people for their help and expertise. First, for technical issues: to David Studley and his son Kevin for helping me understand midget car racing, and to Jerry and Tom Sneva, whose names will be familiar to Indianapolis 500 fans as contenders back in the 1970s and 1980s, for their comments on why they still love to race midgets. Also to Mark Meko, of Earl's Indy Service Shop, who helped explain the technicalities of midget racing engineering and how people find ways around the rules. The Plainfield Police Department has always been helpful in going over procedures with me. I'll name Chief Darel Krieger, Assistant Chief Carri Weber, Captain Jill Lees, Lieutenant Gary Tanner, and Captain Scott Arndt, but really, so many of the officers have been helpful that I apologize to those I haven't named. Any mistakes or misinterpretations I made of the information any of these experts have given should reflect on me and not on them. We fiction writers are expected to make stuff up, and so while I do try to be accurate, I fudge occasionally in the best interest (I hope) of the story.

Second, for reasons unstated: many, many thanks to my aunt, Nancee Brock Margison. The development of this series would not have happened without her.

Two people's names I borrowed for characters in the story need to be called out. First, Joy McQueen, who won a contest I ran when *Saintly Remains* came out. Joy, I hope you enjoy reading the exploits of your namesake. Second, my cousin Jacob Maehler, whose name just fit perfectly for me into this story, although he shows no signs of becoming a race car driver at this point in his young life.

None of my stories would have made it to print without my author friends who are kind enough to read my work and offer thoughts, suggestions, and advice. I first want to mention my friends at the Indiana Writers Workshop, who were with this story from the beginning. They are Teri Barnett, Pete Cava, John Clair, June McCarty Clair, Lucy Schilling, Steve Wynalda, and most recently, David Ballard and Sylvia Hyde. Also thanks to writer Phil Dunlap for his comments. Jess Lourey, a wonderful writer and friend, introduced me to Terri Bischoff, who eventually bought the novel for Midnight Ink. Finally, a special thanks to Julie Hyzy, a good friend who offered much support over several iterations of the novel and never lost faith in it or me as a writer, even when I doubted my own abilities.

—Tony

First, I would like to thank God for providing me with this opportunity. Next, I'd like to thank Dad for inviting me to collaborate with him on this project. I'm looking forward to more collaboration as we work on the next two books in this series. Finally, I'd like to thank my husband, Tim, who encouraged me to jump on board with this venture.

—Liz

ONE

FRANCINE MCNAMARA LOITERED BY the pool alone. It was around midnight, pitch black, and though the Summer Ridge Bridge Club had gathered here to skinny-dip, no one was close to being wet. In fact, she was the only one close to the pool.

Seventy years old and we're all still too wrapped up in our body images to slip off our robes and get in the water, she thought. But she supposed she was just as guilty. Though she exercised regularly and kept herself in good shape, she wondered if she wouldn't look better with a few less pounds. *It's the media.*

Fellow club members Alice, Joy, Mary Ruth, and best friend Charlotte had been here since early in the evening. Francine had almost convinced herself to be the first one to skinny-dip when Mary Ruth approached her. Of all the Bridge Club members, Mary Ruth was the one who most needed to lose weight. Her plump body was wrapped in an extra-large pink cotton robe and its hem bunched on the surface of the pool deck.

"Something smells wrong," she announced. She breathed in deeply with her discriminating nose, analyzing the odor through the filter of her many decades as a chef. Then she wrinkled in distaste. "It's a rotten smell, but I can't pinpoint it."

Francine raised an eyebrow. She viewed this charade as yet another attempt to divert the five-member club—Mary Ruth regularly stepped in when a substitute player was needed—from their intended purpose. They had carefully chosen this warm July night to help Joy McQueen check item #10 (Go Skinny-Dipping) off her bucket list.

Francine gave a half-hearted sniff. "Sorry, I don't smell it. Have you checked with Alice to see if she sprayed anything? She seemed to be obsessed with the idea that mosquitos carrying the West Nile virus will show up."

"I think she's more obsessed with the threat of being discovered. I don't see how, though, not on Alice's watch. She seems to have thought of everything to make it as dark as possible."

That was certainly true. Alice had been nervous about skinny-dipping from the start. Though her house was the only one with a pool and she'd agreed to host the event, she'd insisted on waiting until her husband was away at a real estate convention. She'd also made sure there were no outside lights. The women had to navigate by a trail of citronella candles spaced around the pool deck. There were lights within the pool, but those only gave a soft, eerie blue glow to the water.

Alice, clad in an expensive robe pulled tight around her body in an effort to look thinner, ferried replacement candles around the large pool. The taut robe wasn't working for her, Francine thought. *Another victim of the perfect body-obsessed media.*

Joy trailed Alice, collecting candles that were spent. Joy was the irrepressible president of their Bridge Club. Though she was thin as a stick, Joy didn't appear to be any readier than anyone else to disrobe. Tonight she was enveloped in a powder-blue terry cloth robe heavy enough to be used in winter. She complained of being cold despite the fact it was the warmest night they'd had all summer. Francine wasn't sure what Joy's insecurities were, but the closest she'd come to the pool had been an hour ago when she was referencing her bucket list, accidently caught it on fire with Alice's propane lighter, and raced to the pool's edge holding it aloft, saying "Ow, ow, ow!" She'd let the list go and it caught the wind, which sent it back toward her. Joy fled from the pursuing paper, producing squeals of laughter quickly hushed up by Alice so as not to attract any undue attention.

Realistically, Francine knew the only hope of getting the party back on track was her usually reliable pal Charlotte. She glanced around, looking for the tightly curled silver wig Charlotte wore. She spotted her short friend off in the distance studying the stars like there might be an astronomy test tomorrow.

"What do you think, Charlotte?" Francine called as quietly as she could. "Do you have any idea what Mary Ruth is smelling?" She touched her nose and made a shallow sniff to demonstrate.

Charlotte heard and walked over using her cane. "Well, it's not me." She turned her chubby butt toward them as she said, "My system's been behaving itself tonight."

Mary Ruth chuckled. "That's not what I smell, although the odor does have a faint outhouse bouquet to it." She checked to see her bathrobe was securely fastened before she toddled a few steps in the direction of the house. Detecting nothing, she went the other way, shuffling past Charlotte out of the candlelight toward the darkness by the pool shed. "It's stronger over here."

"I haven't even been over there …" Charlotte began, a little testy.

Francine interrupted. "It's the citronella," she said, while simultaneously thinking it was likely the wine, of which they'd all had one too many glasses over the course of the evening.

Charlotte mimicked Mary Ruth's sniffing process. "No, she's onto something. There may be enough candles to make this place look like a nighttime prayer walk, but citronella's not that potent. If it were, the mosquitoes would have packed up and fled Brownsburg like vampires fleeing from garlic, and we know that didn't happen." She scratched her legs. "I'm getting bit on my thighs. I didn't think mosquitos fancied cottage cheese," she said, aiming the comment toward Alice. She gave Francine a mischievous smile.

Alice heard the criticism. She stopped her dalliance among the candles and moved toward the group. As she reached the pool, its blue glow caught the edges of the large crucifix hanging from her neck, making it glint. With the robe wrapped practically to her neck, Alice almost resembled a nun, albeit one who didn't practice fasting. She swept her arm over the twinkling candles. "Perhaps you'd rather I replace these with smelly candles that *attract* insects."

"At least it would cover whatever that smell is Mary Ruth has detected," Charlotte said.

Francine needed to nip this in the bud. "You can all stand around and play guess-the-odor," she said, "but I'm getting in." She walked back toward the shallow end of the pool, disrobing as she went. She threw the robe over a nearby deck chair. Naked except for the large, black-framed bifocals she couldn't see without, she waded into the pool.

The women all tittered in excitement. They stared at Francine.

She tried hard not to feel conspicuous. She moved farther into the water so it covered her body up to her shoulders. "Mary Ruth just has an overly sensitive nose," she said, trying to divert their attention with the earlier topic of conversation. "It's probably the chlorine."

The atmosphere was charged now, the woman uncertain whether to follow Francine's lead. "Maybe you were just a nurse too long," Mary Ruth stammered. "Maybe your nose has become impervious to bad odors."

"Move away from the pool shed and I bet you don't notice it any more. Better yet, join me in the pool. The water's warm!"

"That's good to hear," said Charlotte. "I sure wouldn't want to go skinny-dipping if it were freezing. Then we'd be the Frigid Ridge Bridge Club."

Joy erupted in nervous laughter. "You've been waiting all night to use that line, haven't you?"

"I was beginning to think no one would set me up."

Francine decided to call Joy out. "It's your turn to follow me in, Joy. This party was set up for you."

Joy hesitantly dipped a toe in, still clutching the robe around her. "Speaking of chlorine, has anyone put any in this pool recently?" She asked it a little too loudly, prompting a "shhh" from the rest of the women.

Mary Ruth rushed over and assumed a bent-over position, examining the water. *Great*, Francine thought, *just what we need. Our resident germaphobe to take up the cause.*

Alice scurried next to her. She squinted at the water, looking for anything that might have caused the comment. "Well, no, I kind of forgot about the chemicals. Larry usually does that. But I know he put them in the last time we used the pool about a week ago."

"A week!" Mary Ruth continued. "You know how I am about germs! Do you know what could be living in this pool after a week without a chlorine shock?"

"No," Alice said, offended. "Do you?"

"Well, not exactly. Algae, I think. But I'm sure it's awful. Makes me not want to get in the pool."

Joy took this as a way out. She backed up toward the pool shed instead of getting in the pool. "Perhaps we should get the chlorine out now, although we'd need a little more light back here."

Mary Ruth followed Joy, stepping carefully so as not to land on something she couldn't see, got within two feet of the shed, and stopped. "There's that smell again. Maybe a raccoon died in there. I once had a raccoon die in the crawl space under my kitchen. I took the trash out three days in a row before I figured what the smell was. I'll never forget it."

Joy wrinkled her nose. "Ewww. Did you clear it out yourself?"

"For heaven's sake, no. You hire people for that. If there's something dead in there, we need to know so Alice can have it removed. Think of all the germs teeming inside a rotting animal." She fumbled with the door latch.

Francine swished the warm water over her shoulders, thinking this may not be headed to a happy conclusion. Mary Ruth successfully conquered the latch and the pool shed's door flew open.

Something large and stiff thumped onto the concrete with a sickening thud.

The women began to talk excitedly at once.

"What was that?" Joy asked.

"I don't know. I can't look." Mary Ruth's hand was over her eyes, but there was a small gap between two of her fingers where she was peeping. "Whatever it is was, was propped up against the door. Now my foot is almost touching it."

Joy crept a little closer. "Can you make it out?"

"Not as dark as it is."

"It's not my fault something got locked in there," said Alice. "I'm not responsible."

"It sounded bigger than a raccoon," Charlotte observed.

"I'm pretty sure it is," said Mary Ruth. "I'm poking it with my toe and it's not moving."

"Is it furry like a raccoon?"

"No, it's stiff and kind of humanlike. And it smells like a ... like a porta-potty. Can you not smell that from there?"

This is surreal, Francine thought. She had a bad feeling about where this was going, yet her friends maintained an intellectual curiosity as though they were playing Twenty Questions.

Francine swam a quick few overhand strokes to the edge of the pool. She gripped the ladder rails and climbed out. The air was cool and it chilled her. She glanced for her robe and remembered she'd left it at the shallow end. She grabbed one of Alice's large fluffy pool towels and covered herself as best she could. As she scrambled to the spot Mary Ruth was backing away from, she tried hard not to breathe in the odor she recognized from her days as a nurse. She squinted, trying to be certain it was what she thought it was—a man-sized thing that flopped out of the shed and landed on its side.

Mary Ruth, normally short of breath, was now gasping. "Don't touch it, Francine."

But Francine felt she had to do something. She couldn't imagine it was anything other than a body. Propped up by a stiff arm, it faced away from her. She braced herself for what she might see, then nudged it with her toe. The body teetered over onto its back. She bent over and was pretty sure she could make out a face. A stiff, dead face. "Call 911. Quick!"

Alice made the sign of the cross. She clutched her satin robe and ran for the house.

Joy grabbed a citronella candle and rushed over. "What is it?"

Though she was afraid the group would plunge into hysteria, Francine answered honestly: "A dead body."

Remarkably, the intellectual calm held. "Really?" Joy used the candle to get a closer look at the head. "Are you sure it's dead? Shouldn't you try something, like CPR?"

"No, I'm confident he's dead. Likely a day or so."

"I'll go look for a flashlight." She handed the candle to Francine and hurried off after Alice.

Charlotte hobbled toward them, excited by the mention of a dead body. She leaned over it. "He certainly looks dead."

Francine flashed back to the last time Charlotte had said that to her, an incident that had become legendary in their hometown of Brownsburg—which was not too difficult considering the Indianapolis suburb had a population of just over 20,000 and the article had appeared in the *Indianapolis Star.* The two of them had visited Charlotte's uncle's house across from the Indianapolis 500 racetrack, which is located in the Town of Speedway. They found him deceased, supposedly of a heart attack. Charlotte believed it was murder and proceeded to prove it, nearly on her own. Since she didn't feel she'd tied it all together neatly, she refused to count it against her #1 bucket list item, (Solve a Murder Mystery), even though Francine insisted she should. Charlotte spoke in her know-it-all tone. "You're practically right over him, Francine. Tell me everything you observe about the body."

Francine felt a knot growing in her stomach, but she knew better than to put this off. "Well, he's hairy, so I think we can safely say he's a man. Plus, he's wearing boxer shorts. And he's stiff, so he's still in a state of rigor mortis. What more do you really need to know?"

"Is he short or tall? Wounded? Is there blood anywhere?"

Francine moved the candle over him, looking for the answers. "He's short. Kind of skinny. I don't think there's any blood." She let out the breath she was holding and backed away, waving a hand in front of her nose.

"Shouldn't we cover the body or something?" asked Mary Ruth, carrying a pool towel she'd picked up on the way back over.

Charlotte straightened up and gave her a withering glance. "Of course not. We should have left it undisturbed until the police got here. Technically, Francine shouldn't even have flopped him over."

"I didn't know for sure he was dead until I could get a good look at him!"

"Don't get defensive, Francine. I'm just saying..."

Joy returned with a flashlight at that moment but stopped several feet short of the body. She tried to shine a light on it, but her hand shook so badly it was like watching a TV game show where a spotlight dances over the audience before they call up a contestant.

Mary Ruth snatched the flashlight. She widened her stance so she could bend over closer to the body. She shined the light into dead man's face. "Oh, my God! I know who that is. That's Friederich Guttmann!"

Charlotte leaned over the body again. "Really? Who's Friederich Guttmann?"

"He's a race car mechanic."

Alice came running out of the house waving a portable phone. She stopped short when she saw the dead face revealed by the flashlight. She made the sign of the cross again. "That's Friederich Guttmann."

"Does everyone know who this guy is except me?" asked Charlotte.

"I didn't know who he was," Francine admitted. "What was it you were going to say, Alice?"

"Oh. Dispatch is sending an ambulance and a squad car. They should be here any minute."

Jostled by all the activity, Alice's robe fell open. The women stared at her nude body underneath. Then they stared at each other.

Mary Ruth looked under her robe and screamed. Then they all screamed.

"Keep it down out there. It's twelve fifteen in the morning," came a shout from next door. Francine recognized the disapproving voice of Darla Baggesen, the nosy homeowners' association president who lived beside Alice. *This isn't good*, she thought.

She scurried to find her robe. Everyone fell in behind her like they were the Keystone Cops.

At least they're not screaming any more.

"We need to get our stories straight about what we're doing out here in the pool this late at night," said Mary Ruth.

"Never mind that," Alice said. "What am I going to tell the police when they ask me what a dead body is doing in my shed?"

"Decomposing," suggested Charlotte.

"We're going to tell the police we were swimming. Nothing more," Alice insisted.

Francine shook her head. "We can try to avoid the skinny-dipping part, but my guess is it'll come out somehow. I think we should tell the whole truth from the beginning. Otherwise we'll get ourselves in trouble."

Mary Ruth gasped. "No, no skinny-dipping. We just went for a midnight swim. Everyone agree?"

"Don't count on my silence," said Joy. "This'll land us on the front page of the *Indianapolis Star*. Number six on my list." (Be on Front Page of Major Metropolitan Newspaper.)

Squabbling over what to tell the police, the women scrambled into the house.

TWO

CHARLOTTE HERDED THE WOMEN, still straightening their clothes, into Alice's living room. She peered at them through the thick lenses of her white-framed glasses. "Focus, ladies!"

Francine knew what was coming. Charlotte fancied herself a sleuth. It would take everything she had to keep Charlotte out of trouble now that a dead body had been found.

Francine took one side of the sofa. Alice sat in her usual place, a blue paisley upholstered chair. Joy sat by the window.

Charlotte remained standing but leaned on her cane. "You hear those sirens?" She put her right hand to her ear for emphasis. "They'll be here any minute. Francine is right. We need to tell the truth, because five people can't keep a lie going for that long. And if it comes out we've lied once, they'll wonder what other things we've lied about. So we tell the truth, agreed?"

Alice smoothed her white linen pants, trying to make them look neat. "I disagree, and I know Mary Ruth would too, if she were here."

"Is Mary Ruth *still* getting dressed?"

Alice pointed a finger at Charlotte. "It takes her a little longer than the rest of us in the best of circumstances. And these are far from the best."

"I'm here now." Mary Ruth bustled into the living room, running her hands through her short brown hair, trying to get it under control. She normally used a straightener to keep it flat. She wore a loose flowered blouse that billowed out over navy blue elastic waist pants. "Do I look okay? What's happened?"

"Nothing yet," Alice said. "But Charlotte is about to bully us into agreeing to tell the police we were skinny-dipping."

"Oh, must we?" Mary Ruth's face was red, and she mopped her forehead with a handkerchief.

Charlotte stared them down. "No, of course not. Feel free to tell them whatever story pops into your head. Technically, you hadn't gone skinny-dipping yet. But know that Francine and I intend to tell the truth. At least our stories will agree. Once they've heard it from us, they're bound to recognize that's why we were here and that you simply chickened out."

Joy stopped brushing her hair and pointed the brush at Mary Ruth. "You *can't* tell them you *didn't* skinny-dip. Then it might come out that I didn't either, and I won't get on the front page of the *Star*." Francine recalled Joy's #6 item specified a Major Metropolitan Newspaper, which ruled out the local *Hendricks County Flyer*.

"I guess you don't leave us any choice." Mary Ruth flopped onto the other side of the couch from Francine, grumbling. She pulled a small mirror out of her purse. "But I don't look presentable enough to be on the front page of the *Star*."

Alice fingered the cross on her necklace. " None of us do. And God forbid it gets out that I host nude parties."

"Maybe you just think that," Joy said. "Maybe once the word gets out, other people will be doing it and you'll look like a trend-setter."

Alice did not look convinced.

"This will all blow over," Francine said. "Once the police start focusing on the dead body, no one will remember what we were doing here."

Charlotte continued in her authoritative voice. "Speaking of the dead body, I know how this investigation is going to go down. First, they'll send a patrolman to check things out. He'll no sooner see the dead body and then he'll call for a detective and probably the coroner. Eventually we'll be separated for questioning. Fortunately, Alice's house could host a bed and breakfast convention. Alice, be thinking of rooms they can put us in."

Francine slipped her cell phone out of her purse. She thought the comparison to a bed and breakfast wasn't far off. Alice's house had five bedrooms, all themed, like the Blue Room, the Tea Rose Room, and the Queen Anne Room. Plus, her basement with its half kitchen could house a family of four.

Alice gripped the arms of the leather club chair she was sitting on. "Five rooms! But the housekeeper hasn't been here in a week, and the basement..."

"Not to worry, dear," Joy said. "Just use the four bedrooms upstairs and your master suite on this floor. No one even has to go into the basement." She patted the pockets of her pants. "Has anyone seen my phone? I want to text my grandniece about this."

Francine thought the sirens sounded like they were just outside. She touched an app on her own iPhone and typed a name in the search bar.

Charlotte stood behind her. "What are you doing?"

"I'm Googling Friederich Guttmann." She made a selection and the web page loaded. "You want to hear what I've found?"

Joy perched at the large bay window. "Three squad cars! They sent three squad cars. Isn't that overkill?"

"For heaven's sake, it's a murder, Joy. In Brownsburg, Indiana!" said Charlotte. "I'll bet there'll be more here before this is over."

"How long will this take, do you think?" Mary Ruth asked, still looking into her handheld mirror. "My eyes are already so bloodshot you can't tell if they're brown or I'm one of those vampires on *True Blood*. I need some sleep. I have a catering job at lunch."

The doorbell rang. Everyone froze.

When the silence continue a few seconds too long, Francine pulled herself to her full height, which at 5'10", was taller than the others. "You should get that, Alice," she prompted, trying to gently take command.

"Oh. Oh, yes." Alice got up and started for the front door. As she crossed in front of the window, red and blue flashing lights streamed in, rotating across their faces and splashing against the walls.

The sirens stopped, leaving an eerie silence. Then the doorbell rang, shattering the quiet. Alice tentatively opened the front door. An authoritative voice issued some kind of identification and she backed away, letting the officers in.

The lead patrol officer turned out to be female, but she was very no-nonsense. As soon as she determined the body was indeed dead, she called for a detective to take over the investigation, just as Charlotte had predicted.

It seemed like only minutes before the detective arrived. The patrol officer stepped outside to brief him. The women were nervous, but they exhaled in relief when they saw Detective Brent Judson enter.

Jud was a Brownsburg native, still boyishly handsome in his mid-thirties. He'd received his degree in criminal justice from Indiana University before landing a spot on the Brownsburg force. He and Francine's boys had played football together. He was dressed in civilian clothes.

"Jud!" Charlotte said, coming to life. She hobbled across the living room. "Great to see you."

"Your reputation precedes you, Mrs. Reinhardt," he said. He spotted Francine and walked past Charlotte. "When they notified me and I recognized whose neighborhood the call came from, I hurried over. I'm sorry to see you're one of the people who discovered the body, Mrs. McNamara. And you, Mrs. Jeffords. Are you okay?"

Alice nodded, but not convincingly.

Francine patted his forearm. "We're fine, Jud. But you must remember to call me Francine."

Charlotte poked at him. "Hello, Jud."

"Ah, Mrs. Reinhardt…"

"Charlotte."

"…Charlotte, good to see you as well." He spoke to the group. "If you will all please follow the instructions the officers will give you, we're going to get this investigation under way as quickly as possible. He turned to Alice. "Mrs. Jeffords—Alice—if you'll please show me where you found the body?"

Alice finally spoke up. "Well, actually I didn't find it."

Charlotte couldn't contain her excitement any longer. "Plopped right out of the door to the pool shed when it was opened. I'll show you."

Jud gently restrained her.

She glared at him. "Don't you want to hear the story?"

"Oh, indeed, I do. We're going to want to hear it from each of you. But for now, I'm going to ask you to not discuss it further. Just do as the officers ask, and we'll try to get you back to as much normalcy as we can, given the circumstances." He took a breath. "And now, Alice, the body, please."

————

Charlotte and Joy were in the process of telling the police officers which rooms they wanted to be questioned in when a second sleepy-eyed detective arrived. He told them to quiet up and dispatched them to rooms of his choosing for questioning.

"I don't know what the pecking order is," Charlotte told Francine under her breath, "but I don't want to be interviewed by the backup detective."

"No talking," he said.

Francine ended up in the blue bedroom, upstairs at the back end of the house. She'd heard of it but had never been in it, despite having known Alice for twenty-five years. Blue Room was not an understatement, either: the walls were sky blue, the carpet a turquoise, the bed comforter navy, and the pillows—of which there seemed to be a dozen—spanned the spectrum from a light aqua to teal. Alice's only consent to non-blue seemed to be the white frames on a series of race car photographs placed around the room. Francine spotted a CD player on the dresser and hoped for a Ray Charles collection. *Alice wouldn't catch the subtle humor, though,* she thought.

She'd been in the room long enough to discover how uncomfortably the daybed served as a couch when Jud opened the door. He crossed the room and sat opposite her in an office chair one of the policemen had rolled in. "Now, Francine," he said, "please tell me again what you and the other women were doing when you found the body."

There was simply no way to soften it. And besides, by the amusement in his eyes, Francine was fairly certain he'd interviewed someone else first and knew the answer. *Probably Charlotte, but possibly Joy.* "Skinny-dipping," she said. "It was on Joy's list."

"List?"

"Her Sixty List. Her bucket list of sixty things to do before she dies. We made them when Alice turned sixty. She was the first. Sixty at sixty. We thought that was significant. Each of us has our own list, although some of them have overlapping items. You know what bucket lists are."

He nodded. "I saw the movie with Morgan Freeman. You've been working on these a long time, then?"

"Twelve years. Alice is seventy-two now. The rest of us aren't far behind."

"Are you close to finishing your lists?"

"Goodness, no. We did the easy ones first. Then it got harder. We dropped it for a long time. We only came back to them recently."

Francine didn't tell him why. Joy's recent bout with breast cancer and then Charlotte's difficult knee surgery had them worried about their health. Now the lists seemed more important. "You're probably too young to have a bucket list."

He didn't reply. "So have you had this skinny-dipping event planned for some time?"

"Six weeks."

He seemed surprised. "Six weeks for that?"

"Alice wanted Larry to be gone so she wouldn't have to create an excuse to get him out of the house all night. We didn't want anyone else to know. Well, at least she didn't."

"What did you tell your husband?"

"That we were having a Sunday-night slumber party. Which, I should add, is not a lie."

Jud didn't comment one way or the other. "Why was Larry out of the house?"

"Alice and her husband are into real estate and rental properties. He's at a convention in Las Vegas. He left on Friday."

"You kept this slumber party from everyone?"

She nodded. "I didn't tell anyone. I can't vouch for the others."

"You seem to have gone to a great deal of trouble to make it dark. The security light in the Baggesens' back yard…"

"I don't know anything about how that happened." That also was true. Francine had heard something about Charlotte using a shotgun, but she didn't see the incident herself.

Jud made more notes. Francine tried to sit up straight on the daybed and keep her hands in her lap, prim and proper. Even though she knew Jud well enough that she had almost given him a hug instead of returning his handshake in the living room, he was keeping the interview very professional, and she felt she should treat it the same way.

But the daybed was uncomfortable. *This thing must be hell to sleep on.*

"Tell me how Mary Ruth found the body."

She stopped twisting and focused on the thirty-six year-old detective's hazel eyes. "She smelled something unusual coming from the shed. She said it had the bouquet of an outhouse, but then you should hear her describe a wine. We thought maybe it was a dead raccoon. She opened it and Friederich Guttmann's body fell out."

"We haven't identified the deceased yet."

"Everyone who knows auto racing in our group seems to be pretty sure it's Friederich Guttmann. He looked to be about fifty, which matches his bio, and his face matches the image I pulled up on Google before you got here." She held up her cell phone.

Jud chuckled at that. "You have a smartphone."

"And why should I not have one? Doesn't your mother?"

"Mom's not very tech-savvy," he replied. "So Mary Ruth both found the body and identified him?"

"You say that as though it's suspicious. According to Google, he was pretty well known."

"Let's go back to when Mary Ruth opened the shed and the body fell out. What happened after that?"

Francine gave up trying to look dignified on the uncomfortable daybed. She went into a half-lounging position. It didn't help. "I was in the pool at the time. By the sound it made when it hit the concrete and the way the others were reacting to the smell, I suspected it was bigger than a raccoon and probably dead. So I swam over to the side and got out. By then I suspected it was a body. I felt

I had to check on it—him—because I'm still a nurse, even if I am retired, and if there was any way to save him…"

"Commendable."

"But he was stiff to the touch, and when I saw his face I became certain he was dead. I told Alice to call 911, and then we all rushed into the house to get dressed."

Jud scribbled in his notebook. "And what time was that?"

Francine didn't have to think long. "About twelve fifteen. A neighbor shouted it at us when she told us to be quiet." She sat up and yawned. Now that the adrenaline rush from finding the body was over, fatigue was setting in. She checked her cell phone. It was nearly two a.m. Perhaps it was a good thing the daybed was uncomfortable.

Glancing around the room, she noticed a grouping of framed photographs just above the dresser. She could see they had race cars in them. She wondered what the significance was. She was so absorbed that Jud's next question startled her.

"How do you suppose Alice was able to prepare the pool this weekend without smelling anything?" he asked.

"Wouldn't it depend on how long he'd been dead? I'm no coroner, but I'm not sure he's been dead all that long. He was still in the grips of rigor mortis, and he didn't smell like he'd decomposed much. It was mostly his waste products that caught Mary Ruth's attention." Francine suddenly realized she was not helping Alice's cause. If he'd been killed recently, how would he have gotten into the shed without her friend seeing it or somehow being responsible? She quickly amended her answer. "But really, Alice is allergic to everything that exists. Her nose is perpetually clogged. And she

21

said she forgot to add chemicals to the pool, so she never got into the shed."

"If it was as dark as you ladies insist it was, how could you be certain it was Friederich Guttmann?"

"With a flashlight. Once we knew we had a dead body on our hands, Joy ran into the house and got a Maglite. So we had better light at that point."

"You have to admit this obsession with darkness makes your group look suspicious."

"Alice and Larry have a privacy fence, but it's not that tall. Nearly every house around here has a second story. Anyone who wants to see into the back yard, could do it."

"Did you really think someone would be up after midnight spying to see if the pool was in use?"

Francine was starting to get annoyed. "Jud, for someone who graduated as high up in his class at Brownsburg High School as you did, you ask terribly naive questions. We're old. Most of us have body issues. Do you really think we want bright lights shining on these bodies?"

"If I may say so, you are in terrific shape. You have nothing to worry about."

Francine blushed. "That's kind of you. But I still wouldn't want to take the chance someone might catch me skinny-dipping."

"But weren't you up kind of late? Would the neighbors have expected to see you ladies in the pool at that hour?"

"Just because we're old doesn't mean we don't stay up late," she said, even though she couldn't remember the last time she'd seen midnight. "The pool's heated. Alice and Larry could use it at any time."

"Did they?"

"I don't know, Jud. Why don't you ask Alice?"

"I already have."

"Then why did you ask me?" She realized she knew the answer. "To see if what we said matched. I get it. What did she say?"

"She said they really don't use the pool that much. She said they hadn't used it for a week or so."

"I'm not surprised. Do you mind if I get off this daybed? I think it was brought here straight from Guantánamo Bay."

Jud had a bemused look on his face. "You can walk around if you want." He looked down at his notes. "This won't take much longer."

Francine strolled over to the grouping of five racing photos over the dresser. The outside four were action shots of midget cars going around a track. Midget cars were small, stripped-down cars that looked like rolling cages just big enough for the drivers. The center photograph, however, had a regular-sized NASCAR vehicle in it. In front of it stood Alice and Larry and the driver of the #51 car, Brownsburg's own racing success story, twenty-four-year-old Jake Maehler. At least, most everyone in Brownsburg regarded him as a success, even though she knew he hadn't won a NASCAR race yet.

She took hold of the ornate white frame and lifted the picture from the wall to get a better look. Clearly it was taken at a racetrack, though Francine didn't know which one. The palm trees revealed it was not in the Midwest.

"Do you have any idea how the body got into the pool shed?" Jud asked. "Could any of your friends have had something to do with it?"

"Absolutely not. We've all known each other for at least twenty-five years. If we had any secrets, Charlotte would have pried them out of us by now."

Jud laughed in spite of himself. "I'm saving the interview with her for last. She'll probably try to interrogate me."

Francine thought back to Charlotte's dealings with the Town of Speedway police force. "I'd watch your step. Ever since she helped the Speedway police prove her uncle was murdered..."

"I have friends who work there. I've been warned. But what were the odds she'd be involved in another murder case?"

Francine lifted her hands, palms up.

Jud cleared his throat. "Now, please don't get upset. We're asking everyone this question: Can you account for your whereabouts on Saturday?"

A clue, Francine thought. *He must've disappeared on Saturday or they wouldn't be asking.* "Let's see. Saturday morning we got up around seven. I fixed breakfast and we read the paper. I did some house cleaning. After lunch I gardened while Jonathan mowed the grass. Then in the afternoon I picked up Charlotte and we went grocery shopping. She has physical therapy on Saturday mornings, which wipes her out, so I come over after her nap and get her going again. Then she, Jonathan, and I went out for dinner. Charlotte likes the Bob Evans out by the interstate so we went there. I'm sure you can verify all of that."

"Did you know Friederich Guttmann?"

She shook her head.

"Did any of your friends know him?"

"You mean like Mary Ruth or Alice? They recognized him, but I'm not sure they knew him personally. I'd never heard them mention him before."

Francine stared at the photo in her hands. She learned in her Google search that Friederich had been Jake Maehler's longtime mechanic when Jake had been younger and involved in midget car racing. Alice and her husband had been longtime fans of Jake's. Was there a connection there? She didn't know, and she wasn't going to bring it up. She tried to hang the picture back up, but in her affected nonchalance, it slipped out of her hands.

BAM! The frame hit the floor, face-side down. In an instant Jud was there, picking it off the floor. He helped her rehang it but studied it when he noticed who was in the photograph.

"Do Alice and Larry know Jake Maehler?"

"I really don't know." He continued to look at her the way policemen do on cop shows when they don't believe someone. "That's the truth," she protested.

"I believe you," he said, though Francine thought he sounded unconvinced. "But I am going to check my notes to see if Alice mentioned it. If she didn't, I'll ask her about it."

Francine hoped she hadn't gotten her friend in trouble.

"You can go now," Jud said, gathering up his notes. "But if you think of anything else, please get back in touch with me."

"Okay." She left the room hoping Charlotte would be interviewed soon so the two of them could start comparing notes before it got much later. She also wanted to tell her about the ugly blue bedroom.

THREE

CHARLOTTE CAME DOWNSTAIRS GRIPPING the handrail with one hand and her cane with the other. She moved both feet to one step before progressing to the next. Francine waited at the bottom step.

"I tell you, Francine, that Jud was a real horse's ass, practically accusing me of the murder and asking for my alibi on Saturday. Although," she said, dropping her voice conspiratorially, "that must be the day Friederich disappeared."

"I figured that out too. We all got asked for alibis."

"When I offered my help, he flat out turned me down."

"You know it's not good for you to get involved in murder investigations. That needs to be left to the police."

"You sound just like him."

Francine dangled the car keys in front of her. "It's three a.m. I think it's time we just went home."

"You can't mean that! We all came prepared to spend the night. Or what's left of it. If we go now, we'll miss watching the police do their procedures."

"All the more reason. You won't sleep, and if you don't sleep you'll keep me up too. Besides, I think this is between Alice and the police."

"Maybe I don't want to go home with you."

"Listen to her, Charlotte," Jud said. The two women turned and looked back up the stairs to where Jud stood on the top step. "We need for all of you but Alice to leave."

He descended the stairs. Francine tried to help Charlotte out of the way, but it took some doing. She seemed intent on standing her ground.

When Jud stepped off the bottom stair, Charlotte advanced a step. "Jud," she said, just loud enough that the three of them heard, "don't you think it had to be someone in the neighborhood who put the body there? Someone who knew the Jeffords, knew they hadn't used the pool in a while and weren't likely to use it anytime soon?"

"Why do you say that?"

"Think about it, Jud. The person who killed Friederich was clearly in a hurry to get rid of the body. Otherwise, you drive west out of Brownsburg and you've got cornfields all the way to Pittsboro. Dump a body there, no one's gonna find it till harvest time. They must have needed somewhere close where no one would think to look, at least for awhile. Someone who knew Alice and Larry certainly would see their pool shed as a good bet."

He nodded. "That's a valid point. The shed is inside the privacy fence, so someone doing a casual drive-by wouldn't notice it. But if you want to restrict this to people who knew the Jeffords, it would make you and your Bridge Club, who knew them best, strong suspects."

Charlotte snatched up her cane and waved it at him. "Jud, I've known you since you were in diapers. If you don't stop accusing us of the crime…"

"I know, I know, you'll call my mother up and have her slap me in the face until my cheeks turn red. You already threatened that."

Francine turned to Charlotte. "Tell me you didn't say that."

Her friend shrugged.

"The point," Jud said, seizing control of the conversation, "is that it doesn't clear you. However, I'll keep it in mind."

Despite Francine's best efforts to get her to the car, Charlotte wouldn't leave until she'd made a go at the evidence tech, the coroner, and the uniformed policemen who protected the crime scene. None of them told her anything, and Alice was in no mood to deal with her, either.

In the meantime, Francine responded to a text that came in from Jonathan. She learned Alice's house was cordoned off with crime scene tape, attracting attention. Jonathan was among the throng of people on the sidewalk across the street.

Francine went to the front window and looked out. Sure enough, a mob of neighbors had gathered under a streetlamp. Apparently it hadn't taken long for news of the dead body to spread after the sirens sounded and the police cars arrived in force. Jonathan wanted her to come home right away, but she texted him that she had to drop off Charlotte first. He wasn't happy, and neither was she. She texted him to go on home, and she promised she would be there soon.

This is like a train wreck, she thought, marveling at all the people outside. *They think they don't want to see it, and then when it happens, they all do.*

She went to find Charlotte, took her firmly by the arm, and, helped by Jud, moved her to the front door.

"Remember, don't say anything to the press until we're ready to make a statement," Jud said. "And say nothing of substance to your friends."

Francine assured him they wouldn't and took it from there. She hauled Charlotte down the driveway and into the car as fast as they could go. Charlotte sputtered in defiance, but Francine was firm.

"Well," Charlotte said, twisting in the slick leather passenger seat of the Prius after the doors were shut, "we need to talk in the morning."

"*Late* morning." Francine yawned. "Maybe afternoon." She put the key in the ignition.

"You sure you're gonna be able to sleep after seeing Friederich's dead body?"

"I will if you'll quit talking about it." The car started with that dead quiet Francine had come to associate with the hybrid vehicle. It rolled away from the curb noiselessly.

"Why would somebody shove Friederich Guttmann into Alice's pool shed?" Charlotte asked, ignoring Francine's request.

Francine was grateful she didn't have far to drive. Charlotte lived a few streets over at the opposite end of Summer Ridge, but since she had a bad knee, no one expected her to actually walk.

"Charlotte, I know what you're thinking. You're thinking this murder is a godsend. You think you can solve it and finally check the number-one item off your Sixty List. Well, I'm here to tell you not to get involved. It's dangerous, you know it, and you also know you should have checked that top goal off your list a year ago. You *did* solve your uncle's murder. The police were the first to credit you with that."

"I was soooo close," Charlotte said, shaking her head. "But I didn't quite have the motive right."

"Close enough for anyone else. You know what I think? I think you've got a morbid curiosity you can't control. It's why you like Dean Koontz. If gore had weight, his books would have to be stored on reinforced shelves at the library."

"Seriously, now, that location has *got* to be the key. If we figure out why, of all the outdoor sheds in Brownsburg, Friederich's body got dumped in Alice and Larry's, I bet we can narrow down the suspect list to just a couple of people."

"*We*," Francine said, and she paused to let that sink in, "will do no such thing. *We* will let the police do their job."

"They need our help. We were the witnesses, after all."

"We didn't witness anything. All we did was discover the body."

"They don't know Brownsburg like we do."

"Sure they do, Charlotte. Jud has lived here all his life. His mother's family was one of the founders of St. Malachy's Catholic Church."

Charlotte fussed for a couple of moments, tapping her cane on the floorboard. "I hope you won't be so cranky in the morning."

"We're not going to discuss this anymore," Francine said with conviction, aided by the fact they were pulling up to Charlotte's house. She helped her to the front door and made sure she got inside safely. Charlotte thanked her for the ride, which Francine appreciated. Charlotte could be difficult, but they were best friends.

Jonathan was waiting up for Francine when she got home. He hugged her and they talked for half an hour until she felt she had finally let go of the image of Friederich's lifeless body. When she was tired enough to sleep, they went to bed.

But Francine slept fitfully, her body snatching only occasional sleep from her too-active brain. How much later she had the dream, Francine didn't know, but that gray lifeless face she'd seen when he flopped onto his back suddenly reappeared in her dream. Then someone nudged her.

She sat up and screamed. Bright sunshine invaded her world.

Jonathan backed away, gripping the portable phone.

"Sorry," Francine said, pulling herself together. "Bad dream."

"I guess," Jonathan said.

She pulled the sheet around her and shivered, even though it was summer. She remembered Friederich's face. His eyes had been closed. Had the murderer closed them, or had Friederich closed his own eyes before death? She didn't remember seeing any blood. That was curious. "This couldn't be a nightmare, could it?" she asked Jonathan, hoping her heart rate would slow soon. "It really happened, didn't it?"

Jonathan nodded. He held the phone with one hand and covered the speaker with the other. "Worse yet, your discovery was a big hit on Channel Eight's *Sunrise* this morning. The phone's been ringing off the hook. I've been fielding questions and fending off reporters since seven o'clock. But it's eleven now, and it's your turn." He held out the phone to her. "Plus, it's Joy. You never know with Joy."

She knew what he was talking about. A call from Joy could mean she was alerting everyone of a bargain at the grocery store or advising them she was taking up tap dancing. Francine took the phone. "Joy?"

"Ohmigosh! I wish I had that scream on tape!"

"Sorry if I startled you," she said, though she didn't think Joy sounded all that startled.

"Don't worry—it's going even better than I'd hoped for!" Her chirpy voice occasionally got on Francine's nerves, but never so much as it did now, right after being awakened out of a bad dream. "We were on after the happy news on *Sunrise*, and I got a tip we're leading off the noon news on all the stations."

"I'll be sure to tune in."

"Don't be sarcastic. I've already had enough of that from Charlotte. We were too late to make this morning's *Star*, but I talked to the editor of the *Hendricks County Flyer*, and I think we're good for Wednesday's front page. That's their next issue. Tuesday's *Star*, maybe not. We might be page-two news by then."

"Too bad you ruled out the *Flyer* in your Sixty List or you'd be set."

"Oh, I've already checked it off. Being on TV is way better than the newspapers. Do you think the police will let us be interviewed eventually?"

"Have they made a statement yet?"

"Well, they confirmed the body was Friederich Guttmann's, but they've not said much else."

"I don't think that puts us in the clear. You should check with Detective Judson. Did they say how he died?"

"They said the death was not natural."

"How unsurprising. I'm sure Charlotte will be thrilled."

"We're both over here at Alice's house. You want to talk to her?"

Francine lay back and let her head sink into the thick, plush pillows. *It keeps getting better and better.* "Not really. What is she doing there?"

"Pacing around the blocked-off crime scene. She's got a notebook and she keeps scribbling things in it."

"Great. Where are the police?"

"They worked all night and finished up everything but the shed. There's a policeman blocking off access there, but other than that, they've gone."

"Well, as long as a policeman is there…"

"I know you just got up, but Alice wants to know if you can come over."

"Technically, I'm not even up yet. I haven't gotten out of bed." Francine rubbed her left temple. She could feel a headache coming on. She scanned the bedside table for her glasses. "Why does Alice need me? Is Charlotte misbehaving?"

"No, Charlotte's fine. It's all the neighbors traipsing around. Alice is trying to keep them at bay, but they're coming through the bushes in the back yard now. Plus, Charlotte persuaded Mary Ruth's grandson Toby to drive her over, the one who doesn't have a job. He thinks Alice should charge admission and has offered to set something up."

"Let me take a shower and get dressed, and I'll be over."

"Thanks, Francine, you're always the levelheaded one. You'll know how to handle this. By the way, watch your step on the way over. The traffic is backed up all the way to the subdivision entrance. Summer Ridge Drive wasn't designed to handle this many cars."

She remembered that Alice's husband was still away on business. "Is Larry coming back from Las Vegas today?"

"No. He tried to get away from the convention, but he can't get a flight home, and he was scheduled to leave tomorrow anyway. Should Alice be charging admission?"

"No, she shouldn't. Toby should be helping keep the neighbors out. Does Mary Ruth know he's there?"

"I don't think so. She has a catering job at noon and Toby says she left the house before he did."

Despite her fatigue, Francine tossed back the sheet and got out of bed. This did not sound good. "I'll be right over."

FOUR

FRANCINE WAS GRATEFUL JONATHAN decided to walk her over to Alice's house. He'd been good with their own three boys and would know exactly how to handle Toby. When had Mary Ruth's grandson become so enterprising? He'd been freeloading in her basement for five years and going to the University of Indianapolis. So far he'd had four majors, showing no signs of graduating anytime soon. Francine couldn't remember when he worked last. Mary Ruth said his favorite thing to do was sit at home and play video games.

"It's a good thing Joy cautioned you about the traffic," Jonathan said. He eyed the cars parked on both sides of the street. "This reminds me of race time in Speedway."

She knew what he meant. Though she hadn't grown up in Speedway like he had, she'd been to enough races to know how tough it was to navigate the streets made narrow by densely packed cars parked along the curbs. Most residents didn't attempt to go in or out of Speedway on race days.

"They should have a policeman stationed at the subdivision entrance."

"I'm not sure they need to." Jonathan pointed to the line of vehicles that ran all the way to the entry point. "I don't think anyone can get in now."

They watched a small Hummer try to squeeze by the first few cars, finally giving up and backing out. The frustrated driver drove away.

"Case in point," Jonathan said.

She laughed, even though at the moment her concern was how many people they'd find at Alice's house. Based on the number of cars, it had to be plenty. She put her arm in Jonathan's and leaned in to hug him. His presence always reassured her. He was smart and funny and solid, not just in physique but also in his common sense approach to life. And handsome. Charlotte said Jonathan was how James Garner would have turned out if he'd been an accountant instead of an actor.

When they were three houses down from Alice's, they came across the end of an orderly line of people. "Will you look at that?" Francine whispered. "It's like they're waiting to get into Disney World."

"Hey, you," a stern-looking woman about Francine's age exclaimed when they passed. "Don't think you're going to be able to cut in line when you get up there." Francine recognized her from somewhere, maybe a homeowners' association meeting.

"I'm number fifty-five," said the older woman in front of her, waving a cane. "That fat young man comes by every once in a while to take names and issue numbers. You just better get in line now."

"Yeah," said the first woman. "He'll just chase you back here. He's ruthless."

Someone farther up the line turned around to see what the commotion was about. "Hey! I recognize you," she said. "You're Francine McNamara, one of the skinny-dippers. Don't you ladies have any shame?"

The crowd began to murmur. "Maybe we'd better make a run for the house," Jonathan whispered in her ear.

While she was grateful that they'd kept themselves in shape, a run was probably not a good plan, especially with the espadrilles she had on. "Let's just walk fast and cut across the lawns."

Francine and Jonathan sped up, but as people began to take notice, they found themselves moving faster and faster to make it to Alice's yard before the crowd got any more unruly. They had barely reached the edge of Alice's property when they were accosted by Toby.

"The end of the line is back there," he said, aiming a pen in that direction. He held a clipboard against his stomach. Francine hadn't seen Toby in some time and was surprised to discover he was not just overweight, but also mohawked and multi-tattooed. A ring pierced his left eyebrow. He looked like a bouncer at a biker bar.

She threw him a withering glance, taking a moment to catch her breath. "I'm not going to stand in line to get into Alice's house, Toby Burrows, and if I find out you're charging these people to see the scene of the crime…"

He took a step back. "I'm sorry, Mrs. McNamara, I didn't recognize you at first! Of course you don't need to wait in line. Let me get you into the house."

"Are you charging admission?" Jonathan's voice held a great deal of disdain.

"No, sir. Alice—I mean Mrs. Jeffords—told me not to and I haven't. But she couldn't have people running all over the house and back yard, so I set up a system for entry. No more than five at a time."

Toby ushered them through a gate in the privacy fence and closed it behind them. He started to guide them around the side yard.

Francine patted Toby's beefy forearm. "We know the way from here, dear. I think you'd best get back out front in case we've started a stampede."

"Good idea." He turned away and reopened the gate to find a middle-aged woman with heavy makeup trying to push through with a camera. "Hey, get back in line," he said. "I told you earlier, no special privileges for the press." He nudged her back as he closed the gate.

"Let me know if you need help," Jonathan called after him.

"Could you believe that woman's comment about having no shame?" Francine was still miffed by the hostility they'd encountered. "Like we're a bunch of out-of-control Internet strippers."

"What's out of control is this situation," he replied. "Look over there. Is Charlotte giving guided tours?"

She spun around. He seemed to be correct. Charlotte patrolled the crime scene tape, five people in tow. A policeman with the demeanor of a Buckingham Palace guard stood behind the tape, preventing access. Charlotte used her cane to point this way and that with great animation. Then she saw Francine.

"Thank God you're here!" she called, waving. "Stay right here," she ordered her group. "I'll be back."

Charlotte hurried over as quickly as she was able and pulled them into a huddle. "Can you finish up these five so I can go back and get the next group?" she asked Francine. "Maybe we could work as a team. I could start the tour and you could finish it. We need to process these suspects faster."

"Suspects? What suspects?"

"All these people. The murderer always returns to the scene of the crime! I've got Toby taking their names, and this gives me a chance to question them while they're here. We've got to help Alice."

"I don't think tours are the way to help Alice," Jonathan said.

"Alice understands why we're doing this, even if it does creep her out to have people she doesn't know marching through her house. And if you have a better idea, let's hear it. I'm told the police will be here any minute to pick her up. Something about Friederich renting space from Larry."

"Head on back to your group, Charlotte," Francine said. "I'll help you out in a minute." She waited until Charlotte was out of earshot. Jonathan was Larry's accountant, and this sounded ominous. "Do you know anything about this?" she asked him. "Is this something to worry about?"

"If I told you, it'd be breaking confidentiality."

"But I'm your wife!"

"And you have a lot of cronies who will try to get it out of you. Better you know nothing, so you can say so in all honesty."

She gritted her teeth. "Just tell me if Alice and Larry have anything to be concerned about."

"There's one little thing that could be a problem," he said, his face grim. "I don't think it will be, but, well, I don't think I should say any more."

Francine was momentarily angry, but then she decided he was probably right to handle it as he was, at least for now. She was pretty sure she could get the information out of him later if she needed. "All right. I'm going to try to keep Charlotte out of trouble. You'd better go talk to Alice. If the police are coming over, they might try to get into Larry's business records. You should be there if they try."

"I'll offer, but she doesn't have to accept my help."

She gave him the sigh she usually reserved for Charlotte. "She will. We both know that. Now get."

She turned her full attention to Charlotte and the tour group. Alice's lot was nearly an acre, more narrow than wide, with a good portion of it in the back yard. When Larry's real estate business boomed in the late '90s, he'd added the inground pool behind the house. The pool shed, where they'd found Friederich's body, was at the end of the long pool's concrete apron, beyond the deep end. Police tape surrounded the outbuilding, extending ten feet beyond the shed.

An elderly neighbor parked herself in the lounge chair outside the tape. Charlotte was busy coaxing them toward the house. "You can't just stop now, Cornelia," she said, yanking on the woman's elbow, "we've got people waiting."

Francine hustled to the chair. "I'll take care of her. You go get the next group."

"Nope. Only five at a time in one area. We let too many people in and we'll have the same situation we had earlier, with people traipsing all over the yard and trampling any evidence."

"If the police have opened up the yard, there's probably no evidence there. And I don't think Cornelia is going to be doing a lot of traipsing."

Charlotte eyed the neighbor. "She better not."

Cornelia struggled to get off the lounge. "My hips just aren't what they used to be."

"Tell me about it," said a younger woman in the group, smoothing the shorts that hugged her shapely hips. "It's called childbirth."

Francine threw an annoyed look at Darla Baggesen, the forty-year-old divorcee whose house bordered the Jeffords's. She'd been the one who'd announced what time it was last night when everyone screamed. In addition to being the homeowners' association president, she was also flighty and self-absorbed. Francine was certain the mention of her hips had only been designed to attract attention to them.

"Cornelia is well past childbirth and what it does to hips, Darla. But since you're so concerned, why don't you help her to the door?"

Darla shook her shoulder-length, sunny blond hair that Francine knew was a dye job. She sniffed. "I was just about to offer."

Charlotte and Francine ambled along with the group as it traversed the length of the pool, the patio, and through the French doors that led into the house. They entered into the family room with its two-story ceiling, bathed in sunlight through the massive Palladian window. Cornelia stopped to stare along with Darla. Summer Ridge was a subdivision of custom built, all-brick homes, most of them Colonial, but the Jeffords's house was the most expensive and everyone knew it. Charlotte had to nudge the rubberneckers past the staircase into the foyer. Toby had the next five people waiting there, so he escorted them into the front room to let Cornelia's group out.

"What does the line look like, Toby?" Charlotte asked when he returned.

"Still long. It's going to take us more than an hour to get all these people through. And that's if nobody else gets in line."

"Go get another five. Francine here will take that group. That'll double our coverage."

"Coverage?" Francine put her hands on her hips. "These people are the curious and the gawkers, not suspects."

"Shows what you know," Charlotte said, pulling her in close. "Cornelia Brown packs heat."

"Her purse?" asked Toby.

"That bag's a treasure trove of torture devices, truth be known."

"Stop it, Charlotte," Francine said. "Stop it right now before I go out and tell all these people to go home. Cornelia is not a criminal."

"I wouldn't put anything past Darla Baggesen, though," Toby whispered. "She's a cougar. She scares me."

From up the stairs, Joy's shrill voice rang out. "Reuters is on the line, Alice! They want to know if you'd make a statement."

Alice stuck her head out of the first upstairs room and shouted back down the hall. "Who's Reuters? Oh, never mind, it doesn't matter. No statements."

The doorbell rang. Toby went to the door and jerked it open. "I told you, only five at a—oh, hello, officers."

He backed up to let a disheveled Detective Judson and a uniformed policeman step into the foyer. Francine noticed dark circles under Jud's eyes.

"Is Alice here?"

"I'm here." She came down the stairs, Jonathan behind her. "The study looks out onto the street. I saw you pull up."

"Hi, Jud," Jonathan said. "I'm glad you're on the case."

Jud smiled. "Thanks. I'm sorry you and Francine got mixed up in this. I'm sorry it happened at all. But we get need to get to the bottom of things. Alice, did you locate the keys to the building?"

"They were right where Larry said they were."

"Good. Then let's go take a look."

She indicated Jonathan. "Do you mind if Jonathan comes with us, since Larry's not here? He's our accountant."

"I've been in the building from time to time, so I'm familiar with it," Jonathan said. "I'd like to be there in case I can help."

"It's kind of irregular, but it's your building, Alice," Jud said, but he was clearly not happy.

"Where is this place you're going to?" Charlotte asked.

He glanced at the tour group of five standing nearby. "I'm not at liberty to say."

"It's on Adams Street between US 136 and College," Alice answered. "Friederich was renting a garage from Larry. The police want to look through it. I'm sure it's nothing."

"Can I come, too?" Charlotte asked.

"No, you can't," Toby said. "I'm not gonna get stuck with a bunch of unhappy people who don't get tours when you said they would."

"He's right," Francine said. "You need to stay and process the suspects." She turned to Jud. "Charlotte thinks that the murderer always returns to the scene of the crime. She's making a list of all the people who've come through to gape at the pool shed where we found the body."

"Actually," he said, "I'd like to have a copy of that list."

Charlotte aimed a triumphant smile at her.

Alice reached out a hand to Francine. "Would you come to see Friederich's garage with us? I don't want to be the only woman along."

"Of course," she replied, knowing without looking that Charlotte had dropped the smile and was fuming with jealousy. But she knew she'd be questioned later.

Jud frowned at the idea.

"You don't mind, do you?" asked Alice.

"As I said before, it's your building. Do you want to leave the house open like this while you're gone, though?"

Toby stuck up his hand like he needed permission to volunteer an answer. "We could lock up the house and let people in through the privacy fence gate. It means people would be walking over the grass, but we wouldn't have to turn the neighbors away."

"That's a great idea," Alice said, sounding relieved. "Everyone'd be mad if they didn't get a chance to look, but I do want them out of my house." She turned and called upstairs. "Joy, just let the phones go to voicemail! You can catch up with any messages later. I need you to help Charlotte with the tours."

For a moment, there was no response. "Do I have to? The Associated Press is on the phone."

44

"Tell them the same thing you just told Rovers, or whoever it was. No statements."

Joy stuck her head out of the entrance to the study. "Okay. I'll be down in a minute."

"And she is doing what?" Jud asked.

"She's my press secretary today. She was a secretary for Lilly Endowment and used to draft press releases for them sometimes."

Charlotte eyed the uniformed policeman with Jud. "Is he here to help? Because we could use him. If he can manage the gate, Toby can start giving tours, too, and with Joy working, that'll triple our productivity."

The policeman looked at Jud, who rolled his eyes. "We live to serve," Jud said. He looked at the others. "Let's go."

FIVE

FRANCINE HAD NO IDEA that Larry owned the old white brick building along Adams Street. It was virtually unnoticeable, one that had been around so long it faded into the mixed-use downtown neighborhood. On the opposite corner was the new Brownsburg Public Safety Building, and next to it were an old two-story apartment and a small vacant lot. Before Larry bought the building, it was probably some kind of machine shop. A few parking spots were in front, but weeds had grown up through the asphalt and the yellow lines delineating the parking spots had faded. There was a double door opening that let out onto the front parking lot, but the doors had no way of being opened from the outside. Along with the boarded-up windows, they gave the appearance the place had been abandoned.

Alice pulled her Cadillac STS behind the building using a narrow alleyway. There were two spots in the rear, far away from the busy Public Safety building, where a car could park and a person could access the building without being seen from the street. The door in the back was fairly new and in good repair. It had two locks and a security camera mounted above the door. Jud got out of his police car, and Francine, Jonathan, and Alice got out of the Cadillac. They entered at the north end.

The interior of the building stood in direct contrast to the exterior. Inside was a pristine auto mechanic's workshop. Immediately to the left of the door were a large number of tools, exotic-looking machines, and what appeared to be testing equipment. Farther beyond was an open space that held two engines and two midget cars. The cars were hovering about a foot off the floor, so Francine concluded there must be stands underneath them. Everything was spread over a shiny floor with a bright blue finish. From one end to the other was probably forty feet, but it was narrower across, maybe twenty-five feet wide. Francine didn't know a working garage could be so clean.

Jonathan saw her staring at the floor. "This is Armorclad epoxy coating," he said, bending down and running his hand across it. "Beautiful, really. Friederich had it installed."

Jud took a few steps into the garage and looked up at the ceiling. He pointed to a dome mounted about a quarter of the way into the space. "Can either of you tell me about the video surveillance system?"

Alice and Jonathan looked at each other. "I don't know a thing about it," Alice said. She sounded testy.

"I think we should wait for Larry," Jonathan said.

Jud cleared his throat. "Catching a killer means moving quickly. We don't know exactly how long Mr. Guttmann has been dead, but the longer we wait to investigate, the more difficult the case becomes. And you said Larry wanted you to cooperate with us."

"I'm certain we have nothing to worry about," Alice told Jonathan.

"Okay. Larry bought a four-camera security system that has two exterior cameras with infrared night vision. One is by the back door and one is out front. The two indoor cameras," he said, pointing to the dome Jud had noted earlier, "are less noticeable and mounted on the ceiling."

They all looked straight up. The small black dome above Francine's head hugged the bare ceiling in an area between two sprinkler heads. After studying the ceiling across the room, she spotted the second one.

"Where is the video recorded?" Jud asked.

"On a personal computer."

"What about storage? Does he save all the video?"

"Larry's told me he downloads the data once a month to an external hard drive."

"So this computer would have some of the most recent video? I'd like to take a look at it."

"I don't know where he keeps the computer, and I don't know the access codes. Only Larry can give you that."

Jud nodded. "Let's get him on the phone. I'd like to see if he'll do that for us."

"We can try," Alice said. "I'm not sure where he's going to be today. He said he had meetings. But I'm sure he'll call us right back." She got out her cell phone.

Jonathan wandered over to the two midget cars on the stands. Each was about ten feet long and five feet wide. Compared to a real car, a midget car looked like a skeleton with an exposed tubular frame on the outside. As its name implied, it was also short. Jonathan would have to squat low and compact himself to get into the seat.

Francine followed him over. "How much do you know about Friederich?" she asked quietly.

"He was a sought-after mechanic for midget cars, but after he helped Jake Maehler advance to the NASCAR circuit, he never worked with any one driver exclusively again. He kept his hand in the business, though. Supposedly he had the magic touch." He examined one of the midget cars, mallard green with decals on it. "Jake's number is fifty-one," he added, touching the car. It moved. "These must be rolling stands."

"How did Jake get the money to pay someone like Friederich?"

"I'd say their relationship was more like protégé and teacher. Jake was Friederich's project. Friederich got paid, but not at the rate he could command now. He was a great mechanic and Jake a great driver. They sort of made each other what they are today."

"Why didn't Friederich move over to NASCAR with Jake?"

"Jake got on at one of the big teams. They have their own mechanics."

"Was Friederich upset?"

Jonathan shrugged. "I doubt it. Both of them knew what would happen when Jake finally got a chance to move up."

Living in the Indianapolis area, Francine had been exposed to racing for a long time. She knew the difference between an Indycar race, like the Indianapolis 500, and a stock car race, like the Brickyard 400. They got all the attention. But other kinds of racing, like sprints, midgets, and Silver Crown, still baffled her. She knew Jake had appeared at the Night Before the 500 midget car race in May and would be at the SpeedFest midget car race on Thursday. "If

Jake is driving for a NASCAR team, why is he back racing midgets? Wouldn't that be below him?"

"Not at all. Race drivers love competition. But from what I hear, this is all about redemption. Jake hasn't won a race in so long he's afraid he's already washed up at twenty-three. He needs to get back to winning. The Night Before the 500 race was supposed to show he could still win a race—any race. Except he didn't. He came in fifth. Car-related issues. He's back for SpeedFest and he's got something to prove."

Francine pointed to the number on the green midget car. "And Friederich was working for him again?"

Jonathan nodded. "Part of the getting the magic back. Jake publicly blew up at Friederich after his car mishandled during the last race and he quickly dropped from first to fifth, but they reconciled."

"So these cars must belong to Jake."

"One does, at least." He pointed to the lack of a number on the other car body. "Not too sure about that one."

Francine examined the second car. It was painted a matte black and looked very ordinary without a number or the logos of sponsoring companies. "Did Friederich have another client?"

Alice came over before Jonathan had a chance to answer. "Larry says he's in a conference and can't talk, so I sent him a text message. Here's what he sent back. He said you would understand."

She handed Jonathan the cell phone. He read the text and handed it back to her. "If that's what he wants."

Jud stood next to Alice. "So, can you access the footage for me?"

He blew out a breath. "Yes, I can. Follow me."

They walked to a corner of the shop where Friederich had placed his clean-up tools. Jonathan moved a Shop-Vac out of the way and knelt on one knee. First he felt around the floor, which looked solid. Then he ran his hand over the tiles on the corner walls, going out about three feet along the side. One of the tiles had a black smudge. Jonathan focused on the tile. He pressed the smudge and the tile popped back.

"This is a false wall," he said. He swung the tile away on its hinge, stuck his hand in the opening, and felt around. "Here it is." He pulled on a latch and a section of the wall about five feet tall by three feet wide opened like a door with the tools still hanging on it.

Alice gasped.

Francine stared in disbelief. It wasn't just that Larry had hidden the system, it was how he had hidden it. And was this really her husband doing this cloak-and-dagger stuff?

Three shelves had been built into the narrow, closet-like space, only about two feet deep. The computer tower was on the bottom shelf and above it was the monitor. Jonathan switched it on and the display came to life. "Let's see what we've got."

A minute passed while he negotiated his way around the security screens until he could access the cameras. He clicked on one of the outside cameras and the back parking lot filled the screen. Francine knew it was current time because she could see Alice's Cadillac and Jud's squad car sitting there.

"Can you run it back to last week?" Jud asked.

"Maybe," he said reluctantly. "This doesn't seem to be a very intuitive menu."

"I've worked with similar systems. Mind if I take over?"

Jonathan shrugged. "Alice, it's your call, not mine."

"Please continue," she said. "I'm fascinated. I never knew any of this was here." She seemed ticked that Larry had kept her in the dark about this. *He'll have some explaining to do,* Francine thought. *Jonathan too.*

Jud located the menu that had the various days on it. It went back to Thursday afternoon. After clicking around, the detective turned and put his hands on his hips. He looked at Alice. "Either your husband downloaded the video feed to an external hard drive on Thursday or someone who had access to this computer erased everything that came before it."

"I'm trusting he just downloaded it," she said.

"So am I. But let's see what we've got from that point." Using the mouse, he divided the screen into four sections, one for each camera, and called up the feed from Thursday afternoon and Friday. He started the video going. For a long time there was video feed but no action. "If there's a motion detector on this system, Larry doesn't seem to be using it." Jud ran the video at the fastest speed possible until something happened. On Saturday afternoon a truck with a utility trailer hitched to it pulled into the front parking lot. The truck backed up the trailer to the double doors. A young man got out.

"That's Jake Maehler," Alice said.

Jake eased the drop-down gate to the concrete so that it formed a ramp up to the trailer. He went around back, unlocked the door, and went to the where the midget cars were located. This time there were four cars, not two, each on a set of rolling stands. Two of the midget cars were emblazoned with Jake's number, 51, and two were unmarked. Using the stands, Jake pushed the first of his cars out the double doors at the front of the building and up the ramp onto the trailer. He secured the car on the bed and then raised the gate, locked up the workshop, and drove off.

Just two days ago, Francine thought. *And that's the day the police think Friederich disappeared.*

"So Jake took one of the cars," Jud said. "Let's see what happened to the other."

At ten o'clock that night, the outside cameras went dark. The situation reversed itself shortly after midnight. Jud ran it back and forth a couple of times. The inside cameras were still recording, but the outside ones showed nothing. "Interesting," he said. "I wonder what happened outside. But the three race cars are still inside."

He continued to run the playback. Just twenty minutes later, the feed from the front outside camera blanked. Jud slowed it to real time. One by one, each of the other cameras blanked. The monitor showed nothing for awhile, and Jud fast-forwarded again. Roughly fifty minutes later, the feed returned all at once. This time an unmarked car was gone. Jud fast-forwarded it again, but there was no more interruption of the video. He checked today, Monday, up to the present time. The video cameras were all operational, and other than daylight passing, the video showed no change. No one pulled into the parking lot and no one entered the workshop.

He turned off the monitor. "A two-hour outside shutdown late Saturday night followed by a fifty-minute gap inside and outside early Sunday morning. The missing unmarked midget car was removed during the gap."

"Who did that, and how did they do it?" Francine asked.

He turned to her. "You're leaping to the conclusion that the same person did them both. It may be likely, but we have to keep an open mind."

"The unit came with a remote that enabled Larry to shut down one or more of the cameras," Jonathan said. "But he kept it secure."

The detective cocked an eyebrow. "Just how secure did he keep it?"

"Larry is very good about things like that." He ran a finger over his lips in thought. "However, remotes operate on radio frequencies, don't they? Someone *could* have figured out the frequency by trial and error."

Francine knew he was trying to think up ways Larry could be innocent. "When did Larry leave for Las Vegas?" she asked Alice, trying to help. "It was Friday, wasn't it?"

Alice fidgeted before she answered. "Yes, he left very early on Friday. I dropped him off at the airport. He would have been in Las Vegas when the cameras were tampered with."

"I suppose someone could have figured out the frequency of the remote," Jud mused. "It would take awhile, but it could be done. I need two things. I need this computer, and I need access to Larry's backed-up video files."

"Let me get hold of him again," Alice said.

Jonathan placed his hand over her smartphone before she could text. "Could I talk to you privately for a moment?" He took hold of her elbow and guided her across the room.

Jud watched them with suspicion. Francine wondered if he could read lips. Moving in front of the monitor and turning it back on, she said, "Can we go back to that fifty-minute gap? There was something interesting about the order those cameras went out. Did you notice that?"

Her fiddling with the computer got his attention. "I'm sorry, Francine, but I have to ask you to step away from the computer. I plan to take it for evidence."

"Okay, but the video blanked out in a specific order, didn't it? First the front outside camera, then the back outside, then the inside camera on the entrance side of the building, followed by the camera on this side."

"The person obviously shut them off as he came to them."

She searched for something else to say. "And it took them fifty minutes to get the car outside and onto some vehicle? How long did it take Jake? Couldn't have been more than ten."

He paused before answering. "Your point is?"

Until now she'd been making things up, but a piece seemed to lock into place. "That either they were incompetent in getting the car out to the front of the building, or they were looking for something else in addition to the car. Maybe you should treat it like one of those puzzles where you have to ask yourself, what's different from one drawing to the next? What if you could get a still shot from each camera *before* it went dark and then one *after*? It might be an interesting comparison. What they were here to do besides take the midget car may be apparent."

"Actually, that's a brilliant observation."

Jonathan and Alice returned. "You may have the computer, Jud, but I'm going to follow Jonathan's advice that you wait for my husband to get home before we give you anything else."

Jud looked at Jonathan. "The purpose being?"

"You're a good guy, Jud," he answered. "I watched you grow up along with my boys. But at this point, you know why it's not a good idea. As this thing unfolds, there could be circumstantial evidence uncovered that implicates Larry. We need to let him get home before any more coincidences get unearthed."

SIX

As ALICE PULLED HER Cadillac into her driveway, Francine was pleased to see the crowds had left. Using the policeman as a gate-keeper must have enabled Charlotte and the group to run through the tours pretty quickly. Jud's police car followed them into the driveway.

Charlotte yanked open Alice's front door the minute they all got out. She hobbled out to meet them. "I have Toby's list." She waved a sheet of paper at Jud. "It's got all the people who were here."

He smiled at her and took the sheet. "Thank you."

"I made copies for us," she told Francine. "The tough part will be separating the merely curious from the guilty party who re-turned to the scene of the crime."

"*If* the guilty party returned," she reminded her.

Jud glanced through the names. "I promise I'll take a thorough look at this later." He folded the paper and pocketed it. Seeing Alice head for the front door, he took off after her.

"I sure hope he's not humoring me," Charlotte muttered. "I hate being humored."

Francine avoided eye contact. She often humored Charlotte.

Alice went through the front door, cell phone in hand. The others followed.

Her voice was tense as she paced in the foyer. "You've already hired an attorney? When? This *morning*? You did that without telling me? Yes, I know Jonathan thinks it's a good idea. He only just suggested it to me. As busy as you've been, I didn't think you'd have thought of it, let alone had time to do anything about it. And you want to tell me what that secret door thing is all about?" She listened, then gave a sideways glance at Jud. "I agree. This isn't a good time to discuss it. I'll call you back later." She took steps away from Jud into the living room, lowering her voice. "Yes, I'll try not to worry. I believe you that it's all circumstantial."

But Francine heard strain in her voice as she said it.

When Alice turned around to see where Jud was, she practically bumped into him, he was following so closely.

"Would you ask your husband what time he gets in tomorrow?" he asked, recovering quickly.

Alice took a step backward. She held the cell phone close to her mouth and mumbled into it. "What time do you get home tomorrow? I know you've told me a hundred times, but tell me again." She looked up. "Three o'clock."

He wrote it in his notepad.

"There's a lot going on here, but I *will* pick you up," Alice continued into the phone. "Don't you worry about that." She ended the call. "Where's Joy?" she asked Charlotte.

"She went home for lunch and hasn't come back. The rest of us ordered Jimmy John's."

The news seemed to deflate Alice. "I don't know that I can eat, but I wish she'd waited."

Francine wasn't surprised. The five of them were good friends, but much as she and Charlotte were close, so were Joy and Alice. After what they'd seen at Friederich's garage, with Larry's hidden security camera and missing coverage, she probably wanted to be alone with Joy.

"I was kind of glad to see her go," Charlotte whispered to Francine. "Her excitement over making the morning news was getting on my nerves."

"Even if you aren't going to let me look at the business records yet," Jud said to Alice, his voice full of resignation, "please don't be out of touch today. We need to move on this investigation, and we may have additional questions for you."

"I know you don't like this," Jonathan said, "but Larry isn't here to make informed decisions. His interests have to be protected."

"If he's innocent, then he has nothing to fear."

"In your heart, you know that's not true. People can be made to look guilty. That's why the legal system is structured to slow things down, so there's no rush to judgment."

"Thank you for letting me have the video surveillance equipment," Jud said, a bit stiffly. "I'll be back in touch soon." He shook everyone's hand and left.

"What—" Charlotte began.

Francine put a finger to her lips and shook her head. She walked into the front room and checked the detective's progress through the bay window. Finally she exhaled in relief. "He's gone."

"What surveillance equipment?" Charlotte pulled a notebook out of her purse and opened it to a blank page. "And don't stall. I'm not Jud."

Jonathan raised his eyebrows at Alice. She nodded for him to answer.

"Larry had a four-camera monitoring system in Friederich's garage, but he had already downloaded to his hard drive everything up to Thursday. Jud wants us to give him the video footage."

"What's wrong with that?"

"There's nothing wrong with it."

"Then what's the big deal?"

He went mum. Alice opened her mouth to speak, but he cautioned her with a shake of his head.

There was fire in Alice's eyes, and Francine was pretty sure it was the situation making her mad, not Jonathan. "Oh, for heaven's sake. It's only Charlotte," Alice said, "and she's good at this kind of stuff." She pursed her lips. "Saturday, Jake Maehler came in and took one of his midget cars. Then later the system went blank twice. Once, just the outside went dark. It lasted about two hours. Then the system came up but someone turned all the cameras off for fifty minutes and took a second car, one that was unmarked."

"Ohhh. And I bet Larry had the means to do that."

"Yes, he did, but he flew to Las Vegas on Friday. What we *don't* know is what's on the video Larry downloaded Thursday. Jud is suspicious, and Jonathan recommends that we don't give up the video until Larry is back in town. He says we need a chance to watch it first and have a lawyer advise us on what to do."

"Evidence *can* be made to look one way or another," Charlotte said, jotting notes. "Larry should protect himself, I agree. Can I watch the video?"

Alice shook her head. "We don't know where Larry keeps it, and our lawyer, who I didn't even know we *had*, has advised him not to tell anyone until he gets home. That way we can honestly say we don't know."

Francine let the lacey window sheer fall back into place. "Did Larry tell you the lawyer's name?"

"No, and I forgot to ask."

"The problem," Jonathan said, "is that the police are going to be pressured to solve this quickly. Brownsburg *isn't* the murder capital of Indiana, and the town council will want this cleared up."

Francine nodded in agreement. "I thought Jud looked very tired."

"Still, we can't let this get rushed," Jonathan said. "We need to make sure anything that comes to light does so in a way to protect Larry."

"And Alice." Francine walked over, put her arm around her, and gave her a hug.

"I appreciate all of you," she said. "Charlotte, thanks for getting rid of the tourists."

"It was my pleasure, believe me."

"Do you need us to stay?" Francine asked.

Alice waved her off. "That's okay. You've done enough, and I'm sure you're all hungry. I just need to be by myself for a while. I'll lock the door, retreat upstairs, and pretend no one's home."

"I'm not hungry," Charlotte said. "Remember, I had a Jimmy John's sub—at least the half Toby didn't eat. I could stay."

"Please don't be offended, but I'd prefer to just wait for Joy to come back. She helped all morning dealing with the press, and I need her right now."

Francine moved quickly to take any sting out of Alice's words. "Do you have a way home?" she asked Charlotte. "I could get the car and drop you off at your house."

"No need. Toby took me home and I drove my car back."

Jonathan started up the stairs. "Alice, I'll just gather up the financial records and head home."

"Thanks for looking them over. I know we're going to need guidance from both you and the lawyer."

Charlotte still had out her notebook. "What financial records?"

"I can't tell you. Client confidentiality." He disappeared into the study.

The doorbell rang. Francine stared at the door. She'd just watched Jud leave, and she hadn't seen any other cars outside. Who was it now?

SEVEN

ALICE LOOKED THROUGH THE peephole. "It's Darla."

"Don't let her in," said Charlotte. "She's already had the crime scene tour."

Alice took a step away from the door. "She's carrying a clipboard. You know what that means."

The women groaned. "The homeowners' association," they said in unison.

Francine had dealt with Darla before in this capacity. "Better let her in and head off any trouble now."

Alice opened the door. Darla sashayed in with her clipboard and an iPad. "Hi, Alice." Then she noticed the others. "Well, it's probably best you're all here together." She exhaled noisily, like this was an unpleasant thing she needed to get out of the way. "Can we sit down?"

"Sure. Would you like some tea?"

"No, I won't be here that long. Thanks anyway."

Alice indicated the front room. Francine couldn't help but remember that fourteen hours ago they were sitting in this very room waiting for the police to arrive. It felt less ominous in the daylight without whirling red and blue lights shining in the windows, but Darla's visit was likely to stir up more trouble. She was the perfect homeowners' association president, since she liked to be in everyone's business. Those who had been on the receiving end of a visit, however, had a different opinion.

"If it were up to me," Darla said, "I wouldn't be here. It's not like you *intentionally* violated the homeowners' agreement. But I've gotten lots of calls, and I want to be able to say that we've talked about it."

Charlotte took a seat. "About what? The dead body? I don't think there's anything about dead bodies in the homeowners' agreement."

"Technically, there is. Don't you remember the roadkill clause we added a year ago? We had to put it in when Denise Faulkenberg hit that squirrel and the furry thing made it up to her lawn before it died? She wouldn't touch it and birds pecked at it for three days?"

"I recall the incident," Alice said, "but I hardly see how it applies."

"The membership overwhelmingly approved the idea that a dead carcass on a homeowner's property must be removed within twenty-four hours of its death."

Francine could scarcely believe what she was hearing. "This was a dead body, Darla, not some unfortunate woodland creature trampled on the street. Alice didn't even know it was there."

"Technically," Charlotte added, "we don't know yet how long Friederich had been dead. She might not be in violation."

"Look, I'm on Alice's side here. But as the president of the Summer Ridge Homeowners' Association, I'm required to report back that I've talked to you about it and that you've received your first warning."

"Warning?" Alice was incredulous.

"I guess this means you'll get no leeway for the next dead body," Charlotte said. "Better check the shed more often."

Darla flipped over a sheet of paper in her clipboard. "That leaves us with two other issues: the public indecency clause and the guest vehicle clause."

"Public indecency? I defy you to prove that one!" Alice said.

Darla pushed a few buttons on her iPad, then turned it around so they could see it. "You admitted it. We don't need pictures."

Charlotte moved closer to the little screen. "Is that the *Indianapolis Star*?"

Darla turned it back around. "In tablet format, yes. 'Skinny-dipping Grandmas Find Body.' But it's not just the *Star*. It's all over the Internet."

"Joy will be so happy!" Charlotte told Francine.

"The vast majority of my callers were not. And then you gave guided tours of the crime scene, which brought traffic to a halt in the subdivision. While it wasn't strictly a party, it did have a party-like atmosphere and there were too many guest cars on the street, which is the heart of the problem. You're not allowed to stage that kind of an event without written permission from your neighbors."

"Her neighbors were here all morning," said Charlotte. "Including you. I think that's implied consent."

"I'm not saying it wasn't kind of exciting to be here. I'm saying the traffic flow was an issue when your neighbors needed to get out."

"What neighbor needed to get out?"

"My daughter, for one. She had to get to the gym for a session with her personal trainer. In the end, I let her walk over to a friend's house where she could catch a ride. Sara has to get ready for Speed-Fest, you know."

This was news to Francine. Sara Baggesen was sixteen and a handful. Though Francine knew Sara raced midget cars, she also knew that Sara's father, Darla's ex-husband Vince, didn't allow her to her to race in nationally televised events. Francine wondered if he was still Sara's mechanic. She was fairly sure the SpeedFest race would be on TV.

Alice waved her hands dismissively. "I'm sorry, but it's really not my fault. I didn't invite all those people to come."

"You let them in. I don't see a difference. I came over to talk to you when Sara tried to drive out, but you weren't here. Charlotte said you were with the police at Friederich's garage. What were you doing there?"

"My lawyer advises that I not talk about it."

"That sounds ominous."

"It's not what you might think. But I'm not going to talk about it."

Darla sat there for a moment deciding how to proceed. "The important thing is—and I always say this to first-time offenders—warnings are just a way to make sure everyone knows what's expected so it doesn't happen again."

"I was one of the first people to move into this subdivision thirty years ago. We've been neighbors for what, fifteen years, Darla? I've seen Sara grow up, for heaven's sake. This is the first murder in the subdivision. I think it's safe to say the likelihood is small that there will be another one in the next thirty years."

"I certainly hope so. You don't seem like the type who would attract dead bodies on a regular basis. And that's what I told the neighbors who called."

"Thanks for the vote of confidence."

"You're welcome." Darla removed a sheaf of papers from her clipboard and handed them to Alice. "I'll just leave these with you then. You can fill them out anytime, but I'll need your action plan before the next homeowners' association meeting."

While Alice was still sputtering, Darla let herself out.

"Action plan?" Alice's face turned a purplish-red.

"Next time she's not getting the tour for free," Charlotte said, straining to see the papers Darla had handed her.

Alice threw the papers on the floor and burst into tears.

"Don't you mind her," Francine said, rushing to provide comfort. "Darla's just a first-class busybody."

"Is everything okay down here?" Jonathan descended the stairs carrying an inch-thick folder of what looked to be memos and ledger paper. He stepped into the front room.

The women looked up, startled, having forgotten he was in the house.

Francine was first to recover. "I'll tell you about it on the way home."

"Do you have what you need?" Alice asked.

He held up the folder. "It's all here."

Charlotte stared at it for a moment, then maneuvered to her feet. She started across the room. "What is it you have in there?"

Francine intercepted her on the way. "Let me walk you to your car."

"It's okay. I can manage it."

"No, I insist. Jonathan and I are headed out anyway." She took Charlotte by the arm, knowing it was best to leave her no alternative.

The three of them said good-bye and made their way outside. Charlotte's eyes never left Jonathan's folder. "Now don't forget, if you need my help, you just call."

"I won't. Forget, that is," he added dryly.

They reached Charlotte's car, a big black Buick she'd had for nearly fifteen years. She gripped the car door for balance and lowered herself into the driver's seat. "Let's talk later," she said. "I'll have lots of questions." She closed the door and started the car.

I bet you will, thought Francine. She and Jonathan walked hand in hand back home. Charlotte's car passed them and Francine waved, but the wave was not returned.

So Charlotte is ticked. She'll get over it.

"Do you need to go to the office this afternoon?" she asked Jonathan.

He squeezed her hand. "No, I think I'll use the time to review these records. And to watch Larry's video."

"What video?"

"Larry keeps his surveillance video archives in his home office. I didn't tell Jud. I copied a week's worth of data off the hard drive to a blank DVD."

"You didn't!"

"I did."

"What will Larry say if he finds out you did that?"

"He texted me privately and asked me to do it. He wants to know as much as anyone what's on there."

EIGHT

FRANCINE AND JONATHAN WERE famished by the time they got home. The crime scene tour fiasco with Charlotte, the trip to Friederich's garage with the police, and the homeowners' association incident with Darla had pushed them way past lunchtime. They threw together a midday meal of ham sandwiches, baked potato chips, and grapes and took their plates upstairs to the sitting area off their master bedroom. Not a big believer in television, Francine only had two places where TV could be watched: the sitting room and the great room. The sitting room was intimate and perfect for just the two of them, while the great room could hold a crowd watching a sporting event.

Francine balanced the plate on her lap after propping her feet up on the ottoman. She nibbled at the sandwich. Jonathan put the DVD into the player and returned to the love seat, mimicking her position. He aimed the remote at the television. A split screen with four panels, just as they'd seen at Friederich's shop, filled the display. The top left showed what the camera at the front of the garage had recorded; the top right revealed the back lot; the bottom left held the front of the shop; and the bottom right the back end of the shop. A time stamp had also been embedded in the video display. The date was a week ago Saturday, the fourteenth of July, at eight a.m.

"Based on what you deduced from Jud, I started the copy a week before we think Friederich disappeared," Jonathan said. "It's the weekend, and I'm pretty sure Friederich doesn't work weekends at his regular job. It shouldn't be long before he gets here." He crunched on a couple of chips.

"I didn't know he had a regular job."

"He works—worked—for Excalibur Racing as their chief mechanic."

There was no activity on three of the split screens. The one at the front of the building showed cars passing by. Jonathan fast-forwarded.

"Whoa, wait a minute. There's Friederich," Francine said.

Friederich got out of his vintage Corvette in the upper right panel. Jonathan pressed a button and the recording returned to real time. The time stamp showed it was 9:47 a.m. Friederich vanished from the top right and moments later appeared in the lower left as he went into the shop. He transitioned to the lower right, picking up his coveralls from a hook outside the restroom. He went in and emerged shortly afterward in the coveralls. Because the camera had a wide view, Francine couldn't make out Friederich's face, but she could tell his full attention was on one of the racing cars on the stands. He worked on the area where the right front tire would be located.

They watched him work for two or three minutes.

"Do you know what he's doing?" Francine asked.

"Something with the shock absorber. Let me speed this up."

Friederich worked until about noon, when he received a call on his cell phone. He seemed animated by the call. He went over to a workbench where his tools were stored and organized. Suddenly the entire screen went dark.

Francine and Jonathan sat up.

"A remote?" Francine asked.

"Let's watch it again." He backed the video up to where the call came in and slowed down the action. As Friederich approached the workbench, he picked up something and aimed it at the corner where Larry had hidden the computer that recorded the video input. Almost immediately afterward the darkness hit. The time stamp showed it was three minutes after twelve. Jonathan backed it up one more time, and this time zoomed in on the workbench right as Friederich reached it.

"Look at that," he said, freezing the action.

"It *is* a remote."

"Exactly. We suspected Friederich had one."

He stepped through the sequence until the darkness appeared. The time stamp remained. Jonathan sped through the period of no input until the shop appeared again. Friederich placed the remote back on the bench. It was two thirty. He resumed work on the shock.

"It's like nothing happened," Francine said.

"But something must have, something he didn't want anyone to see. That's a two-and-a-half-hour gap."

Jonathan sped through until shortly before five, when Friederich wiped his hands on a shop towel and then went to the restroom. He returned with his coveralls in hand. He hung them up, then exited the building. The camera feed remained on. The top right panel showed Friederich as he got in the Corvette and drove away.

"I wonder how long he's had a remote?" Francine asked.

"We might be able to answer that by going back further, but we should wait until Larry gets home. I need to get hold of him, tell him what we've seen, and ask what he wants me to do."

"Can we watch the rest of the video?"

"Sure."

They settled back in, finishing their lunch while speeding through the video until Friederich reappeared the next day, Sunday. He got an earlier start, before nine o'clock. This time he had a brown sack with him. He worked on two of the other shocks. After a while, he reached for the sack, but then stopped himself. He reached for the remote and the screen went dark.

"Earlier, this time," Francine said. "Nine thirty."

"Let's see how long it lasts."

Jonathan sped up the video until the feed resumed. "Wow. Much later. It's five in the afternoon." He slowed the video to real time.

"Wait a minute. There's no one there."

Together, they stared at the four panels. Friederich's Corvette was gone. No action on any screen except the one that showed the front lot. A few cars drove past, the light traffic one would expect at that time of day. "How did the cameras come back on?" she said.

"Let me zoom in on the workbench."

Francine watched as he did that. They both searched but saw nothing other than Friederich's organized tools. "It's gone," she said.

"Yep. Whoever unblocked the feed was out of camera range. And that person took the remote with them."

"Jonathan, I'm thinking that there's a reason Larry's pool shed was chosen as the place to leave Friederich's body."

"Because the person who did it knew he could be made to look suspicious?"

"Exactly. And while I hate to sound like Charlotte, if that's the case, the person responsible for Friederich's death may not be finished yet."

The phone rang. Francine got up and looked at the caller ID. "Speak of the devil." She answered the phone.

"You need to come over to Alice's house right away. There's a situation here," Charlotte said.

"Is she having a breakdown?"

"She will if Joy gets her way. She came back from lunch with a reporter in tow."

"I'll be over."

NINE

THIS TIME FRANCINE DROVE her Prius over to Alice's. The situation merited a quick response. *If I had a Transporter Room like on the old* Star Trek *series, Alice's house would be on my "frequently beamed" list,* she thought. Alice opened the door before Francine had climbed the last step. Alice looked like she'd had time to pull herself together. She was dressed in black Michael Kors slacks and a white crewneck top. Her ever-present silver cross necklace glittered against the white fabric. "Thank heavens you're here." She pulled Francine into the foyer, closed the door, and nudged her into the corner where they couldn't be seen from the living room. "I don't know what to do. Joy's hired a public relations consultant."

"Consultant? Charlotte said it was a reporter."

"You know how Charlotte only hears what she wants to hear sometimes."

"I do. Why would Joy hire a PR consultant?"

"Exposure, fame? Who knows? None of us has been able to figure out her need for attention. She wants to use this dead body discovery, combined with our Sixty Lists, to get articles written about us. The consultant even asked me point-blank what was number one on my list."

Francine grimaced. "I'm sorry. I know how protective you are about it." Alice wouldn't tell any of them what her #1 was, not even her best friend Joy. And she wasn't sure how long Joy would continue to be a best friend if she kept up this nonsense.

"The PR consultant thinks we could hit national airwaves with our story."

"Bet the lawyer doesn't like that."

"I haven't told him yet." Alice slipped her hand through the crook of Francine's bent arm. "I'm still hoping we can talk some sense into them."

"With Charlotte involved, that may be difficult. Are they in the living room?"

Alice snorted. "That room's seen more company in the last twenty-four hours than it has in the last twenty-four years. Let's go."

They stepped through the double French doors into the expansive living room.

"There you are," Charlotte said. "I was just telling Marcy here that we've been involved in murder investigations before."

The PR consultant crossed the room, shook Francine's hand, and thrust a business card toward her. "Marcy Rosenblatt. Nice to meet you." She looked Francine up and down.

Like she's trying to decide where to filet me. Since the woman was being rude, Francine assessed her as well. Despite being in her fifties, the woman wore her hair long and straight, down to her shoulders. It was pure black, obviously dyed, and she had bangs that started a good four inches north of her eyebrows and flopped down into her eyelashes. The woman desperately wanted to look young and vital, *desperate* being the operative word.

"I love the big glasses," Marcy said. "Makes you look smart. I hear you're the sensible one in the group. Have a seat, let's talk."

They all sat.

"Tea?" Alice asked.

"Please."

Alice sailed out of the room and into the hall.

Marcy sat next to Joy and, like her, was perched on the couch so that her knees touched the coffee table. *Eager.* "Tell me a little about yourself, Francine. I already know you were the first one in the pool skinny-dipping."

"I was just trying to put everyone at ease. I'm really not an exhibitionist."

"Ha-ha," said Marcy, faking a laugh. "It would be better, though, if you were."

"Better for who?"

"For us. For the publicity," said Joy. "We're trying to think of angles that Marcy can use to get TV shows interested in us."

"I'm not sure this is a good idea. For one thing, it's a murder investigation."

Marcy doodled with her smartphone. "I've already thought of the murder investigation angle. We're maxed out on that one. The *Hendricks County Flyer*, the *Indianapolis Star*, all the local stations. They've all signed on. They'll continue to follow the story until it's resolved. What I'm looking at is the Sixty List thing. I think we can hang the whole campaign on that and get national exposure. Skinny-dipping is fun! It makes a nice place to start. What else was the group planning to do? Or maybe we should look at what you've done in the past."

Joy had a stack of three photo albums sitting in front of her on the coffee table. She picked up one of them. "Well," she said, starting to flip through it.

Marcy's phone rang. "Hold that thought," she said, looking at the phone number. "I've got New York on the phone." She took the call. "This is Marcy. Yes, I represent the skinny-dipping grandmas." She got up and paced. "Uh-huh, uh-huh. *The Today Show* is offering us Hoda and Kathie Lee on their last hour, but we view this as more newsworthy. We'd certainly prefer to work with *Good Morning America*. Can you give us an earlier time slot?"

At first Francine thought she was joking. But as Marcy continued to argue, she realized this might actually be happening.

"Can you be more specific? We'd love between eight thirty and nine. Uh-huh. Uh-huh. No, you'll love them. They're very colorful. They went skinny-dipping, for heaven's sake, and the Convention & Visitors Bureau is trying to get them to do a nude calendar as a county fundraiser. They've still got more than fifty bucket list items each to finish."

Francine stood up, shaking her head. "No, no calendar."

Marcy shushed her. She indicated the cell and listened a bit more. "It's a deal. You'll have a producer from the local affiliate call? Great. We'll get it arranged. Thanks."

Alice came in carrying a cup of tea. Marcy beamed at them. "It's a done deal. You're all going to be on *Good Morning America* tomorrow."

Alice dropped the teacup. It hit the hardwood floor and shattered. Tea and ceramic shards spread everywhere. "*Good Morning America*?"

Francine rushed to clean up the mess because Alice was still staring at Marcy. She headed into the kitchen to get a sponge.

"Ohmigosh!" Joy said, a huge smile evident in her voice. "It's exciting, isn't it?"

Alice's voice pitched high. "No! No, it's not."

Francine grabbed a handful of paper towels and rushed back into the living room. Marcy was tapping her right foot on the floor. Her arms were crossed. "Well, that kind of attitude is not going to get you any subsequent segments."

Joy was delirious with enthusiasm. "Are you serious? It might be a series?"

"No promises. They want to see how tomorrow's segment goes. But they're considering it. Might make a great recurring story about how senior citizens live their lives, having no regrets."

"I have regrets," said Alice. "I regret letting you in the house. Joy, how could you do this?"

"But Alice, this is great exposure. Haven't you ever wanted to be on national television?"

"I don't think I've ever wanted that."

Marcy patted Joy on the shoulder. "I'll leave you to straighten all this out. I've got to make arrangements. We can leverage this into even *more* publicity. I'm thinking we need to do the *GMA* broadcast out by the pool." She turned to Alice. "Make sure you've got your cell phone with you the rest of the afternoon. I'll probably have to show a producer the remote location as soon as national gets this straightened out with the affiliate." Then, to Joy, "Make sure everyone is here by seven tomorrow. I know it's early, but we'll have a lot to go over before we go on at eight thirty. I'll see myself out."

And with that she was gone.

A moment of calm passed as though the women couldn't believe what had just happened. Then they went to work. Francine mopped up the liquid. Charlotte gingerly picked up pieces of the teacup. Joy helped Alice to a chair.

"Sit down," Joy said. "It's going to be all right. Trust me."

Alice was breathing hard. "I don't want to be famous. I don't want people to know my name. Right now, I just want the police to find out who did this horrible thing so that my life can go back to normal."

Charlotte straightened her back while holding on to a couple of bigger shards she'd picked up. "You can't beat national attention for keeping the public interested in figuring out who did it. We'll probably get lots of tips that will lead us to the killer."

Francine held a mass of wet paper towels in her hand. "You mean lead the *police* to the killer. The only thing we're likely to get with national exposure is more visits from Darla telling us it's a violation of our homeowners' agreement." She headed out toward the kitchen, cupping one hand under the paper towel to keep it from dripping on the floor.

"You and Alice need a new outlook," Charlotte said, following her.

The other rooms in Alice's house may have had kitschy themes, but the kitchen was modern all the way, with stainless-steel appliances, quartz countertops, and a big preparation island in the middle. Francine had no shortage of commercial-like trash cans to dump the soggy towel into. "No, you need to get a grip on what's happening here. This isn't a book you're reading. This is a real murder investigation."

Charlotte moved carefully across the hardwood floor without her cane. "Someone knows something. Media attention will encourage that person to talk." She dropped the broken teacup pieces into the same trash container.

"It's more likely to bring out the cranks. The police will probably get plenty of false leads from people who believe in conspiracy theories rather than real leads. If anything, it'll slow them down."

"If that happens, it'll be all the more important for us to solve the crime."

"If that happens, it'll be all the more important for us to support Alice. It's possible someone is trying to frame her husband."

"What are you saying, Francine?"

"I can't tell you what I know, so don't ask that. But Jonathan says Larry could be made to look suspicious. Maybe even more than he looks now. If that happens, it will be hard on Alice. She'll need us."

Charlotte grinned triumphantly. "What she'll need is for us to solve the crime! It's the only way to protect her and Larry. I've got some ideas on how to gather background information too. Let's go back out and talk with the others."

"We are *not* getting involved, other than to support Alice."

"If you're not going to help, Francine, I'll just go around you."

The two women faced each other. Charlotte had a bull-like expression on her face. Francine thought her curly silver wig looked like smoke that had risen out of her nostrils and gathered above her head. "Okay, but we can't let her know what we're going to do. She stays in the dark."

"The first thing we'll do is hold a meeting of the Bridge Club tonight."

"Without Alice," Francine insisted.

"Yes, without Alice. Mary Ruth ought to be available this evening. What are we going to do about the *Good Morning America* interview tomorrow?"

"I'm hoping it won't come off."

Charlotte disagreed. "We either do it voluntarily or they'll show up and ambush Alice. Joy's publicist may have hooked them with the bucket list angle, but trust me, it's the murder that's reeled them in."

"I'm confident Larry's lawyer will have something to say about this."

"Let's just focus on the Bridge Club meeting tonight. We'll have it at my house, say eight o'clock. You persuade Mary Ruth to come, and I'll work on Joy."

Francine grabbed another wad of paper towel as they left the kitchen. When they got back to the living room, Alice was sitting on the couch, her elbows propped on her knees, her head in her hands. Joy was gone.

Francine put an arm around her. "Are you all right?"

She didn't remove her head from her hands but made a nodding motion.

Charlotte looked around. "Where's Joy?"

Alice pulled out of her stupor. "I told her it was okay."

"To do the *Good Morning America* interview?"

"It's so important to her. And she's my friend. I couldn't say no. But I told her I won't appear on camera, and they have to stick to the bucket list angle. That's the only way we'll get it past the lawyer anyway. She's gone to talk to the publicist about it."

"Have you even talked to the lawyer?" Francine asked.

"I'm going to call him after I get his name and number from Larry."

"Do you need us to stay?"

"No, thank you. Really, I just need to be alone."

"You've made a good decision to let *Good Morning America* come," Charlotte said. "It'll help us—I mean, the police—figure out who did it."

Francine glared at her. "We'll be leaving then." She stood up and put a hand on Charlotte's back. "Won't we?"

"If you say so."

"Call me if you need me," Francine told Alice.

"Or me," added Charlotte.

Alice leaned back into the couch and put her forearm across her forehead. "I will," she said, but Francine thought it did not sound sincere.

"I hope you don't come to regret what you said," Francine said, when she finally got Charlotte out of the house.

"About what?"

"About it being a good decision to let *Good Morning America* in."

"It's a morning show. How bad can it be?"

"Once you let the genie out of the bottle …"

"You are such a naysayer, Francine."

Francine sighed audibly as they headed down the sidewalk toward their cars.

TEN

When Francine knocked on Charlotte's door that night for the Summer Ridge Bridge Club meeting, she was greeted by an eye checking her out through the peephole. Francine understood. It had been a difficult afternoon. If she wasn't so tired, she'd have found it difficult to believe not twenty-four hours had passed since they found the dead body.

The door creaked open, and Charlotte hustled Francine in, shutting the door behind her. "Can you believe the promos for our *Good Morning America* appearance were running by the evening news?" Charlotte said. "It's been nonstop madness since."

"I wouldn't answer the phone after the first one ran."

Charlotte beckoned her into the family room, slid back a red paisley curtain panel, and peered out. "I guess so. I must've left a hundred messages for you."

"Didn't you get the phone call from Jud not to say anything? It wasn't long after that the phone started ringing off the hook. I didn't recognize the numbers, so I stopped checking to see who was calling."

"It wasn't just the phone calls that bothered me. It was the reporters who camped outside my house. At least they're gone now." She straightened the curtain.

Charlotte's house was one of the smaller ones in the subdivision, a three-bedroom ranch with a small family room to the right off the front hall, the kitchen and dining room straight ahead, and a screened-in porch off the back past the dining room. She led Francine to the right toward the bedrooms.

"Joy says Darla Baggesen was out at her house telling the reporters it was against the homeowners' agreement to park on both sides of the street and narrow traffic to one lane," Francine said. "They didn't pay much attention, but they did try to interview her. I'm guessing what she told them won't make it past the censors."

Charlotte had long ago transformed the third bedroom of her home into a library. Well-organized shelves full of alphabetized books lined the walls from floor to ceiling. They were all mysteries or thrillers.

But the room was not tidy. A dozen partially-read books lay open, scattered throughout the room. Sticky notes protruded from their pages. Francine had to move one off the padded rocking chair she usually sat in.

Charlotte pulled a thin white cardigan around her. "Do you want any brandy? I feel like I need a nip of it."

Francine debated whether it was the coolness of the air conditioned room or the bizarre day that fueled the brandy comment. She wasn't crazy about brandy—it burned all the way down her throat. But she knew Charlotte wouldn't drink alone. If she took a tiny bit for herself she could always knock it back if the others showed up early. She was fifteen minutes ahead of the agreed-upon eight o'clock meeting. "I'll pour us each a little. You just have a seat."

She went to the liquor cabinet, took out a couple of crystal aperitif glasses, and poured a tiny amount into hers, then a bit more in Charlotte's, while her friend eased herself into her favorite reading chair, an apricot-colored recliner. It was getting threadbare but was still the most comfortable chair in the house. Charlotte thought the apricot added a splash of color against the dark blue flowered wallpaper. Francine would have ditched the wallpaper two decades ago.

She distributed the brandy glasses and took a seat in the rocker. In spite of all that had happened that day, she relaxed. Just being in a familiar place with a friend felt good. "Are you really going to go through with it?"

"With what?"

"The *Good Morning America* interview tomorrow. You know how nervous you get when someone shoves a microphone in front of you."

"Pshaw." Charlotte took a swallow of the brandy. "Joy's going to do all the talking, which is good because she can really talk. Besides, I'm better than I used to be about stuff like that."

Francine doubted the latter, but she did hope that Joy would do the talking. "Still, don't overburden your digestive system in the morning. Okay?"

Charlotte didn't answer the question but picked up an open notebook and pen sitting on top of an open mystery book. "I've been looking at this Friederich Guttmann murder from different angles, trying to figure out who could have wanted him dead. Larry is hardly the best candidate."

Francine touched the glass to her lips and pretended to sip. "I agree about Larry. We've known them since they moved in a couple decades ago. Seems like we'd have noticed something odd about him if he were the killer type."

"I've been looking to draw a parallel with one of the cozy mysteries I read sometimes. They almost always have a killer you'd never suspect. Although, I can usually spot them from the beginning now."

"The papers seem to favor Larry. Either him or Jake Maehler."

"Jake Maehler is more likely in my opinion. Here's a guy who became a NASCAR driver, gets branded a loser because he can't finish in the top ten anywhere, and returns to Brownsburg. His back is against the wall. He's desperate. And he had a dustup with Friederich two weeks ago."

Francine had done a little research that afternoon, so she knew about it. The sports section of the *Hendricks County Flyer* had covered it extensively at the time. Jake had wrecked at the Night Before the 500 race in May and blamed Friederich's work. "But they patched things up. They announced they were going to work together at SpeedFest."

"You realize that announcement was just Thursday? Friederich disappeared on Saturday. It might have been a ruse."

Francine took her first sip, a tiny one. "Or someone didn't like their decision to keep working together."

"I do like the way you think. That's another good angle. You've hardly touched your brandy. Don't you like it?"

The doorbell rang. Francine looked at the glass. The others were probably here, and she didn't like them seeing her drink outside of dinner. She tilted her head and drank it down. It burned, making her cough. "I'll get the door," she choked out. "I assume we're going to meet in here."

"Thanks, Francine. It saves me from having to get up and come back."

She took her aperitif glass and detoured to the kitchen to set it in the sink before she answered the door. Mary Ruth, Joy, and Alice were on the doorstep together.

"Why is the door locked?" Mary Ruth said, breathing heavily. "I rushed up the sidewalk thinking I was late and tried to get in, but the door wouldn't open."

"You had a catering event today, didn't you?" Francine answered. "The rest of us have been hounded by reporters all afternoon. Jonathan and I hid upstairs in his office, but they still didn't leave until Jud showed up and told them to disperse."

"It was awful," Alice said.

"It was wonderful," said Joy. She looked at Alice. "Sorry. I know it was awful for you."

Francine wondered how Alice had learned of the meeting. "I didn't think you'd be coming," she said. "You have a lot to deal with."

"All the more reason to be here. Plus, I need to talk to all of you."

Mary Ruth handed Francine a small square cake. "Here, this is my famous flourless chocolate cake. I made an extra one for the event today but didn't need it." She stepped into the house, flapping her arms and trying to get a breeze going under her pink *Mary Ruth's Catering* t-shirt.

Joy tapped Mary Ruth on the shoulder. "You're available tomorrow morning, aren't you? *Good Morning America* is going to interview all of us at Alice's pool near the scene of the crime."

Mary Ruth's stared in fear. "I don't think so!"

"It won't be so bad," Joy said, taking her by the arm. "Alice can't be on because of the lawyer, but the rest of us will be there. It's not so much about the murder as it is about the skinny-dipping and our Sixty Lists."

"That's supposed to make me feel better?"

The two walked back to the library, Joy speaking soothingly. She must have been effective because by the time Francine took the cake to kitchen and got back to the library, Mary Ruth had agreed to participate.

The five women sat in a circle, the latecomers having unpacked folding chairs from the library closet. Joy, as president of the group, tried several times to start the meeting but everyone kept talking. Just as she got the group quiet, Alice interrupted.

"I'm sorry, but I've got something I've got to get off my chest and if I don't do it right now I think I might burst." They all leaned in a little closer. "Larry hasn't been in Las Vegas, like he said. He came back on Saturday, and he's been staying in a hotel on the east side of Indianapolis. The police located him an hour ago. He's down at the police station with his lawyer." She burst into tears.

ELEVEN

THE ROOM WAS DEATHLY quiet but for Alice's sobs.

Finally Joy spoke up. "You ... didn't know this?"

Alice tried to talk but the tears kept flowing. She shook her head.

The women acted on reflex. Joy went to comfort Alice. Charlotte went to get her a glass of water. Mary Ruth went to get some tissues. Francine began massaging Alice's shoulders.

"How did you find out?" Francine asked.

She took a minute to pull herself together. "He called me from the police station. Told me not to come down. Whispered a few excuses. Said he'd try to explain it later."

"I bet that middle part really hurt," Charlotte said. She set the glass next to Alice. "Why would he not want you to come down?"

The remark made her start her crying again. Francine glared at Charlotte while they waited for Alice to become calm. Mary Ruth came back, yanked out a couple of tissues, and handed them to

Alice, who wiped her eyes. "I don't know. Would the police even let me see him?"

"Did he say he was arrested?" Charlotte wanted to know. "If he wasn't arrested, he doesn't have to stay for questioning. He can just walk away."

"He didn't say."

Francine tried to mentally step back from the situation so she could analyze it. From what little she knew about the law, Charlotte was right. If Larry was only being questioned, he didn't have to answer. He could just walk away. Larry had his lawyer there, though. What did that mean? She hoped it meant he was getting good advice.

Charlotte was still talking. "I know it looks really bad, Alice, but I don't think you should leap to conclusions. You haven't heard his side of it." It was surprisingly sympathetic of her to make the point, and it would have stayed that way had she stopped. "Of course, the fact that Larry came back the day Friederich disappeared makes me want to connect the dots. But it doesn't have to be that. He could just be an accessory to the crime."

To which Alice resumed crying.

Francine steered Charlotte out of the library.

"I know what you're going to say," Charlotte said when they were out in the hall, "but it's true. It would be better if he was guilty of something other than murder."

"Accessory isn't a lot better."

"Well, he's guilty of something. You don't do stuff like that unless you have something to hide."

"While I agree with that, we don't need to go announcing it in front of Alice. We're her friends. We're supposed to lift her up, give her hope."

"She knows what we're all thinking."

"Not unless she reads minds."

Joy came out into the hall. She shut the door to the library behind her. "Thanks for nothing, Charlotte. Alice is now talking about backing out of the *GMA* interview tomorrow."

"How can *she* back out? *She's* not going to be on camera."

"She's talking about not letting anyone onto her property tomorrow. We're supposed to film by the pool."

Francine wanted to scream. Was no one thinking about poor Alice?

"We could film in front of the police station," Charlotte suggested. Then she thought a moment. "No, that might cause Jud to go crazy on us. What if we set up in front of Matthew's Funeral Home? Do we know where the funeral's going to be?"

Joy paced in the hall. "Might work. Or we could do it at a church. Did Friederich go to church? Who would know that?"

The door to the library opened and Mary Ruth's head popped out. "With no help from you, I've managed to calm Alice down. She wants to talk to us all together." She nodded her head in Alice's direction.

They filed back into the room. Charlotte regained the apricot chair, but the rest stood. Tissues littered the floor around Alice. She blew her nose with a fresh one.

"Charlotte's comment reminds me that I'm not necessarily telling you the whole truth as I know it," Alice began. "At first, I didn't want to tell you this because it made Larry look like a suspect. Now I guess that doesn't matter."

"What didn't you want to tell us?" Charlotte asked, surreptitiously retrieving her notebook and pen from the end table.

"Six months ago Larry threatened to throw Friederich out of the garage space."

"Why? And what made him not follow through?"

She took a deep breath and closed her eyes. "Friederich was having money problems. At least that's Larry's take. At the time he was way behind on the rent. Larry told me he was thinking about taking Friederich to small claims court, maybe try to garnish his wages."

"That would take a court order," Charlotte agreed, making notes.

Alice shrugged. "I don't know why Larry put up with it. He should have just dumped him and written off the rent. But with the economy being bad, Larry said he doubted he could get another tenant, and he hoped to work it out with Friederich. Really, it's one of our lesser properties. I don't think Larry paid much attention to it."

"So he never sent an eviction notice?"

"Not that I know of."

"Did Friederich ever start paying again?"

"I don't know. Larry never brought it up."

Charlotte turned to Francine. "Jonathan is his accountant. Wouldn't he know about this?"

She lifted one eyebrow. "You know I can't comment on things that are client confidential."

Mary Ruth squatted into a folding chair. "I wonder if the police know about Friederich being behind on the rent. It makes sense that they would want to question Larry if they discovered that."

"They didn't know until earlier today. Jud tricked me into talking about the incident. He called about an hour before Larry did, and what he said made me think he knew. So I let it all out. Now I'm not sure he knew at all."

Charlotte chuckled. "That Jud, he's a good bluffer. You could tell him a flying saucer just landed in Arbuckle Acres and he'd act like his department filed the flight plan. You never know if he really knows anything or not."

"They'd probably been over to Friederich's house and gotten the information there," said Francine soothingly. "All they'd need to find would be a checkbook or his computer files to figure out he wasn't paying Larry."

Charlotte put down her pen. "I hadn't thought about Friederich's house. We need to get in there."

"We can't do that!" Mary Ruth said. They all looked at her. "I mean, I'm sure it's illegal."

Charlotte waggled her eyebrows. "Not if there's no crime scene tape barring the door. And anyway, if Jud is prying information out of Alice to gain circumstantial evidence pointing the finger of guilt at Larry, we should be able to access Friederich's house to prove otherwise."

"And just how do you think you're going to get in there?" Joy asked.

"I have connections," Charlotte replied. "Just leave it to me. Remember what's at stake here."

"So, what is at stake, anyway?" Mary Ruth said. "Sure, the police are investigating Larry and Alice, but they're innocent, or at least Alice is. This is all about *you* solving a mystery, isn't it?"

Charlotte sat back, affronted by the accusation. "We all know of cases where justice has been perverted."

"No we don't. Not personally. And you only think there's a lot of it going on because of those creepy thrillers you read."

"How about we have some cake?" Francine stood up, hoping to defuse the tension.

"It's my cake," Mary Ruth said.

"Yes, it is," she replied. "It's your wonderful flourless chocolate cake."

"Make sure you wash your hands before you cut into it."

Francine took a deep breath before she responded. "We need to have some cake and cool off, but let me make this observation before we do. As bad as it sounds, it's not just a murder that's been committed. It may well be that the killer is not through yet. He may be actively working to frame Larry. Jonathan and I have reason to believe that."

"Really?" Mary Ruth said, sounding doubtful. "You need to stop encouraging Charlotte like this. You have some kind of proof?"

"I hate to be mysterious about this, but I can't say more until Jonathan talks to Larry."

"That could be awhile," Charlotte said. "In the meantime, the more we do to uncover the real facts of this case, the sooner the police will be able to find whoever killed Friederich. I have a plan. After everyone gets cake and coffee, I'll lay it out. Then we can discuss it."

TWELVE

THE MEETING OF THE Summer Ridge Bridge Club moved from the library to the dining room table, where Francine had to stack randomly scattered mystery novels to clear enough room to cut the cake. "Research," Charlotte told her, though Francine thought it was just an excuse; the table always looked that way. Charlotte made coffee. When everyone had their plates and cups, the five women took their seats at the round table just big enough for four.

Charlotte didn't let too much cake disappear before she spoke up. "We need to get this underway before anyone lapses into a chocolate stupor." She unfolded a map of the neighborhood on the table and forced the women to move their food. "You'll all recognize this as our Summer Ridge subdivision."

The map was an old one from when the subdivision was in the development phase. The semicircular Summer Ridge Drive, which bounded most of the subdivision, was the dominant feature. The smaller Trail Ridge Court, where Charlotte lived, ran beside the southern section of Summer Ridge. Charlotte had scribbled all over the map in red ink. "I've noted on each lot the name of the family who lives there," she said, pointing to the map, "and if the house is being rented, who the owner is."

"What's the blue circle mean?" Francine asked.

"It means Toby recorded that person as having come to check out the crime scene."

Francine smoothed out one side of the map that was trying to curl. Charlotte placed her empty cake plate on the corner to hold it down. "Remember my observation that the killer always returns to the scene of the crime. The thirty-eight names you see circled constitute our best set of suspects."

Mary Ruth looked at Charlotte over her reading glasses. "Your *observation*?"

Francine put up a hand. "I don't want us to quibble about this. Yes, Charlotte has *not* had a lot of experience. But she did solve her uncle's murder *and* she reads a lot of mysteries. Whatever her plan is, it's as good as any we have right now. Besides, it makes sense that the killer could have come back to see what, if anything, the police found. He would naturally be curious. With the police scrambling to find clues and a motive, a killer would feel safe returning as a part of an organized tour."

"However unsettling, wouldn't it be exciting if it were someone in our neighborhood?" Joy said.

Charlotte pointed to Larry and Alice's house, which was on the corner where Summer Ridge Drive turned west. "I've been over the logic before, but maybe it's better if we all see it. Here's where Larry and Alice live. If it was someone from outside the subdivision, why not plant the body in a house closer to the entrance? Or better yet, why not drop it in a field on the way out toward Pittsboro?" She moved her hand well off the map in a westerly direction. "Who's going to find it until fall? One possible reason would be because they needed to put the body somewhere quickly and the shed was not likely to be used for a while. But that says two things: one, it was someone who lived in the neighborhood; and two, it was someone who knew Larry and Alice didn't use the pool much. Am I not right on this?"

There was a general murmur of agreement.

"But," Francine said, "it could also be premeditated, that the killer wanted to frame Larry, which would also explain the choice of the shed. That would mean that they knew Larry was renting the garage to Friederich, and that he'd threatened to throw Friederich out."

"I don't know that it means they live in our neighborhood," Mary Ruth said. "Lots of people know Larry, especially since he's so active in the community. And if the purpose is to frame him, they could have come from anywhere."

"Good point. But it still doesn't account for their knowledge of the pool shed, which any neighbor would know about but a casual observer wouldn't because of the privacy fence. So, it would have to be someone who knew Larry and Alice well enough that they had been invited to the house and knew about the shed." She turned to Charlotte. "You said you had a plan?"

"Wait a minute," Joy said. "I don't mean to complicate things, but what if the killer had help? I mean, it could be someone *inside* the neighborhood helping someone *outside*."

Charlotte blew out a breath. "Well, that would complicate matters. We'll just have to keep alert to that possibility as we unravel the mystery thread by thread. Here's what we know: In addition to reneging on the agreement he had with Larry, Friederich also was recently blasted in public by Jake Maehler, the midget driver."

"I keep telling you, he races midget cars," Mary Ruth said. "He's not a midget."

Francine choked back a laugh. Someone snickered.

Charlotte glared at her. "Okay! Point taken. Maybe you'd like to tell the rest of the story?"

"Well, I know racing a little better than you, but go ahead."

Charlotte bristled but continued. "Jake and Friederich had a long history. Friederich took Jake from a competitive fifteen-year-old racer to a big name in midget car racing, which then earned Jake a NASCAR development contract. Except that he hasn't been doing so well there. So he hooked up with Friederich again to help him get back to his winning ways. Then the midget car Friederich built for him had issues on the final laps of the Night Before the 500 race, and Jake went from first to fifth. Jake was really PO'd. Financially, he needs to be seen as a winner to keep his sponsors happy and to stay on the NASCAR circuit. Publicly, they made up. Friederich was supposedly rebuilding the car for him to race at SpeedFest. But there may still have been a lot of tension between them." She took a breath. "We need more inside information. Francine, you know Crystal the Pistol?"

"Yes, but how is that important?"

"Crystal's son is Jake's personal trainer. The papers said Jake and his trainer are pretty tight. So he probably knows something. We need for you to get to Jake's trainer."

Francine frowned. "Through his mom?"

"It's the best we have. And don't you go to the same gym Jake does?"

"When he's in town. I've seen him *maybe* a couple of times. I have no idea when he works out."

"Crystal might. Or she can find out."

"I don't know about this, Charlotte. Even if I can get to him, the trainer may not talk to me."

"Sure, he will. People love to show off how much they know. Especially when it comes to the famous—or in this case, nearly famous. It's all in how you approach him."

Francine grumbled, but she knew how Charlotte could get. "I'll try."

"That's the spirit. Now, another thing we need is to figure out is who in the neighborhood has a connection to Friederich, other than Larry. Any ideas?"

Francine collected the empty dishes that weren't holding down the map and took them into the kitchen. She already had one more assignment than she wanted. She knew if she waited them out, someone would come up with an idea. No one in the group could go very long without talking.

Mary Ruth spoke first. "This is kind of self-serving, but hear me out. Brownsburg has a lot of people working in the motor sports business now that Eaglepoint business park is attracting racing-related companies from all over the country. A number of people in our subdivision work in the racing business or are connected to people in the racing business. I think it's possible any of them could have known Friederich in some way."

Joy picked up Toby's list. "There are thirty-eight names on this list from the neighborhood. You want us to ask each of them if they knew Friederich?"

"Well, actually, yes. These racing companies have money. They hire caterers to handle their parties and serve them food at Lucas Oil Raceway. I'd like to capture some of that business for myself. Perhaps if we invited neighbors to a luncheon that featured my food but was themed around neighborhood security, we could use it to gather information about the neighbors and who might have known Friederich—"

Charlotte snatched the list. "That's brilliant, Mary Ruth. Most of these people want to gossip about the murder, or else they wouldn't have been at Alice's house for the tour. We'd get good attendance on just the hint that the murder would be talked about. If they were able to come in the middle of the day to see the murder scene, they'd probably be available for lunch."

"The problem is where to have it. I can't accommodate that many people at my house."

Charlotte's face swung toward Alice.

"Oh, no, not my house. We've had enough going on there."

"Then we'll do it at Francine's."

Francine had the deer-in-the-headlights look. "My house?"

"Next to Alice, you have the biggest house. Plus, you've got experience. You've hosted lots of Sunday school parties with that many people. We'll just expand onto the deck if we have to."

"I'm not sure we can throw it together that fast."

"Sure we can." Mary Ruth peeled a sticky note off a stash Charlotte kept in the kitchen and began to write on it. "Today is Monday. We can have the luncheon on Wednesday. If I fax in an order tonight, my supplier can deliver food tomorrow. We won't get the full thirty-eight neighbors, but I'll bet we get twenty-five. That's a high percentage."

"I don't know if I can get the house clean in time."

"Oh, please, Francine," Charlotte said, interrupting. "Dust bunnies are an endangered species at your house. It would pass a Board of Health inspection on an hour's notice."

"That's not true. And Jonathan—"

"Jonathan will grump about it, but in the end he'll do what you ask. He doesn't even have to be there if he doesn't want. He can hide out at work."

"Well…"

"Can we all agree we'll help Francine put this on?" Charlotte held up her hand like she was asking for volunteers.

The others were extraordinarily agreeable since it wasn't at *their* house.

"See?" she said. "We'll all help. Just make sure Jonathan knows who's catering. He'll be okay with it."

"To make this legitimate, someone should invite the police to talk about a neighborhood crime watch program," Francine said. The women nodded in agreement. "I nominate Charlotte to contact them."

"Good idea," said Alice. "She's always calling them anyway."

"That's not true…"

"I have a question for you, Alice," Joy said.

"What is it?"

"Who would know Larry had rented that garage to Friederich? It didn't seem to be general knowledge. If I understand correctly, the police didn't know until Larry told them."

"Good point. I'm not sure how many people even knew we *owned* that building. We bought it ten years ago as an investment, but no one seemed interested in renting it. Larry finally had to close it up to stop the minor vandalism. I guess he took the For Rent sign down when Friederich leased the building, but I'm not sure anyone noticed. I didn't."

"Neither did I," said Charlotte, "and I must cut through there fifteen times a day to avoid the stoplight at the corner. That's a great observation. Larry was being secretive. How would someone find out who owned the property and who had rented it?"

"What are you two getting at?" Francine asked.

"Think about it. If Larry is being framed, then either the person who killed Friederich knew him well enough to ask him who he rented the garage from, or that person had to dig out the information. If they did, then how did they do it? They would have left some kind of trail, wouldn't they?"

"Isn't Larry active in the Chamber of Commerce? Would someone there know what rental properties he had available?"

"So someone could have asked at the Chamber," Charlotte said. "Joy, you're the reporter. Could you find out if anyone did, and if so, who it was?"

"Okay, but not until after we do the *GMA* appearance tomorrow. And you all will be there, won't you?"

Mary Ruth looked horror-stricken. "I don't have to say anything, right? I mean, you promised..."

"I walked through this with the producer this afternoon, and I think I may be the only one talking."

Mary Ruth still seemed hesitant.

"It's all good," Joy assured her.

"I guess," she said.

"Don't forget now! We need to be there by seven a.m."

"At least we'll get it over early," said Mary Ruth. "I can get back to my kitchen and work on the luncheon in peace."

Francine hoped for all of their sakes it would go like that. But ever since Friederich's body fell out of the shed, nothing had been quite like she'd expected.

THIRTEEN

Francine and Charlotte arrived at Alice's house at exactly the same time the next morning, ten before seven. Charlotte seemed to be much more excited than Francine. "Do you think we'll get to see that handsome George Stephanopoulos?" she asked.

Francine rang the doorbell. "Not in Brownsburg, Charlotte. He'll just be a face on this little television monitor like you see him every morning."

"Of course I know George won't be here in person. I meant, do you think we'll get to talk to him?"

"Not likely. I think Joy will do all the talking. Good thing, as far as I'm concerned. I don't even want to be seen. I'm only doing this for Joy."

"We're *all* only doing this for Joy." Charlotte stepped back and regarded Francine. "You shouldn't have worn that yellow sundress if you didn't want to be noticed. You look smashing in it."

"Thanks. I wonder what's taking Alice so long to answer the door." She rang the doorbell again and this time added a knock.

"They say the camera adds ten pounds. I wore a girdle under this to counteract that. It's pretty tight."

Francine took a critical look at Charlotte. She was wearing a white dress with red and blue polka dots on it. She'd seen it on her before, but now it hung more loosely on her frame. "How tight did you make that girdle?"

Charlotte bit her lip. "I don't look good?"

"No, you look fine. The dress fits well. I only worry because…" Francine contemplated how to tell her the girdle was so tight she was afraid either Charlotte would pass out or the girdle would give out. Both would make for bad TV. Before she said anything, the door opened and Joy stood there. She was wearing the same sundress as Francine, only in a lime green pattern.

Joy's eyes narrowed on Francine's dress. "I worried this might happen. We shop at too many of the same places. Fortunately I brought a change of outfits." She spun on the ball of her foot and marched into the foyer. Francine followed with Charlotte behind her.

"It'll be fine," Francine said. She glanced around. "Where's Alice? How is she doing this morning? Is Larry…? Did he…?"

Joy pulled them closely together. "He came home last night. They had words, and he slept in the blue bedroom. That's all Alice would tell me. He left early this morning because he didn't want to run into Jud or any reporters."

Charlotte said, "Jud? I didn't know he was coming."

She shrugged. "Coming? He's already here. He showed up on the half hour and chased away everyone but the camera crew."

Francine looked at her watch. "Who else was here this early in the morning?"

"The curious and the paparazzi. They're still here, just moved down the street. You can see them camped out on Darla's second story balcony with binoculars and cameras with long-range lenses."

"Wow," said Charlotte. "After yesterday, I would think Darla would be angry, not helping them."

"Could be she's charging them."

Someone coughed. Francine looked up to see a tall balding man. He coughed again. She wondered if he was trying to get their attention or if he just coughed a lot.

"There you are," he said to Joy. He indicated Francine and Charlotte. "Are they part of your Bridge Club?"

Joy introduced them. "I'm the assistant producer," he said. He looked from Francine to Joy. "Same dress."

"A little snafu," Joy said. "We should have talked about outfits. But I brought a backup."

"Good. Go change now. We need to mike you and run some checks."

"I didn't think we were on for an hour and a half."

"Don't mess this up for me, okay? I don't get to work with the national morning shows that much."

"I'll get on it." Joy marched up the stairs.

"You two, let's get you out by the pool. I was told there would be three of you. Where's the other one?

Francine disliked the way he put his hand on her back and moved her along. "Her name is Mary Ruth, and I'm sure she'll be here soon."

"If not, you'll need to call her." He ushered them through the family room and out the back French doors into the pool area.

Jud had squatted down outside the pool shed where Friederich's body had flopped out. He had a roll of yellow tape in his hands.

Charlotte waved at him. "Jud!"

He looked up for a moment, then returned to taping.

"Well, how do you like that?" Charlotte said. "He's ignoring us. He's a public servant. He can't do that."

"Keep away from him," the associate produced warned. "We need him to re-create the crime scene."

"I thought this was all about the Bridge Club."

"This is a multifaceted story." He looked at his watch. "Where's Joy? I need her here."

Francine was growing tired of his self-important edicts. "You ordered her to change."

"So I did." He broke into a coughing fit. "Go check on her, will you?" He turned away and went to talk to the cameraman.

"Yeah. Go check on her," Charlotte said, mocking.

"Did he give us his name?"

"No."

"I may start referring to him by the first three letters in 'assistant producer.'"

"I'm with you."

Joy came out of house at that moment in a khaki skirt with a light blue polo shirt. She joined them.

"That looks better on you," said Charlotte. "You look more ESPN."

"You think so?"

"That's the kind of thing you would see on trackside reporters at car races."

"I hadn't thought of that. I wonder what their pool crews wear when they cover big swim meets?"

The assistant producer whistled at them and motioned them over. Francine and Joy obeyed but Charlotte hung behind. She turned and started for Jud, but the tight girdle made it difficult to move. Francine heard her cane thunking on the concrete and changed directions herself.

The two reached Jud at the same time. "I thought they only wanted to talk to us skinny-dipping grandmas," Charlotte said.

He continued taping the head of the body's outline. "I was invited. They apparently also want the police perspective on what we're doing to solve the crime."

"So what do you have on Larry?"

"I haven't said anything about anyone."

"You hauled Larry out of a hotel room on the east side and brought him to the police station for questioning. You must have something on him."

"I'm not going to respond to that." He stood up, stretched, and noticed Charlotte's dress. "Have you lost a lot of weight recently?" He sounded concerned.

"It's the dress," Francine said. "Doesn't it look nice?"

He nodded in agreement, but his eyes still held doubt. "Don't you have something to do over there?" He motioned toward the assistant producer.

Francine coaxed Charlotte around and headed her in that direction. "Indeed we do. The ASSistant producer is going to have a heart attack if we don't get over there."

Jud chuckled at her thinly veiled assessment.

Charlotte looked like she was about to resist when Marcy hustled over. Francine hadn't seen her that morning, but from the wetness of Marcy's espadrilles, she guessed the publicist had been in somebody's grass. "What are you two doing?" she asked, waving her hand frantically to emphasize her displeasure. "Are you deliberating trying to sabotage our shot at morning TV? This is the keystone in my PR plan. No *Good Morning America*, and we might as well kiss the spread in *People* magazine good-bye."

"You've got us in *People*?" Charlotte's jaw practically dropped.

"Got them considering it. I'm telling you, we just need this one domino to fall and there's really no stopping the media coverage. But this has got to work."

"Sabotage is certainly tempting," Francine said dryly. "But it means too much to Joy."

Marcy frowned at her. "Let's get back over to the pool area. Kurt is about to go over the details of the shoot." She swept a lock of unruly hair back from her forehead.

Francine looked at her watch. "But it's not even seven thirty yet."

"They need you to be ready to go at eight. They've notified us the segment could come anytime after that. It's a slow news morning. Could work out really well for us."

While Marcy urged them along, Francine saw Darla waving from the second story balcony of her home, which rose above the privacy fence. "Knock 'em dead!" she shouted in encouragement.

"That woman," said Marcy, "is dangerous."

"Only if you break a homeowners' covenant," Charlotte said. "Otherwise she's just annoying."

"No, she and the paparazzi are a wild card. They need to back off until after we've filmed." Marcy smiled a fake smile and waved at the crowd on Darla's balcony. "Just remember what we talked about," she yelled at them.

Catcalls ensued.

"Keep walking and don't look at them."

Joy was snaking a tiny microphone through the front of her polo shirt. The cord was connected to a small transmitter attached to the back of her skirt. "Testing, testing," she said. The cameraman, wearing a headset, nodded.

"Where's Mary Ruth?" Charlotte asked her.

"Don't know. Alice went in to call her. If she doesn't get here soon, we may have to go on without her."

The assistant producer, who Marcy had called Kurt, motioned the women toward the deep end of the pool. They grumbled among themselves.

"Ladies!" he said. "Please be quiet! I want to see all of your eyes looking at me so I know you're listening." The effort of this speech made him cough.

Charlotte groused. "I feel like I'm in second grade."

"Then stop acting like a seven-year-old," Marcy said, giving her a sharp elbow in the side. She felt the tautness of the girdle. "What do you have under your dress?"

Kurt glared at them. "This is the monitor where you'll see the feed from New York." He pointed to a television screen they'd set up. "You won't be able to hear anything, because we don't want feedback. Joy will be your spokesperson. She's equipped with an earpiece so she can hear the anchors and a microphone to respond to them. It would complicate the interview if we miked all of you.

Marcy put on a sunny smile. "Joy will do a fantastic job."

Francine wondered how much the publicist was being paid.

"But I wanted to talk to George Stephanopoulos," Charlotte said.

"That's not possible," Kurt responded.

Mary Ruth came out of the sliding glass doors to the house and rushed over to join the women. The people on Darla's balcony started hooting.

"It's about time you got here," Kurt said.

"I've changed clothes a hundred times. I finally decided to wear black because it's supposed to be slimming on television." She made a twirl to show her black pants and black polo shirt.

The crowd on the balcony continued to be annoying. Marcy motioned for them to calm down.

Kurt tried to keep everyone on task. "You, in the yellow sundress." He pointed at Francine. "Come up here next to Joy."

"Why?"

"Just do it."

"It's because no one in America wants to imagine the rest of us skinny-dipping," Mary Ruth said out loud. "Only you and Joy."

That made Kurt laugh, and he coughed again. He finally cleared his throat. "I want our police detective here," he said, moving to a spot near the shed. "Where's our detective?"

"He's in the house, talking with the lawyer," said Mary Ruth.

"When did he go in there? Has he finished taping the spot where the body fell?"

"I meant to say something about that," Charlotte said. "I don't think that's the right spot. It was closer to the shed."

Francine agreed, but she was pretty sure it was irrelevant for the purposes of the morning show.

"You," the assistant producer said, pointing this time at Marcy, "go get him. You're not in this shot anyway." He tapped his foot until Marcy had retrieved Jud from the house. She pushed him along.

"Over here," Kurt said. "By the crime scene."

Jud moved to the spot where he was pointing. Marcy followed closely behind.

"We need to mike you," Kurt told Jud. "You'll get asked a few questions about the case, after George and Robin have interviewed the ladies. The segment wraps up with you, but we'll pull back to a shot of the women before we end. Ladies, I want you to do something like wave. Remember, you're having fun here! You're on television."

Jud folded his arms over his chest. "Fun? They uncovered a murder!"

"Listen, pal. It isn't every day a group of senior citizens finds a body that didn't die of natural causes. Phone calls to the station were overwhelmingly positive when *GMA* ran our promos. Viewers were excited."

"Murder is not exciting."

"Sure it is. The overnight polls showed the vast majority of America wished *they'd* been the ones who went skinny-dipping and found the body."

Jud shook his head.

Kurt coughed into his hand. "Look, you don't have to pretend it's fun. You can be the serious one. Just don't be too much of a downer." He told one of his assistants to get Jud a mike and an earpiece.

Charlotte burped loudly. "Excuse me," she said. Then she burped again. "Sorry. Maybe I shouldn't have had that frozen waffle."

Francine was alarmed. "You ate?"

"I was hungry."

"We talked about this yesterday. You know how nervous you get when you're on television."

"And remember I told you I'm over that."

"How many waffles did you have?"

"Two. But I had healthy ones. Whole wheat with extra fiber."

"Tell me you didn't use the butter pecan syrup with the artificial flavors."

"Okay, I won't tell you. But they don't taste good without a lot of syrup."

"You know what that does to your system."

"I'm fine."

Francine wasn't so sure. Between the tight girdle and the food, Charlotte was as much of a wild card as the paparazzi on the balcony.

The cameraman called to the assistant producer. "They're too close to the cop and too far from the pool."

Kurt checked the monitor, then herded the group backward. Francine, Charlotte, Joy, and Mary Ruth shuffled obediently toward the pool.

"I can't swim," Mary Ruth told Kurt. "I don't mind the shallow end, but being this close to the deep end makes me nervous."

"We're not asking you to get in." He clapped his hand over the ear that had the earpiece in. "Ohmigosh. We're going live in less than two minutes. Places everyone!"

Charlotte belched. "Whew. I hope I don't do that on camera. Maybe I shouldn't have had the tofu sausage."

Francine was aghast. "You had sausage with the waffles?"

She nodded. "Tofu. Have you had it before? It's not very good. I had to drench it in the syrup to make it edible."

Kurt waved his arms. "One minute. I want to see energy, ladies!" He danced around behind the cameraman, animatedly pointing at his exaggerated smile.

Marcy moved out of camera range, but she was no less animated. "Remember, you're the skinny-dipping grandmas everyone wants to know about!"

"Don't mess this up," Joy snapped at Charlotte. "Look. You can see yourself in the monitor. Smile."

Mary Ruth grabbed Joy by the shoulders. "This is awful! I look like a bowling ball with arms."

Francine checked the monitor. The black catering pants and voluminous polo shirt Mary Ruth had selected were probably not a good idea. Nothing could be done about it now, though.

Suddenly the screen split and the women could see George and Robin.

"It's him!" Charlotte said. She burped and bent over at the waist.

"I don't want to do this anymore," Mary Ruth said. She inched backward.

"Straighten up," Joy told Charlotte. Charlotte did what she could.

Kurt held up three fingers. "We're live in three … two … one." He pointed to Joy, who gave a big, toothy grin.

Francine couldn't hear the questions, but from the monitor she could tell the anchors were enthusiastic.

George must have asked Joy to introduce the group, because she stood to one side and pointed to Francine. Dutifully she put up her hand, waved at the camera, then backed off. That put Charlotte front and center. Mary Ruth, seeming to realize she was next, continued her rearward retreat.

Charlotte held a fist to her mouth. Her eyes were glassy. Francine could hear Charlotte's stomach heave as her name was called. "I need to get to the bathroom," she said.

Charlotte took off without looking. Francine watched in horror as she plowed into Mary Ruth. The caterer teetered on the edge of the pool for a moment, then plunged into the water. Charlotte tried to regain her balance.

Francine glanced at the monitor. The split screen showed a close up of a terrified Mary Ruth floundering in the deep end. On the other side of the screen, the anchors clearly mistook the wild look in Mary Ruth's eyes. They kept repeating something and throwing their hands in the air in encouragement.

"Help me," Charlotte screamed. She stretched out her arms. Francine grasped for her friend's hands but couldn't snag them in time. Charlotte fell in.

Kurt was now in full hysteria. "Jump!" he shouted. "Jump in!"

"Why? What are they saying?" Francine pointed in panic to the monitor where the anchors were having a good time.

"They're telling us to show them our stuff," Joy said. "They want us to get in and pull off our clothes."

Francine recoiled at the idea.

In the pool, Mary Ruth came out of shock. She clutched at Charlotte, dunking her in and out of the water like a sputtering buoy with silver curls. Francine jumped in the water to rescue her friends.

Charlotte managed to escape Mary Ruth and get over to the side, leaving the caterer floundering. Francine went underwater and came up behind her. She pushed her toward the ledge. Mary Ruth saw the ledge coming toward her and seized it, holding on for dear life.

Joy took hold of Charlotte's arm and pulled her out of the water onto the pool deck. Charlotte leaned up on her elbows. Her wig fell off her head and landed in front of her. With a huge belch, what remained of the waffles and tofu sausage came up all over her wig and the pool deck.

The paparazzi went crazy.

Francine climbed out of the water, her drenched sundress clinging to her body.

Marcy started to applaud.

And before long, the balcony joined in.

FOURTEEN

"OH, FOR HEAVEN'S SAKE, Charlotte, it was just your nerves, not food poisoning. No one is seriously trying to kill you, although Jud might be contemplating it." Francine removed the wet washcloth from her friend's forehead.

"Why? I embarrassed myself, not him." She lay on the couch in her family room, one arm flung over the edge in despair. Her backup wig, which Francine had retrieved from the bedroom, was slightly askew on her head. "I may die."

"You won't, but his segment did. After you and Mary Ruth got out of the pool, the whole interview went to pot, and they never talked to him."

"How would you know that? You rushed into the house to dry off."

Francine took out her iPhone and flashed the screen toward her. "It's already on YouTube. You want to watch it? I can call it up. We had ten thousand hits last time I looked."

"Great. It's been all of what, an hour? You'll probably get some kind of lifesaving award."

Francine took the washcloth into the kitchen to wring it out.

Charlotte hobbled after her, straightening the wig. "Would you use your phone to do a search?"

"When I finish here." She stood over the sink squeezing water out of the washcloth. "What do you want to know?"

"I want to know more about the Jake Maehler and Friederich breakup," she said. She moved a couple of books off a chair and sat down at the small dining room table. "I thought about this last night after our meeting. We need a lot more details."

Francine sat next to her and pulled out her iPhone. She Googled "Jake Maehler Friederich Guttmann." After scanning the list, she selected a link to the *Hendricks County Flyer*. "I've found the *Flyer* article that came out after the breakup. It's dated June second." She adjusted her glasses so she could read it. "It's a long article, but here's the pertinent part."

> Brownsburg's hometown favorite, NASCAR driver Jake Maehler, placed fifth after leading most of the race. His car had noticeable problems in the final two laps, enabling four drivers to pass him. Though he initially blamed head mechanic Friederich Guttmann, he later recanted his remarks. He attributed them to his disappointment at being so close and not being able to pull out the win. Guttmann refused to comment on Maehler's initial accusation of sabotage. There's no word on whether the two will work together for the upcoming midget car race at SpeedFest.

"What made Jake call it sabotage?"

She read through the remainder of the article. "Doesn't say."

"Can you find something on when they got back together?" Charlotte asked. "That was more recent. Maybe the reporter added more when he recapped the first part of the story."

Francine went back to the *Flyer*'s website. They'd posted a lead story online about Friederich's death even though the paper didn't come out until tomorrow. The accompanying photo of him was just a head shot, but it still startled Francine. It had only been early yesterday morning that they'd found him dead. It was difficult to imagine. She read the important parts of the article to Charlotte.

> Friederich Guttmann, an employee of Excalibur Racing, has been found dead at the house of Lawrence and Alice Jeffords, according to the Brownsburg police. The 55-year-old man, long known as the mechanic who nurtured local racing sensation Jake Maehler from the midget car circuit to NASCAR, is believed to have disappeared on Saturday. Police checked his duplex on Monday for clues to who might have murdered him. Neighbors say Guttmann's duplex had been up for sale for a month.
>
> "We found the house in order, as though Mr. Guttmann left for the day and never came back," recalled Detective Brent Judson. "There was no evidence of abduction or foul play. His only family lives in Germany and calls to them have not uncovered any clues as to why he was killed."
>
> Guttmann had been in the news following the Night Before the 500 midget car race when Maehler, for whom

he had built a car, accused him of sabotage. The car faded in the last laps and Maehler lost the race he had led virtually from the beginning, placing fifth. Guttmann denied charges that he had tampered with the car, and Maehler later shrugged off his comments as being "hotheaded." The two had reconciled recently when Maehler announced Guttmann was rebuilding his car for the SpeedFest race at Lucas Oil Raceway on July 26.

Maehler's sponsors, which included several Brownsburg retail businesses, declined to comment on Guttmann's death, other than to say how sorry they were that it had happened. However, speaking on the condition of anonymity, one representative said they had all been relieved when Guttmann and Maehler reconciled and Guttmann recommitted recently to being Maehler's mechanic for the SpeedFest event. He had termed them a formidable team. He declined to speculate on Maehler's chances now that Guttmann was dead. "I just hope the car was ready to go."

Police encourage anyone who might have knowledge about Guttmann's death to contact the station.

Charlotte sat back in her chair. "Who wrote that article?"

Francine checked. "The editor. The earlier one was written by Jeff Kramer. I recognized his name. He's the one who usually handles sports stories."

A china cabinet was next to the table. Charlotte got up and rummaged around in a drawer, finally coming up with pen and paper. She wrote down Kramer's name. "I'll call the paper later and see if I can talk to one of them."

The animation in Charlotte's face made Francine think she was running through some kind of scenario. "What are you thinking?" she asked.

"I'm thinking, 'What do we really know about Jake Maehler?'"

"We could check his website." Francine tapped in Jake's name. The website came up. She scooted over next to Charlotte so the two of them could look at it together. The main page showed Jake climbing out of his midget car, helmet off. The biography page showed him in his driving suit, standing next to the car with the helmet in the crook of his arm.

"Boy, he's a handsome one, isn't he?" said Charlotte. "Let's check his publicity photos."

"Wait a minute." Francine scanned the written bio. "Did you know all this about Jake?"

"What?"

She pointed to the screen. "That he had a single mother and that she died of cancer early in his life? That he came here from St. George, Utah, to live with his grandmother and that the two of them eked by on social security? That's so sad. And his grandmother died before he made it into NASCAR." She read more of the bio that covered how Friederich was a friend of Jake's grandmother and how he'd helped mentor the boy in racing. "No wonder Jake was loyal to Friederich."

"Yeah, but imagine how Jake would have felt if he thought Friederich was not being loyal when he came back. He would have been angry. Now let's take a look at those publicity photos."

Francine touched the screen and thumbnail photos of Jake in various settings came up. Several of them had female models. All of them had something to do with a sponsor.

Charlotte reached over and touched one of Jake on the beach. The photograph filled the screen. He was standing next to a woman in a blue flowered bikini, her oversized breasts practically spilling out her top. She had her hands on his bare chest, and he had a smirk on his face like he was used to this kind of attention and enjoyed it. His outfit consisted of surf shorts and flip-flops. They came from a shop in Brownsburg.

Charlotte tapped her cane on the floor. "Boy, I'd like to see that photo on a bigger screen. Look at his abs!"

The two women went through Jake's publicity photos for a few more minutes. His muscular body was captured from virtually every angle. "He doesn't seem to have many sponsors," Charlotte said, "but he does his best to work them into the photos."

"What he knows how to work is the camera. I'm not sure I should be looking at these pictures," Francine said.

"Why not? You read *People* magazine at the beauty shop, and there are always pictures of actors showing off their bodies. I don't think Matthew McConaughey owns a shirt."

"I guess."

"And anyway, it's not like Jonathan isn't a hunky husband. If they had a contest for hot men his age, I'd send in his photo."

"Charlotte!"

"Well, I would. You're a lucky woman."

"Okay, I am. But these photos feel … exploitive."

"Not exploitive. *Sex*ploitive."

"Exactly."

"So Jake has an image to protect. Can we do anything with that?" She pointed at a photo of him in front of a stock car, sans shirt, working on the car's souped-up engine. "If he wants to show he's worthy of sponsorship, he's probably got to do stuff like this."

"But he's a race car driver."

"When Helio Castroneves won *Dancing with the Stars*, it changed everything. Teams need to attract sponsorship money to stay competitive, and Helio proved it doesn't even have to be racing-related. Winning is all about who has the most cash. As long as every team has a *good* driver, money is the differentiating factor. Money buys the car, the technology, the crews."

"I thought you loved Helio," Francine said.

"I do. And he's a *great* driver. With him, Penske has the perfect combination. I'm just saying that having a good driver who can attract sponsorship money is way more important than having a great driver who might be ugly or dumpy."

Francine set the iPhone on the table and mused. "I can see where Jake Maehler would fit into that scenario. So he doesn't have any big sponsors, and he's not winning. We know he doesn't come from a family with money. Far from it. Where's he been getting his money?"

"I'd bet there'd be a few women who'd pay to spend time with Jake."

Francine frowned at her. "It would be so sad to think Jake needed to resort to being a gigolo to pay the bills. In fact, I don't believe it. He seems better than that."

"I didn't say he was a gigolo, but you have to be free-thinking if you're going to be a detective. You've got to keep your mind open to all possibilities. Anyway, I'm just trying to wrap my head around this whole thing. We have so few clues to go on."

"You expected them to just pop up? Do they ever do that in the books you read?"

"Not in the good ones."

"Then you got the first-class mystery you wanted. You know what they say: be careful what you wish for."

"Thanks a lot, Francine."

The grandfather clock in the living room chimed. Francine counted the hours, then double-checked her iPhone. She stood up. "It's ten o'clock! I've got to run. If I'm going to get to the gym in time to catch Jake's trainer before he gets busy, I need to leave now."

"What'd Crystal the Pistol tell you, besides his schedule?"

"Nothing. I played it low key and didn't ask too many questions. She told me the best time to catch Brady was before he taught spin class, which starts in an hour."

"Then you'd best go. In the meantime, I'm going to get hold of Jeff Kramer at the *Flyer*. Maybe he can shed some light on what evidence Jake might have had when he described Friederich's actions as sabotage."

FIFTEEN

Most of the time, Francine was glad Jonathan still had a group of clients and a reason to go to work, even though he could have sold his accounting business and retired. This was one of those days. He had seen the *GMA* episode—he'd sent her a brief text ending with a Groucho Marx emoticon on how sexy she looked soaking wet on television—but Francine was grateful she didn't have to talk about it right then. She changed into exercise clothes, even though she had no intention of exercising. With the excitement of all that had gone on this morning, she felt she'd been through an intense cardio workout.

Clad in her exercise gear, she pushed through the front door of the Brownsburg Fitness Factory, hoping she would be in time to catch Brady Prather before spin class.

The gym was in a former church located north of downtown. The building had been creatively repurposed. Arched front doors led into a vestibule that was now the reception area. She flashed her membership badge at the thin blond attendant and entered onto the main floor. To the right were stairs that led up into an ante-room and choir loft where the free weights were located. To her left was a bank of small rooms containing tanning beds. Directly ahead was a large open area that formerly housed pews, narrowing into a triangular shape that had been the sanctuary. The open area had three distinct segments: one for cardio equipment, another for exercise machines, and a third for stretching and yoga. She scouted all three zones, didn't see Brady, and headed up the stairs.

She hadn't given much thought to figuring out what to say. She had no idea how to break the ice with Brady, let alone get him to open up about Jake. Whatever story she created, it needed to sound truthful. She decided to imagine she was asking about training sessions for Mary Ruth. Of her overweight friends, Mary Ruth was the one who could benefit the most.

She found Brady with a teenage protégé amid the strength training equipment. She didn't want to look like she was loitering, so she picked up a couple of light dumbbells, located a bench, and did a set of ten shoulder presses. While she rested, she watched Brady train the young man.

Brady was tall, his head was shaved, and his body showed the thick, well-developed muscles of a guy who did a lot of weight-lifting. His calves were totally out of proportion. They rose out of his shoes like oversized turkey drumsticks before disappearing into the bottom of his long black shorts. If he hadn't had a soft smile that seemed genuine, he might have come across as scary. Before Francine had to fake another set of shoulder presses, he finished with his client and the young man left the free weight area drenched in sweat. Francine walked over.

"Hi," she said, sticking out her hand, "I'm a friend of your mom's. Do you have a moment to talk about personal training?"

"For you?" he asked.

"Well, actually it's for a friend of mine. She's kind of overweight. She's intimidated about coming in. Do you work with older people, or only with athletes?"

"I've trained clients over the years who've been older. How long has she been overweight?"

"A long time."

"The problem is, it's not just exercise; it's diet too. My clients have to commit to both. It's a totally different lifestyle. Do you think she can make those changes?"

His answers were coming too fast, and he was asking too many questions. She needed time to run them through her story to see if they matched up. Maybe she should have rehearsed with Charlotte.

Francine stared at him, trying to remember his last question. Something about changes. "She'll need a lot of encouragement," she said.

"I can provide motivation here in the gym, but if she can't stick to the diet at home, it's not going to work. Is there anyone who can help with the home part? Maybe you?"

"I hadn't thought of that. Her grandson lives with her, but he's overweight too. I guess I could check up on her."

"If she's willing to put in the work, I'm willing to train her, depending on my schedule. I have a few openings. There's a sheet at the front desk that has prices on it."

"Great," she said. "I'll pick that up." She was momentarily relieved to get Mary Ruth out of the way so she could focus on the next topic. "Aren't you Jake Maehler's trainer, too?"

Brady shrugged. "He's one of my clients. If your friend is willing, you need to move fast before she talks herself out of it. Do you think you could get her in here tomorrow for an evaluation? I have a hole in my schedule at three o'clock."

Francine felt her throat tighten. The more he kept bringing up Mary Ruth, the more difficult it was to keep the lying coherent. "I don't know. That might be a little too fast. It's a shame about Jake Maehler's mechanic, isn't it? How's he taking that?"

"He's handling it. You look to be in shape. Have you considered training with your friend? I could devise a program that the two of you could use together. If you were with her, you might be able to motivate her to stick with it."

Now she was really getting flustered. Not only was Brady giving short answers about Jake, he kept pushing her about Mary Ruth when she had no intention of actually dragging her into it. "I could try. But about…"

"I have to go. I have a spin bike class in a couple of minutes. Let's do this. Bring her in tomorrow at three. I'll talk to her, see where she's at, maybe work her out just a little."

Brady started downstairs toward the cardio area.

Francine stumbled a bit, struggling to keep pace with him and think on her feet. "I don't know if she'll…"

"Don't worry. I'll make her feel good about it. If she really wants to do this, tomorrow's session will make her want to do it more." They arrived in the cycling area, where the bikes were arranged in five rows of five each. About twenty were occupied. The bikers were pedaling easily, warming up. Brady mounted the instructor's bike that faced the class and spoke to Francine. "The first session tomorrow is free, okay? Won't cost her a thing to come. Want to join my class today?"

"Well, I . . ."

He held a hand up to indicate she didn't need to answer. "So, we'll see you tomorrow."

"Sure," she replied, but Brady hadn't waited to hear her out. He was already biking and talking to the class. He picked up a remote and aimed it at the music system. A song blared.

Francine stood for a moment, debating what to do. She suspected Brady wouldn't be surprised if she *didn't* show up tomorrow, and the likelihood he would mention it to her if he noticed her at the gym again was slim. Even if she talked Mary Ruth into this, there was always a possibility he wouldn't be any more forthcoming with information about Jake Maehler than he already had. On the other hand, with two of them working together, they might be able to get him to open up.

Just as she was about to leave, she watched him pick up the remote again, this time dampening the sound so he could talk to the class. Brady and the remote . . . it made her think. But then she dismissed it. She could connect Brady to Jake and Jake to Friederich, but Brady to Friederich?

She shook her head and headed for the exit. Before she'd even left the building her cell phone rang. She checked the number. It was Joy, so she answered it.

SIXTEEN

"Is this not the most exciting day ever?" Joy gushed over the line after Francine said hello. "We were a smash on *GMA*."

"I think that depends on your definitions. I'm betting Mary Ruth and Charlotte would use different terms."

Joy paused. "So right. I'm thinking selfishly." Then she got excited again. "But *GMA* loved the interview I gave them the next hour. They're talking to Marcy about me being a regular contributor to the show, covering senior citizens issues and filing reports on unusual things that seniors do."

"Congratulations. I didn't know anything about a second interview."

"I thought we were done for. Marcy worked hard to get me a second chance. And it worked!"

"I'm glad."

"The Brownsburg Chamber of Commerce wants to give you an award at their next meeting for being a good role model and saving Mary Ruth's life."

"Why would they do that?"

"I'm sure they're just trying to piggyback on our popularity, but I'd go with it if I were you. What are you doing for lunch?"

"I was going to grab something at home, why?"

"I just got out of meeting with the Chamber director, Rob Seneff. That's how I knew about the award you're getting."

"What were you doing at the Chamber?"

"You remember it was my responsibility to find out who might have inquired about the building Larry owns..."

Francine made listening noises. She decided this was going to be a long conversation, so she left the gym and headed for the car.

"...I can't believe Charlotte was so pushy about this. I know she's your best friend, but even you have to admit her single-mindedness can be annoying. Not one word asking how the second interview went. Just insistent that I go to the Chamber and get the information."

Francine figured that Charlotte must've called Joy right after Francine had left to go to the gym. "So what did you learn?"

Joy sounded annoyed. "In some ways, you're like her, you know that?" She didn't wait for a response. "Here's what I know. Larry is a member of the Chamber, but Friederich wasn't. Larry's page on the Chamber website listed all of his properties, even the ones that are already rented, with one exception: Friederich's garage."

"That's curious."

"Isn't it? I had researched the subject a little before I went to the Chamber, so I asked about it."

"Did you get an answer?"

"Not really. But I have the impression there's something unusual about the building. Something that Rob knows, and maybe others."

"Why do you say that?"

"Just a feeling. He was … evasive when I asked about the building. Friendly, but evasive. And then he changed the subject with a crack about us 'skinny-dipping grandmas.'"

"I may shoot the *Indianapolis Star* reporter who coined that phrase."

"With Friederich's murder unsolved, you should probably keep that thought to yourself."

Francine unlocked her Prius and opened the door. "You're right. So why did you ask me about lunch?"

"Oh, right. Getting around to that. I'm heading over to Danville to check the assessor's records."

Danville was the county seat. "For what?"

"To find out how much information about that property anyone could have gleaned from public records, about who owned it and what was in it. For whatever reason, Larry wasn't advertising the property, but Friederich found out that space was available. I want to see if it's anything obvious."

Francine wondered if Joy was on a roll. Earlier she must have impressed the *GMA* producers with her interview, and now she had dug up something interesting about the garage Friederich rented from Larry. "Count me in. I'm not at home, but I'm on my way. You want me to swing by and pick you up?" It would only take fifteen minutes to drive from Brownsburg to Danville.

Joy agreed, and they hung up. Francine switched from her regular glasses to her sunglasses, then started the car. She took a couple

132

of minutes to drive past Friederich's garage on Adams Street, even though it was out of the way. She paused to think about the situation. Outside, the building was boarded up like no one was there. Few people knew it was rented to Friederich. Larry had hidden cameras watching what went on inside the building. And Joy just told her others seemed to know there was something unusual about it.

It looked suspicious. Francine felt bad thinking that way. "Jonathan and I have known Larry for years," she told herself. "He couldn't possibly be involved in something that was … shady."

She stopped speculating and headed home to change and then pick up Joy. A few minutes into the drive she started checking the rearview mirror more often. There was a dark sedan three cars behind her she thought she recognized as having left the gym's parking lot at the same time she did. But the thought that it had taken the same detour past Friederich's garage spooked her.

"I'm not going to let Charlotte's obsession with murder mysteries get to me. I am *not* being followed." When she pulled into her subdivision off Hornaday Road, the car she was watching went straight. She let out a breath she didn't know she was holding. That was also when she noticed her hands were shaking.

SEVENTEEN

FRANCINE DROVE AROUND THE courthouse in Danville trying to find a place to park.

"How is Alice holding up after this morning?" she asked Joy.

"Could be better. I've had to order Marcy to stop asking her about her bucket list."

Francine found a spot next to a truck on the east side of the courthouse and pulled in. "I've never quite figured out why she's so secretive about her top item. Doesn't she know we can't help her make it happen if she won't tell us what it is?"

"I may know a little bit more about that than you. She says we *can't* help her. She says it would take a miracle. You know that cross around her neck? There's a Biblical verse on it that is all about the miracle she wants. I've asked her to tell me what the verse is or let me see it, but she won't. If we could get that cross off her, we could figure it out."

"She was wearing it the night we were supposed to go skinny-dipping, so I don't think it's going to come off without divine intervention or a lot of liquor. And we both know Alice hardly drinks."

Francine and Joy had settled on lunch at the Courthouse Grounds, a comfortable little coffee shop on the square in downtown Danville that the Bridge Club frequented. Mary Ruth said the owners had managed that tricky balance of making the place feel intimate but welcoming. Whether it was your first time or you were a regular, she said, you always felt welcome in their elegant little café.

But that was not how Francine felt this time. This time when they walked in the door, everyone stopped talking and looked at them. *Like we're celebrities.*

Joy smiled magnanimously. Francine reddened.

"Just head for the empty table in the back and act like normal," Joy whispered.

Francine felt she was on a runway, not an aisle. She tried to look as inconspicuous as possible as she made her way past the round, antique Queen Anne tables. Every seat of the first six was occupied, every eye was upon her. Moving purposefully toward the back, she didn't think about Joy behind her when she made a sudden decision to stop at the self-serve coffee area. Joy collided with her just as Francine picked up a coffee mug. The mug sailed into the kitchen and hit one of the owners on the hand. He'd just picked up a plate of food but let it loose in surprise. The plate shattered when it hit the kitchen floor, sending egg salad all over his pants.

"I'm really sorry," Francine said, struggling to keep the table upright. Joy grabbed a coffee urn before it tipped over.

"It's quite all right," said the owner, recovering quickly. "I'd always wondered how these pants might look in yellow." He grabbed a napkin and scraped the egg salad off.

Francine and Joy attempted to reassemble the coffee table's contents. "That was close," Francine whispered. "Good thing we averted that disaster."

Joy looked out over the sea of cell phones taking their pictures. "I think it still might be a disaster. Our graceful photos might be all over Facebook in a matter of minutes."

The owner saw what Joy saw, helped them with the table and got them seated.

"I'm so sorry," Francine said. "I'll pay for that sandwich you dropped."

"Nonsense," he said. "It's just a sandwich. Let me get you both coffee. I'll be back with the menus."

It took a while, but conversation in the restaurant resumed its normal hushed tone. Francine breathed a sigh of relief. The owner brought them coffee and menus. The two women hurriedly ordered.

Rather than make conversation, Francine cast casual glances at the other patrons to see if they were being watched. Every time she looked up, someone averted their eyes. The place was mostly women. She heard male lawyers preferred Frank's Place, an Italian restaurant with a liquor license on the other side of the Royal movie theater from the Courthouse Grounds, but she'd never been there at lunch.

"I think we're okay," she told Joy. "No one has their cell phones in hand."

"That's because they already uploaded their photos to Facebook and Twitter while we were ordering. I saw it out of the corner of my eye."

Francine sighed. She wouldn't have guessed the people who were lunching there would be the types. They were divided between the professionally dressed, probably lawyers from the courthouse, and the older "ladies who lunched." But it wasn't the first time she she'd been wrong about things like that.

Joy whispered, "I wonder if this is what Robert Pattinson faces every day. In a way, it's kind of exciting, isn't it?"

"More awkward than exciting," she said, pretending to know who Robert Pattinson was. She tried to imagine how much more of this they were in for if they couldn't persuade Joy to rein in her publicist. "I don't generally read celebrity magazines unless I'm in the beauty shop, but I see a lot of bad things caused by paparazzi. Are you sure you're not getting in over your head?"

"By hiring Marcy? I don't understand why everyone is so resistant to getting their moment in the spotlight." Joy blew on her coffee and then took a drink. "I've always wanted to be glamorous. When I was young I fantasized I'd grow up to be a Grace Kelly to someone's Cary Grant. Instead I became a skinny Carol Channing who thought she'd married Rock Hudson's on-screen double only to find out she had married Rock Hudson's *in-bedroom* double."

Francine winced. A long time ago, shortly after Joy had moved into the neighborhood and become part of the Summer Ridge Bridge Club, her husband had left her for another man. With much therapy and their support, not to mention a big divorce settlement, they thought Joy had come through okay. Now Francine had her doubts. "This isn't a latent attempt to show Bruno up, is it?"

Joy gave a wry smile. "Well, not really. Although I hope he noticed I did a great job handling the *GMA* segment. He demeaned my role as a secretary at Lilly Endowment. That'd show him."

The owner returned with their food. As he slid the plates in front of them, Francine remembered how large the sandwiches were. She'd have to carry half of hers home.

Just about the time she figured out how to broach the subject again of Joy's sudden need for attention, Joy finished the remaining coffee. She looked in her mug. "Empty already." She got up and went to the coffee station.

Francine picked up her spoon and sampled the chicken corn chowder that had come with her turkey sandwich. It was wonderful; just the right amount of creaminess without feeling heavy. She had a big spoonful in her mouth when someone asked, "Can I sit here with you?"

She looked up. Darla Baggesen, Homeowners' Association Nazi, stood in front of her holding a mug. Francine tried to finish the bite, but Darla didn't wait for an answer. She set her mug at the empty space between Francine and Joy.

"Thanks," she said. She pulled out her chair to sit. The tables were so close that she nearly bumped the woman at the next table. "It's crowded in here," she told Francine. "Good thing I'm thin." She placed her napkin on her lap. "So, not to bring up an unpleasant subject or anything, but how are you faring since the *Good Morning America* fiasco this morning?"

"We're doing okay," Francine responded coolly. "I don't think we violated any homeowners' tenants today. I know you were watching from your balcony. Who was in your group?" She had thought about *not* mentioning the balcony since it wasn't good to be on Darla's bad side. But she guessed the Bridge Club had already crossed that line.

Darla batted her eyes, seemingly taken aback. She sported long lashes so mascara-laden Francine was afraid they might stick together if she closed them for too long. "Some people from the neighborhood. Maybe a few visitors from the local media. It was better having them on my balcony than camped out on Alice's lawn, which would have been a violation."

"I'm hopeful we can put this episode behind us now."

"You can hope, but I wouldn't bet on it after *Good Morning America*. I think we're going to have to get used to having the 'skinny-dipping grandma' celebrities in our subdivision. Rumor has it the Visit Hendricks County bureau wants you to do a calendar."

How did that rumor start? "We would never do something like that."

"You say that now, but wait till you're in *People* magazine." She looked around to see Joy returning from the coffee station. "I heard Joy's publicist is working on them," she said quickly. "Maybe you'll get your own reality show on TLC."

Joy shifted her food so she was seated on the other side of Francine from Darla. She faked a smile. "Hi, Darla."

The owner came by and dropped off Darla's food, a spinach quiche with fruit cup she had apparently ordered when she arrived.

Joy picked at the chicken salad in her spinach wrap but then put the fork down. "I'm too excited to eat," she said. She drank more coffee.

Francine addressed the elephant in the room. "What are you doing here in Danville, Darla?"

She sighed. "I've been at the courthouse. More paperwork on the divorce. Sara turned sixteen last week. Legally, she can now decide who she wants to live with. My ex is trying to get her to move in. It's all a ploy so he can stop sending me support payments. It's not like I need that money for myself, you know. It's all about Sara's racing."

Joy dabbed her mouth with her napkin and sounded polite when she asked, "How's her season going?"

"It would be going better if I could get her to focus more on her driving and less on boys." She laughed, but not convincingly. Francine suspected there was some truth behind it. "Seriously, though, she's doing well. Of course, if we had more money it would help. Racing is expensive."

"I thought your ex-husband was Sara's mechanic."

"He is, but I'd rather have his money than him. Vince is not very good. Everything he does—well, I've always had to make a list and check it twice. Santa Claus should hire me for seasonal help. What do you know about this luncheon Mary Ruth is having tomorrow? I got a voicemail about it."

Though no one cared for Darla, Francine knew was best to rally her behind the idea. "Mary Ruth's trying to get some racing clients for her catering business, so this is really about that. But since we've all been a little shaken over a murder taking place in the neighborhood, Charlotte is arranging for the police to talk to us about a neighborhood watch program."

"Plus, it'll be good for everyone to hear the truth about how we found Friederich," Joy added, "and Alice is anxious to dispel the rumor that we go skinny-dipping all the time."

Darla pursed her cherry-red lips. "Good old Holy Alice. I daresay the tourism people won't be happy to hear that, though." She leaned in. "You mentioned the police will be there. Will they tell us what they know about the case?"

Joy shrugged. "You know how the police are …"

"… but I'm sure they'll tell us whatever they can," Francine said. She didn't want to lose any support Darla might give them.

"As President of the Homeowners Association, I suppose I should be there. And Mary Ruth's food *is* delicious. I just hope the police will be open with us."

"You know a lot of people in the racing business," Joy said. "A good word from you would really help her."

"I guess I do know a lot of people," she said. "Is she licensed to cater at Lucas Oil Raceway?"

"She is, but she hasn't got a single job lined up for SpeedFest."

"I'll see what I can do."

Francine hated herself for thinking that Darla's altruism would come with a price tag. *How cynical I've become.* She tried to remember that Darla was a good mother. Despite the divorce and her snide comments about her ex-husband's effectiveness as a mechanic, she had found ways to work with Sara's father. Francine had a thought. "Does Sara know Jake Maehler?"

"Of course they know each other! Sara is a huge fan. And mark my words, she'll be the next big thing from Brownsburg after Jake. Why do you ask?"

"Friederich was Jake's mentor for so many years. I just wondered how he's doing."

"Oh, that." Darla picked at the last bit of fruit in her cup.

She's dying to spill some gossip, Francine thought.

"Jake's doing fine," Darla said eventually. "Sara said she asked Jake what he was going to do about a mechanic for the SpeedFest Race. He said he thought his own skills were enough to make it work, if he had to. But she said she was certain Jake was looking for another mechanic."

"He hasn't got much time left."

"Not much at all." She pulled out her cell phone. "Speaking of time, I should check in with Sara." She used the touch screen on her phone. "Hmmm. Listen, I need to get moving. Thanks for letting me sit with you."

"See you tomorrow?"

"Yes, definitely." Darla picked up her purse. Francine noted that it was a Coach brand. *Must be taking her ex to the cleaners.*

The center aisle at the Courthouse Grounds was narrow, so Darla could not hurry despite her declaration. She also wasn't exactly thin (again despite her declaration), more like strong and in shape, and she definitely had hips. They swayed from side to side in a Mae West kind of way as she made her way out.

"She knows how to make an exit, doesn't she?" Francine said. "We should make ours now. We'll pale in comparison."

"I don't know. We're becoming famous as the skinny-dipping grandmas. We should show them what we're made of."

Francine rolled her eyes. She gathered up her leftovers and her purse. "Let me go first. You can show them whatever you want."

EIGHTEEN

THE ASSESSOR'S OFFICE WASN'T located in the courthouse but in the county government center a few blocks south. Francine and Joy decided to walk. As they headed down Washington Street, she filled Joy in on her morning encounter with Jake Maehler's trainer, Brady Prather, and how she was now thinking about asking Mary Ruth to go with her to the gym the next day at three o'clock. "It'll be after the luncheon, and she shouldn't have to do the dishes, not after preparing all that food."

"I agree. The rest of us will do dishes. You focus on getting her to go."

"So you think she should? I feel like I'm using her."

"You are, but it's for her own good. We need an excuse to talk to him, and Mary Ruth would feel so much better if she lost weight. The stress of owning a catering business in this economic downturn is partially to blame, but still, if you don't take care of yourself, you can't take care of your business."

That was harsh, Francine thought. Mary Ruth was the only one of their Bridge Club who still worked. Joy dabbled in things that were communication-oriented and the others volunteered at various organizations, but only Mary Ruth had a full-time job. She was a longtime divorcee, and catering was her only source of livelihood. Who knew how any of them might have overindulged under the same circumstances?

As they approached the government center, Francine couldn't help thinking about the center's history. Originally built as Danville's first high school in 1927, the three-story red brick building had served as an elementary school in the 1960s before being remodeled into the Hendricks County Government Center in the 1990s. Now it housed all the non-justice functions because the courthouse could no longer accommodate all the offices.

"The west face looks just like the old high school," Joy said.

"It does, doesn't it? I always have to remind myself that this is where I have to go for county business, not the courthouse."

They located the assessor's office on the second story. A middle-aged clerk with an abundance of pendant jewelry recognized them immediately and came over. She gushed a little about them being on television. Joy basked in the glow for a few moments, then asked how to find out who owned any particular piece of property in Brownsburg.

"If you have the address, it's extremely easy. You don't even need to come in. We have all that stuff online."

Francine had wondered if that wasn't the case, but the thought of going to lunch at the Courthouse Grounds had been appealing.

"Could you show us?" Joy asked. "We're interested in the building at 179 Adams Street."

"Sure." The clerk spun the monitor around so the women could see what she was doing. "You just go to the county's web page, then click the auditor's office." She did that, and another screen came up. "Now you see this area here where you can request information about property taxes? You just type the address and press enter. What was the address again?"

She repeated it. The clerk typed it in, hit enter, and a whole history of the property appeared on the screen. Sure enough, the first record showed who owned it, Larry and Alice Jeffords.

"It's a rental property," Joy said. "Do you have any records that show who rents it?"

"Not that I know of." She scrolled down checking to see if there was something she missed.

The records went back into previous decades. "How far back do the records go?" Francine asked.

"As far back as we can trace them. For some of the properties, we can even track them back to the organization of the county, but those are in a different database."

Without prompting, the clerk returned to the home page and then clicked into an old map of the county. The center of the screen showed the Danville area. She scrolled over to Brownsburg. "If you put the cursor over any of the properties, you can find out if we have any original information on who owned it."

"Interesting," Joy said. "One of the things we wanted to find out was whether anyone had accessed the information on this property recently. We'd hoped they'd have to do that through you, and you'd be able to tell us."

The clerk shook her head. "No, with the information online, anyone could have visited the site and we wouldn't know."

Francine was fairly confident *someone* had the ability to trace it. If the police could track down criminals through their Internet usage, the information they wanted had to be logged somewhere. The question was, who could find it for them and how difficult would it be to persuade that person to do it?

The women thanked the clerk and walked back to the car. Before Francine started it up, she pulled out her cell phone. She called up the county's website and began to scroll through the information on Larry's rental property.

Joy watched her. "What are you doing?"

"I'm looking back over the history of Larry's property. The clerk whipped through it pretty fast."

"It was just a gas station, wasn't it?"

"No. More like a small machine shop of some kind. I have no idea when it was built or what they made or if there was anything on the property before it."

"What for?"

"Just curious." She tilted her head back to read the assessed value through the bottom part of her bifocals. The value last given seemed low for a commercial structure, but she didn't know how those kinds of things were priced. She could only compare it to the assessed value of her house, and she knew the two were very different. She scrolled down to the bottom of the page. "I was right. It says here the property was built as a machine shop in 1928. Its square footage then was less than a thousand feet."

"That's about what it is now, isn't it? It doesn't look very big."

"One addition was made, in 1972. It doubled it in size to something over two thousand square feet."

Joy seemed surprised. "Over two thousand? It doesn't look that big from the outside."

"Nor from the inside. I remember walking through the building with the police the day we found the body. It can't be much bigger than a thousand."

"Then where's the other thousand?"

Francine thought a moment. "Basement?"

"You were there. Did you see a basement?"

"It wasn't obvious."

"How long has Larry owned the building?"

She scrolled through the listing again. "He bought the property ten years ago. No mortgage company involved. The structure's purpose changed to commercial storage. And the property is now classified at a thousand square feet."

"Where did the extra square footage go?"

"Wait. I read that wrong. One thousand square feet is commercial garage; the remainder is commercial storage. But where's the storage and what's being stored there?"

"I bet Jonathan would know. You should ask him about it. Doesn't he prepare the paperwork for Larry's property taxes?"

"I'm pretty sure."

"Well, there you go."

Francine put away her phone and started the Prius. The two women were quiet as she negotiated the heavy traffic on US 36. She reached Dan Jones Road and turned north toward Brownsburg.

In her mind she kept going back over the trip she'd taken to Friederich's shop with Jud, Jonathan, and Alice. She mentally repaced the area and compared it to her home. She was certain it couldn't be more than a thousand square feet. There was no attic,

147

so there must be a basement. But if the owner before Larry had dug a basement for the property, even in 1972, lots of people would remember it. Had there always been a basement, but maybe unfinished, so the original owner never claimed it? But if there was a basement, why hadn't they seen an entrance? And why had Rob Seneff at the Chamber avoided talking about the building?

Francine thought about the videos of the building she'd watched. The cameras only covered the area they'd been in. If there was a basement, why would Larry not have cameras down there?

And then there was the fifty-minute gap. Someone came back into the building to get one of the midget cars and was in there a long time. Could that have anything to do with a basement?

Francine did not want to suspect Larry, even if he was secretly back in town at the time. She was certain there must be a logical explanation that would clear him. Friederich knew about the cameras. He must have told someone else. Otherwise, who would have known how to get past them?

She couldn't help but think that one single event, the mysterious re-entry into the garage, held the key to why Friederich had been killed.

NINETEEN

FRANCINE FOUND THE LIGHT flashing on the answering machine when she returned home. The missed call was Charlotte. She sounded excited about information she'd dug up and wanted to talk immediately. Francine returned the call right away.

"What took you so long?" Charlotte asked. "Did you get a chance to question Brady? What did you learn? I've talked to Jeff Kramer, the reporter. Well, not actually him, but his editor, and I've been to see Jud. We need to talk. When can you come over?"

"Watch your blood pressure, Charlotte. I went with Joy to Danville to find out what we could about the property Friederich rented. I've got more questions now than I have answers."

"Isn't that the way it always goes? The answers I get only produce more questions. The facts in this case fit together like the season finale of *How I Met Your Mother* did with the other episodes of the show. I keep looking at the clues and thinking: How does this make sense?"

Francine wasn't sure she understood the analogy but then Charlotte watched way more television than she should. Her DVR was perpetually 90 percent full.

"So, can you come over?" Charlotte repeated.

"I'm tired of going other places today. Can you drive over here?"

Francine got no argument from Charlotte, who pulled into their driveway five minutes later. Francine watched her hustle to the front door, wielding her cane like a third leg extending from her hand. But by the time Francine had the door ajar, Charlotte had slowed to a crawl. They all knew Charlotte was more mobile than she let on; they just allowed her to maintain the illusion that her handicap slowed her down.

"That was quick," Francine said under her breath.

"What was that? Sometimes I think you mumble on purpose." Charlotte maneuvered around her and made her way into the great room.

Francine's house was one of the Colonial brick homes in the subdivision, two stories with all of the bedrooms upstairs and most of the living areas downstairs. When the three boys were young, it had almost seemed too small. The house was full of life then, with schoolwork and sports and the boys' friends over all the time. Now two of the bedrooms were guestrooms and Jonathan's office occupied the other. They'd talked about moving to a smaller place, but they loved their neighbors. As long as they were healthy and could deal with the stairs, they decided they would stay. They'd remodeled to keep it updated—the great room had been a family room and a living room before they knocked out the wall between them—and it was this room Charlotte loved. She nabbed her favorite Italian leather armchair and set her purse next to it.

"Sit," she told Francine as though it were her own house. "We need to compare notes." She reached into her purse and pulled out a notebook. "You go first."

Francine sat on the couch across from Charlotte. She started at the beginning, with her meeting at the gym that yielded little information from Brady. "The good news is I'm meeting with him again tomorrow. The bad news is, I sort of promised him Mary Ruth."

Charlotte slapped the knee that hadn't been replaced. "That's a good one. Why ever did you promise him that? You'll never get Mary Ruth in a gym unless you tell her there's a chance she could cater an event there. And she'll never believe that. I bet they don't even allow carrot cake in that Brownsburg gym."

"I was thinking of an ambush after the catering event tomorrow. Maybe rush her into the car and whisk her over to the gym before she has a chance to think about it. Joy is in on it, and she's all for it."

"I don't know. Mary Ruth is short and wide and has a low center of gravity. I'm not sure even with all four us working together she could be budged. But it's worth a shot. You're sure that's the only way you'll get him to talk about Jake Maehler?"

"He's all business. We need to dangle the prospect of a new client in front of him if we're going to divert him into a conversation about Jake."

"You said you also saw Joy...?"

Francine recapped Joy's trip to the Brownsburg Chamber of Commerce, and then backtracked to their lunch at the Courthouse Grounds. When she finished covering their conversation with Darla Baggesen, Charlotte stopped her. "Sara wants to go live with her father? Why would she want that?"

"Why wouldn't she want to go live with her father? Maybe she's closer to him than she is to Darla. If I were Sara, I know I'd want to live with my dad."

"True. Darla is obsessive about Sara's racing, worse than a soccer mom at times. I think Darla keeps her on a short leash too. Maybe she clapped one of those bracelets around Sara's ankle like they put on sex offenders, to keep track of her when she's not around."

Francine snorted at the suggestion. "You're exaggerating. Anyway, with these new smartphones, Darla wouldn't need an ankle bracelet. She could just install an app to keep track of where Sara's phone is. Kids don't go anywhere without their cell phones." She thought back to the Courthouse Grounds when Darla said she needed to check in on Sara. She'd looked at her cell phone and left abruptly. *Had Darla seen where Sara was and it worried her?* Francine decided to switch topics. She prompted Charlotte about her trip to see Jud.

"There was something about Friederich's dead body that bothered me, especially knowing he was murdered. Do you know what was missing?"

"What are you talking about?"

"Blood, Francine. There was no blood."

"You're going to tell me it had been drained, like a vampire, aren't you? Have you been reading Charlaine Harris again?"

"No. But it begs the question, how did he die? I asked Jud about it."

"Did he tell you?"

"Amazingly enough, he did. He said he wanted me to understand that this was a murderer who knew what he was doing. Friederich was blood choked."

"He was what?"

"It's like choking a person to stop them from breathing, only they choke the carotid artery so blood doesn't reach the brain." Charlotte touched the carotid artery on the left side of her neck to demonstrate. "All it takes is firm pushing until they pass out, and then holding it longer until real damage is done."

As a nurse, Francine understood what Charlotte was saying, but the act was so heinous. "Someone deliberately stopped the blood from reaching his brain so he became brain dead?"

"That's how a blood choke works. Of course, when someone uses it in a cage fight or a wrestling match, they let up after the person passes out so the blood can get going again to the brain and there's no brain damage."

"But it's so … calculating."

"Or to the killer it came naturally, like in a fit of anger. Jud says he thinks Friederich tried to fight back. There was skin under his fingernails, like he'd clawed at the person who killed him. The coroner is checking for DNA samples."

"I can't believe he told you all that, Charlotte."

"I'd like to say I pulled it out of him with brilliant investigative questions, but he was getting ready for a press conference and I think he was practicing on me. I did soften him up first, though. I told him about our luncheon tomorrow and asked him to be there."

"I thought it was going to be a neighborhood watch program. Jud doesn't handle those."

"Hear me out. At first he tried to push it off on the Support Services division, so I told him he should consider it professional courtesy. I told him the guest list included the people who'd returned to the scene of the crime when we gave tours and that we would be using the luncheon for a dual purpose: showing off Mary Ruth's skills and interrogating a list of possible suspects. That was when he agreed it was a good idea."

"Just like that?"

"Okay, he did get a little angry that we haven't stopped investigating. But after I reminded him that at least I was keeping him informed, he seemed better about it. Still suspicious of my motive, but he said he'd come. Then he drop-kicked me out of there to go to a press conference. Said he was trying to get the press under control."

Francine hoped he could tame the media circus Marcy had created around the Bridge Club and put the focus back squarely on the murder itself. "Speaking of the press, what did you learn from the reporter—I can't remember his name."

"Jeff Kramer. I couldn't get hold of him, but I did talk to the editor. The best thing I learned from her was the reason Jake claimed it was sabotage in the first place."

"Which was?"

"Rumor had it that Friederich was building a car for another racer before he hooked back up with Jake. When Jake's car gave out so close to the end, he believed Friederich had done it on purpose to give one of his rivals a chance at victory."

Francine thought a moment. "Jake came in fifth. Four people finished ahead of him. Were any of those…?"

"…linked to Friederich? My question exactly. The editor said Jeff couldn't uncover a single thread connecting any of those racers to Friederich. All of them had cars that had been built by their mechanics."

Francine was confused about why Charlotte found this somehow significant. "What did he make of the rumor, then?"

"Uncertain. The editor said it could be no one yet understands the connection between Jake's rivals out on the track and Friederich. But for Jake's first thought to be sabotage, Jake must have some kind of information no one else has, information that accounts for him assuming the failure was deliberate and then getting angry."

"I can believe it. But Jake's anger should make him a prime suspect. Wouldn't that give Jake a stronger motive for killing Friederich?"

"Yes, but the reporter argued that if we assume Jake knows more than he's telling, then the question remains, who was Friederich building a car for? Answer that question, and you have another suspect. At any rate, the editor said Kramer told her he wasn't giving up on it yet. She promised to have Kramer call me when he returned to work. I guess he'd taken a few days off and she hadn't seen him."

Francine's cell phone rang. She looked at the number. It was Jonathan.

"Are you alone?" he asked.

"No."

"Is it Charlotte?"

"Yes."

"Get rid of her and then meet me over at Alice and Larry's house. They want to talk to us. Or rather, Larry wants me there, and Alice insists that you be there too."

"Okay." Francine looked up. Charlotte was watching her. This would be a problem.

Jonathan must have read her mind. "Just tell her you have to meet me to sign some papers—personal papers."

Francine told her that. Charlotte gave her a disappointed look. Jonathan said, "Now say, 'right now?'"

"Right now?"

"Good girl. Now see her out. I don't know for certain, but I think Larry and Alice are getting close to being honest with each other. How that involves you and me, I guess we'll learn."

TWENTY

Francine waved from the porch as the big Buick backed out of the driveway. As soon as she was certain Charlotte was gone, she got in her Prius and drove to Alice and Larry's house. Time was of the essence. Jonathan's car was already there.

Alice answered the door and pulled her into a tight hug. "Thanks for being here."

She squeezed Alice back. "How can I help?"

"Just listen, and ask the questions I forget to ask. I'm so frazzled. It's like Larry is someone I don't know."

She did look frazzled. Her hair was normally teased and combed so that it puffed out at her ears and de-emphasized her lengthy face. Today her hair was flat and close to her head and emphasized her nose, which was not Alice's best feature. Francine took a deep breath and put her arm around Alice's shoulders. "Let's go in."

Walking through the familiar French doors into the living room, Francine could see the stress was wreaking havoc on Alice's impeccable housekeeping. Half-empty teacups sat abandoned in saucers on the coffee table and on the ledge of the bay window. Haphazardly folded newspapers lay on the floor beside the couch.

And Larry looked even worse. He looked like he hadn't slept in days. Seated in the recliner by the couch, his no-longer-distinguished gray hair stuck out at all angles. His goatee hadn't been trimmed in a week or more. And for a tall man, he appeared to have shrunk everywhere.

Jonathan sat on the couch in the business casual clothes he'd worn to work. When he saw Francine, he patted the seat next to him. She joined him, but Alice chose a seat across the room from Larry, almost deliberately distancing herself.

Larry wrung his hands. "I don't have an alibi for the night Friederich was killed because I came home from Las Vegas a day early to meet with someone, but that person didn't show up."

"Who was it?" Jonathan asked.

"Good question," snapped Alice. "I hope you get an answer out of him, because he won't tell me."

Larry shook his head. "No one can know. Not yet. Not until I see this person face-to-face."

"Maybe I can arrange a meeting," Jonathan said.

"That's the problem, don't you see? Then I'd have to tell you who it is."

Francine kept her voice soft. "How did you arrange to meet this person in the first place?"

"I sent a letter."

"Why do you want to meet?"

His voice was shaky. "I have some information this person needs to know."

"They were supposed to meet in the parking lot where Friederich's garage is." Alice spit out the information like she was getting rid of a bite of moldy fruit. "Isn't that ironic?"

"But that should be good, shouldn't it, at least as far as an alibi is concerned?" Francine said. "You have all that surveillance equipment. It should have recorded that you were there."

"I disabled it."

The missing footage on Saturday night, Francine thought.

"Whatever for?"

"If this person didn't like the information I was going to give them, I didn't want it to be recorded. I wouldn't ever want to see it again. That's all I'm going to say about that."

Jonathan crossed his arms over this chest. "Does your lawyer know who this person is?"

"Yes, but he didn't know about the meeting. No one knew."

"Why did you ask us here?"

"As soon as I can meet with this person, I will tell you everything. Alice first, of course. I'm going to do that soon. But in the meantime, the police have uncovered something that I partially hid from Alice, and I fully hid from you, and you both deserve apologies before you learn it the hard way. I don't know how to do it other than to tell you together, because it's hard and I don't want to have to do it twice."

Alice looked stunned. Jonathan leaned forward in anticipation.

Larry got up and took Alice's hand. She let him do it. He said, "You remember when my grandparents died?"

She nodded.

"And you remember that they left me some money?"

"It was a nice amount," Alice said. "About two hundred thousand dollars. Our real estate business took off because we had that backing."

Larry bit his lip. "There was much more. Well over a million dollars more. But for reasons I can't explain right now, I moved it to an offshore bank and hid it from you, and from my accountant, who is also one of my best friends, and I'm so sorry. When I can finally tell you the reason, I hope you'll both forgive me."

Alice almost seemed relieved. "Larry, it's only money. I don't love money, I love you. Why didn't you tell me this before? I don't like this secret rendezvous you were planning the night Friederich died, but the money's not important."

"It's not the money, it's how I spent it."

"It's gone?"

"Not all of it, but most of it."

Alice shoulders sagged. Francine thought she seemed more exasperated than angry. "What did you spend it on? Something foolish?"

"I can never call it foolish. But I've been reckless, Alice, and I'm honestly sorry about that."

Alice stood up. "Well, if we're going to apologize for things we regret, let me give you one. I hired a private detective to follow you to Las Vegas. You've been acting strangely for six months now, and when you snatched up this trip, suddenly having to go to Las Vegas, I became suspicious."

Larry narrowed his eyes, almost indignant. "You had me followed?"

"Wait a minute," Francine said, turning to Alice. "If you had him followed, then did you know that he'd come back early?"

"Not until Sunday afternoon when the detective told me. I guess Larry caught him off guard with the second roundtrip ticket Saturday, and he couldn't get one fast enough to follow him home by the time he figured out where Larry was going."

"So Larry lied about being in Las Vegas, and you kept the police in the dark by pretending you were talking to him there, even though you knew he was in Indianapolis?"

"I didn't know where he was exactly, only that he had come through the Indianapolis airport. He could have rented a car and driven anywhere."

"And when you came to Bridge Club last night, you weren't quite truthful with us, either?"

"I'm sorry, Francine. I'd been keeping up the fantasy that Larry was out of town because I believed, and still do, that he had nothing to do with Friederich's murder."

Jonathan slid forward on the couch. "Too bad the detective didn't get back in time to follow you that night. If he had, then you'd have an alibi."

"I guess I would."

"I want to give you that alibi," Alice said. "I really do. The detective called a few friends in the business, but none of them could cover him, so he ended up calling a reporter friend. He swore the guy to secrecy, and he supposedly followed you from the airport for the rest of the night."

"But this is great! He should know I spent most of the night in the parking lot, hoping this person would show up. He should be able to testify to that."

"He might, but no one can find him. The detective's tried to get hold of him but hasn't been successful. It's one of the reasons I didn't get called right away. The detective kept trying to reach the reporter so he'd know where Larry went."

"Who's the reporter?"

"Jeff Kramer."

Francine recognized the name. Charlotte had just told her he'd done the articles on Jake Maehler and Friederich Guttmann. "He's a reporter for the *Flyer*," she said.

And the fact that the editor had told Charlotte he'd taken a few days off and hadn't been seen since made the hair on the back of Francine's neck stand up.

TWENTY-ONE

ALICE ANNOUNCED THAT SHE'D like to talk to Francine alone, so the two of them went to the kitchen. Alice leaned against the marble countertop of the center island and let her head drop back, staring at the ceiling. Whether it was in contemplation or disbelief, Francine wasn't sure. "What do you think?" Alice finally asked.

"I don't know what to think. He doesn't sound like he's fallen out of love with you at any rate. But he has so many secrets."

"I don't have a clue who this person was he was meeting or how he or she relates to Friederich, but I figure it's got to be tied together. I think there must be a connecting reason he chose to meet in the parking lot at Friederich's garage. Why else choose that spot?"

Francine helped herself to a handful of mixed nuts from a bowl on the island. Stress had a way of turning her into a nervous nibbler. "Just why do the police suspect Larry? What could he possibly have to gain by killing Friederich? Just because they argued about the rent doesn't mean he'd kill him for it. It couldn't be that much money."

Alice picked a couple of almonds out of the nut bowl. "I suppose it's all going to come out eventually, but promise me you won't say anything for now. When Friederich fell so far behind in his payments, Larry threatened to take possession of the workshop and everything in it. That really upset Friederich, naturally. Larry had hoped it might make the rent a priority. Apparently it didn't. The police know about Larry's threat."

Francine mentally reviewed what she'd seen in the garage. She couldn't imagine that Friederich's tools and equipment were valuable enough to kill for. But she also remembered something from what she and Jonathan had watched. "Have you seen the video from Larry's surveillance equipment?"

"He showed it to me. It was an attempt to demonstrate he's being as honest with me as he can right now. I'm afraid I don't remember much of it."

"I'm wondering if maybe Friederich was developing some kind of new racing technology. There was a point in the video when he brought in a brown sack that must have had something to do with his work, but he shut down the video feed before he opened it. It was like he didn't want the camera to know what it was. When the video came back up, Friederich was gone."

Alice sounded doubtful. "A new technology would be something Larry would kill for?"

"I didn't say it would be. I'm just saying the police might believe it."

"What part of the car was he working on?"

"Jonathan said it was the shocks."

Alice popped another almond in her mouth. "Larry is *not* a killer, but we can ask him if Friederich was developing any kind of valuable technology. If there's something to it, we need to convince the police Larry wasn't interested enough to kill for it."

Francine found she had another handful of nuts in her hand. She dumped them back in the bowl and gave the bowl to Alice. "Please hide these things."

Alice tucked the bowl in a drawer. "What do you think I should do?"

"About Larry?"

"Of course about Larry! Who else are we talking about? Should I kick him out of the house? I hate to, but a few nights in a hotel with the police breathing down his neck might convince him to either tell me what's going on or meet with this mysterious person and tell them whatever it is he's got to tell them."

Francine tried to think if she'd do that to Jonathan. It was hard to imagine herself in the position Alice was in. "I think you should err on the side of kindness."

The women heard a knock on the door frame. Jonathan stood outside the entry. "Larry left to go see the lawyer," he said.

Alice pushed herself off the bar. "I guess Larry and I will have to talk later, then."

"Do you want us to stay."

"I'll be okay."

Francine gave her a hug. "If you need anything, call me."

"I'll see you tomorrow at Mary Ruth's luncheon."

"You'll be there?"

"I have to have something to do other than stew about this situation with Larry."

Alice saw them out. Since they'd driven separately, Francine had to postpone any questions until she and Jonathan got home. She noticed a couple of cars parked on the curb, but she didn't think anything of them until she passed them and they started their motors. To her alarm, they swung in behind Jonathan's truck and followed them back to their house. They parked a short distance down the street.

Francine was frantic. After Jonathan had pulled in and the garage door went down, she hurried over to his truck. "Did you see those two cars?"

He nodded. "Who do you suppose they are?"

"I don't know, but earlier today I thought I was being followed when I came home from Danville. They went straight when I pulled into the subdivision, so I decided it was my imagination."

They went into the house and looked out the front window of the great room. Francine did it discreetly from the side, but Jonathan defiantly stood in front of the glass. The two cars were still there. "Either we're both hallucinating," he said, "or we were followed." He stepped back so he was no longer in clear view. "What were you in Danville for, or do I want to know?"

"You remember how we decided that someone might be trying to frame Larry? Joy and I went to the assessor's office to try to find out how someone could have learned Larry had leased that property to Friederich. It wasn't public knowledge. It was like Larry was hiding something."

"How do you know it wasn't public knowledge?"

"Joy talked to Rob Seneff at the Chamber."

Jonathan tensed. "What did Rob say?"

"Joy felt he knew something about the building, but he was hiding it." She watched her husband become more and more uncomfortable. "You wouldn't know anything more about that building, would you? You knew about the hidden computer."

He shifted his weight from one foot to the other. "Maybe."

"You want to elaborate on that?"

"Not right now."

She pressed him. "The auditor's records showed the building was listed at two thousand square feet, half of it business and half of it storage. There's no way Friederich's business occupies more than a thousand square feet. Where's the other thousand?"

He didn't answer.

"A basement is the logical answer," she continued. "But I didn't see any stairs."

He squirmed. "I hate to claim client confidentiality, but I'm going to."

"Jonathan. It's me, your wife. Don't go pulling a Larry on me."

"You deserve answers, I agree. And Larry needs to stop stalling." He pulled out his keys. "He said he was going to see the lawyer. I'm going to try to get into that meeting. I'm bothered by a lot of things, not the least that he hid over a million dollars in an offshore account and that he's spent most of it on something he won't tell Alice or me about."

"In the forty-five years we've been married, you've never pulled this client confidentiality thing on me."

"We've never dealt with a situation like this before, where you're asking me for details about someone we both know."

She reached for his hand. "Promise me when this is over, that you won't keep secrets from me."

The phone rang. He moved to get it, but she wouldn't let go of his hand. "Let it go to the answering machine."

"This is Darla Baggesen," the chipper voice said on the other end.

Francine rolled her eyes. *Like she needs to tell us her last name.* But then Darla said something that made Francine wish she'd answered it. "Just wanted you to know I'm not bringing Sara with me tomorrow to the luncheon at your house. Thought you should know so you can get Mary Ruth an accurate count of how many she'll be catering for. Good-bye."

Jonathan crossed his arms over his chest. "What luncheon tomorrow?"

"I was going to tell you about it. Really."

"This is connected to the murder, isn't it?"

"Mary Ruth wants to get more catering jobs, too, so it's kind of yes and kind of no."

"Sounds like kind of yes to me."

Francine felt resigned. "Okay," she said, and filled him in on Charlotte's theory that the murderer's choice of the shed to store the body pointed to a neighbor being involved at some level, and that the killer always returns to the scene of the crime. As she started in on the selection of the guest list and having Jud there to presumptively to talk about a neighborhood watch program, she started to think the plan sounded absurd. But Jonathan nodded his head.

"So you're keeping secrets, too?"

"Not big ones, like Larry."

"I don't keep big ones from you either. Trust me on this. And it's okay. Fran, if we knew each other so well that we could predict each other's moves every time, how boring would that be! I know I'd miss it if you didn't show up on *Good Morning America* every once in a while in a wet sundress."

She hugged him. "Don't ever fall out of love with me."

"Never," he said, encircling her in his arms.

They stayed that way for awhile. "I only wish we could come up with a better suspect than Larry. Charlotte's trying to make a case against Jake Maehler. It's just not very strong."

"Would it help to know Jake Maehler doesn't have an alibi for the night Friederich was killed?"

"What? How do you know that?"

"It was something Larry said before you got there."

"How would he know?"

"I have no idea. He's still a big fan of Jake's, but let's be honest. It's to his advantage right now that Jake doesn't have an alibi either."

Francine's cell phone rang. She checked the number and held up the phone. "It's Joy."

He shrugged. "You better take it. It's risky to not keep up with what Joy and Marcy are concocting."

She answered.

"Have you been on the Internet lately?" Joy asked.

"I just haven't had time…"

"The YouTube video of our *GMA* appearance went over its millionth viewing an hour ago. We're number one!"

"I'm glad you're happy but—"

"So Marcy used that to get the *People* magazine people to agree to do a feature. They're hiring some local talent to interview us on Saturday and then follow us around taking photos."

"Wait a minute. I haven't signed up for this kind of thing, and I'm certain Alice and Mary Ruth won't agree to it, either." She would have added Charlotte, but she was worried her friend was getting accustomed to the attention, even if it didn't always show her in the best light.

"You're wrong about Mary Ruth. Marcy knows Ted Allen—he's from Indiana—and she's talking to him about getting her a guest spot on the Food Network. He thinks they can work her into the next season of *Chopped*. Mary Ruth's convinced it will do wonders for her catering business."

"I don't like the idea of cameras following me around. I thought you didn't like it at the Courthouse Grounds when people pointed their cell phones at you."

"That was before the CBS interview came through. Marcy was right. We nailed our appearance on *GMA*, and now everyone wants us. The CBS morning show is bidding against *GMA* for me to be their senior citizen correspondent. I have to film a sample segment and have it in New York on Monday. Marcy and I are working on a script this afternoon."

Jonathan tinkled his keys and indicated he was going to leave.

"Don't go getting a big head, Joy. And don't forget we have that luncheon tomorrow. No press. I won't let them in my house." She nodded her head that it was okay for Jonathan to go, even if they hadn't quite finished their conversation.

Joy continued to babble. "If you don't let them in, they'll only camp out on the lawn. Haven't you noticed yourself being followed? I don't know if they're official press or celebrity stalkers, but there are two vehicles I don't recognize parked on my curb."

Francine checked to make sure the two she had were still there. "Yep, we've got two as well. Jonathan is getting ready to leave. Maybe one or both of them will follow him."

"Anyway, I'm guessing from your attitude that you wouldn't like a guest spot on *The View*."

"Absolutely not."

"Marcy's already working on it. I'll tell her, but I think it's almost a done deal."

"No. That's my final word." And she hung up in anger.

Neither of the cars followed Jonathan, to her dismay. They stayed put.

Her iPhone rang again. This time it was Charlotte. "What are you doing right now, Francine?"

"I don't even know. What do you need?"

"I got a breakthrough. You remember I said we needed to get into Friederich's house? I got it arranged."

"You didn't! It's illegal."

"The realtor I'm working with thinks it's not. At least not too illegal."

"I don't think there's a spectrum of illegality, Charlotte. It either is or it isn't."

"Then it isn't. There's no crime scene tape around the house, no notice on the front door saying you can't go in. Besides, how much trouble could we really get into?"

"What do you mean, *we*?"

"That's why I asked what you were doing. I need you here to help."

"Charlotte!"

"I know what you're thinking... fingerprints. How can we not leave fingerprints? I'm already ahead on that one. I brought a box of Mary Ruth's food serving gloves for us to wear."

"I wouldn't worry so much about fingerprints. I'd worry that it's broad daylight and every neighbor will see us go in his house."

"Good, you're on board then. I've circled the block and I'm headed down the alleyway to park in the back. No one's in the other

171

side of the duplex, and it doesn't look like anyone in the neighbor-hood is home. As long as the realtor can get us in the rear entrance, we're set. She should be here any minute. Better hurry up, Francine. And watch out for the paparazzi. I had to give them the slip when I left the subdivision."

"Paparazzi?" she said, but Charlotte had already hung up.

She couldn't decide if it was better to have press or paparazzi. They would both be a nuisance. And she had no idea how to give them the slip.

TWENTY-TWO

FRANCINE HEADED INTO THE old area of Brownsburg using several alleyways she knew about and finally lost the two cars. Then she drove over to the duplex Friederich had put on the market.

As Charlotte advised, she used the alley behind the duplex to keep the car hidden from the street. The back yard had a chain-link fence about waist high. Francine let herself in the gate and power-walked across the untended lawn dotted with yellow dandelions. She worried her tennis shoes were leaving tracks in the grass, but there wasn't anything she could do about it.

Charlotte, stationed on the side of the house, motioned her to hurry. "I stood on the back stoop for a little while but the position is too exposed," she said when Francine got close. "Besides, here we can stand in the shade."

Charlotte was dressed in a black shirt, black elastic-waist pants, and a wig that harkened back to Marlo Thomas's hairstyle on *That Girl* in the '60s. She had on dark sunglasses. If Francine hadn't been so nervous, she would have laughed at the disguise. "I can't believe we're doing this. When is the realtor going to show up?"

"Soon, I hope. I feel like I'm the poster criminal for that neighborhood crime watch Jud is going to talk about tomorrow." She hopped from foot to foot.

"Will you quit dancing like that? You're making me nervous."

"You're nervous? That little episode this morning with my stomach triggered my diarrhea, and I've been drinking Gatorade to stay hydrated. It's weighing heavy on my bladder. That bush over there is starting to look pretty good."

"I heard something. Maybe she just pulled up."

The two women watched as the gate opened.

"You didn't tell me the realtor was Emily Barringer," Francine said.

"What's wrong with Emily?"

"She's good friends with Darla Baggesen! This has the potential to be all over the grapevine."

Emily, wearing dress pants, a flower print blouse, and heels, closed the gate behind her and started toward them. There was no sidewalk, so Emily's shoes kept getting stuck in the yard as she made her way to the house.

Charlotte shook her head when the realtor finally reached them. "You're dressed like you're going to show the place. We're here to skulk around, not do a formal viewing."

Emily matched Charlotte's attitude with her own. "It's just in case the police show up. If they do, the party line is that I was unaware we weren't supposed to show it."

"I'm sure that'll work," Charlotte said dryly. "It explains why you came in the back and core-aerated the yard."

Emily took a key out of her purse. "You want in or not?"

"Wait." Charlotte handed a pair of Mary Ruth's gloves to each of them. "Put these on before you touch anything. I'm sure I don't have to tell you why." She waggled her eyebrows.

"What do you suggest we do with them if the police show up?" Francine asked, pulling on her pair. "They're not going to believe Emily's story if we have these on."

"We won't have them on. At the first sign of trouble, I expect you to eat them."

Emily shook her head. "You're such a card."

Francine was amused. *She thinks Charlotte's kidding.*

When the women were gloved, Emily opened the door. It led into the kitchen, which had old appliances and a worn-out Formica countertop but was otherwise clean.

Francine looked around. "It's pretty dated. Was this thing getting many showings?"

"Look at the neighborhood and think about the economy," Emily said. "No. You should try being a realtor under these conditions."

"I'm checking out the bathroom," Charlotte said.

"Why the bathroom?"

"Because I have to use it."

Francine rifled through the kitchen drawers. "Let's check in here first. We'll do this methodically from back to front."

"I'm not doing anything," Emily said. "I'm going to sit on the couch and watch. I agreed to get you in, but now I'm having second thoughts. I don't even know what we're looking for."

Charlotte spoke before she went in the bathroom. "The police have been able to find all sorts of clues they won't share with us.

175

We're looking for reasons someone other than Larry Jeffords killed Friederich. Someone like Jake Maehler."

Emily got more defiant. "You didn't tell me you're trying to find evidence against Jake Maehler. I like him. I don't think he's a killer. He's got a killer body, though."

"I said someone *like* Jake Maehler. Why don't you go look for financial records? See if you can scare up a file cabinet."

"You know, I'm trying not to get in trouble for this."

"If you help, we'll get out of here faster." Charlotte closed the bathroom door behind her as Emily relented and got off the couch.

Francine searched the kitchen. Emily wandered down the hall. Eventually Francine heard the toilet flush. The bathroom door opened and Charlotte came out waving a bunch of magazines. "He read magazines while sitting on the pot," she announced.

"Something scandalous?"

"*Mechanics Illustrated* and *Sprint Car & Midget Racing*."

"No hot button there."

Charlotte leafed through them. "But he's turned down the corners to mark pages in several of the *Sprint Car* issues."

"Anything interesting?"

"They're pages of photos. Looks like they were taken at racing events. I'm taking them with me. They might be important." She put the magazines on the kitchen table.

Francine got up on a step stool and examined the upper shelves of Friederich's cabinets. "This is definitely a bachelor's kitchen. I think he may have four mismatched place settings total, and they're assembled from cheap dinnerware. Lots of empty, dusty shelves."

Charlotte opened the refrigerator and peered in. "Ewww." She recoiled from the smell. "Not too much in here, but whatever it is needs to be thrown away." She closed the door and opened the freezer compartment above the refrigerator. "He had a thing for Marie Callender, apparently. Hey, what do we know about Friederich's love life?"

"Nothing. Maybe we should ask about that."

Charlotte closed the freezer door and checked behind the refrigerator. Francine came down off the step stool and stood behind her, peering over her head into the dark space. "What are we looking for back here?"

"If you were going to hide something important, you'd put it in a place people wouldn't think to look."

"We'd need a flashlight to see back there. And anyway, he'd have to move the fridge every time he wanted to get it. This is a wild goose chase, Charlotte."

"I should have remembered to bring a flashlight. I wonder if Friederich kept one around."

"Probably in the garage."

"Good idea." Charlotte found a door off the kitchen that led into the garage. She flipped on a light and went in.

"Even if she finds a flashlight, there's nothing behind that refrigerator," Francine said to herself. She gave up on the kitchen and checked on Emily. Emily was in the second bedroom, which Friederich had turned into an office.

"Not finding too much here," Emily told her. "Looks like the police hauled out a computer, and a lot of the drawers in this file cabinet are empty. I'm going through a few folders that were left, but I don't see anything important." She held up a folder with a single sheet of paper in it.

"Well, keep trying. I'm going to check his bedroom."

She crossed the short hallway. Friederich's bedroom was small and squarish, maybe ten feet on a side. A window on the west wall had Venetian blinds, partially closed, that let in some light. There were a couple of generic framed paintings on the wall, but no photos on the dresser. A twin bed lined up along the south wall. Between the twin bed and the lack of photos, Francine wondered if Friederich had a love life at all. The police might have removed photos, she mused, but it certainly didn't look like he had a relationship to speak of.

Doors that slid back on one another hid the contents of a closet on the east wall next to the dresser. Francine slid open one of the doors, found a pull cord, and turned on the low-watt lightbulb in the closet. A rod ran from wall to wall with hangers on the rod. About half the hangers had clothes on them. Typical of a man, she thought. Limited wardrobe. There was a shelf above the hanging clothes. Francine was tall enough that she could pat around without having to get a step stool. On one side she found a magazine. The lack of dust on the cover made her think it was a magazine he'd looked at recently. She stood on tiptoes and pulled it down, expecting to find something like *Playboy*. Instead, it was another copy of *Sprint Car & Midget Racing*. There were no marked pages, as Charlotte had found with the copies in the bathroom. It had a July date on the cover, so it must be the most recent issue. She wondered why he would keep it on the top shelf of the closet. She carried it back to the kitchen table and added it to the stack Charlotte had created.

Francine hadn't seen Charlotte since she disappeared into the garage. She opened the door. The light was still on.

"Charlotte?" she said. There was no answer. Fearing her friend had fallen, Francine went in.

Friederich's home garage was spotless, just like the workspace he'd rented from Larry and Alice, but it was small. Taking up most of the single car garage space was his vintage Corvette in immaculate condition. Something about muscle cars appealed to Charlotte, so Francine went to the driver's side and peered in the window. Charlotte was slumped over in the front seat.

Francine yanked open the door.

Charlotte sat up immediately. She had terror in her eyes, then relief. "Ohmigosh, Francine, you scared me half to death."

"What are you doing in there?"

"Imagining myself taking this thing out for a spin. It's a beauty, isn't it?" She put one hand on the steering wheel and the other on the gear shift.

Francine leaned an elbow on the car's roof. "We don't have time for this."

"Do you think the police searched the 'Vette?"

"Of course they did."

"Good. Then I'm taking this." She held up an iPod Touch. "I've always wanted one."

Francine's eyes widened. "You can't take that."

"Why not? I'm taking the magazines. And Friederich's dead, it's not like he's going to miss it."

The door opened and Emily stuck her head out. "Emergency problem. We've got a Channel 59 satellite truck outside. It doesn't look like they're going anywhere anytime soon."

Charlotte said a bad word.

"We'll be there in a minute," Francine said.

Charlotte put out her hand. "Help me out. I'm stuck. That's the problem with these muscle cars, they're not designed for senior citizens."

Francine pried her out of the seat.

"We need to put the cover back on," Charlotte said.

"You took the cover off?"

"Don't lecture me. Just help me put it back so we can see what's going on with Channel 59."

The two of them draped the cover back over the Corvette. In the house, they found Emily holding the curtain back just enough to see outside. "The cameraman is filming the place and there's a reporter that's been snooping around the windows. All the shades are drawn, which is a good thing."

Charlotte stood behind Emily where she could see outside. "She looks like she's headed back to the van."

Emily wrung her hands. "I'm going to get in trouble for this. I knew I shouldn't have agreed to show you this house."

"Okay, here's what we'll do," Charlotte said, talking with her hands. "They're both in front now. We'll slip out the back, the way we came. If we head the long way down the alley we'll come out on a side road, and we can use it to get back to Green Street. From there we scatter, each in a different direction."

"I don't know," Francine said. "If they're smart, they'll have planted another cameraman back by our cars. At least you have a disguise on, with that silly wig."

"It's not silly. I bet you wish you'd thought of it now."

"Quiet, both of you," Emily said. "You're not the ones whose career is on the line. I bet they followed one of you here."

"It's possible, but I tried really hard to lose them," Francine said. "They must be good." She decided from now on, no more doing anything she didn't want on camera.

Charlotte pulled open her pants and stuck the iPod in her underwear. Francine started to say something, but she waved her off. "In case the police show up and we get searched," she said. "Grab the magazines. We can't hide those. We'll have to chance them."

The women gathered at the back door. Charlotte had them slip off their gloves. She opened the back door and let them out and closed it behind her. Then she took off her gloves. They hustled as fast as they could across the back yard, but Emily easily outpaced them, even in heels. She reached the gate first, opened it, and froze. "We've been found," she said.

Francine and Charlotte came up behind her as she took off for her car. Channel 59 had not only stationed a cameraman back by their cars, but also a reporter. The reporter screamed questions at Emily as she covered her face with her hand, got in the car, and drove off. The cameraman stopped filming her and turned his attention to the other two.

"Follow suit," Charlotte said, "only not as fast." She took the magazines from Francine.

As embarrassing as she found it, Francine couldn't think of anything else to do. She and Charlotte tried their best to cover their identities and get to their cars. The reporter asked questions about why they were there and what they hoped to find. Neither she nor Charlotte answered. The cameraman got in their way. They pushed past him and climbed in their cars. Francine drove off first. She hoped Charlotte didn't have any problems.

Francine had tears in her eyes on the way home. She'd never done anything even remotely criminal before. Now she felt like a felon. When she pulled onto her street, she noticed another reporter, this one from Joy's beloved Channel 6, parked on the curb in front of her home. Francine was glad she could open the garage door remotely and get in the house while avoiding him.

Once inside, Francine tried to calm down but couldn't stop the shaking. She eyed the clock. She wondered if they'd make the five o'clock news in a half hour. One way or another, she was pretty sure Jud would be visiting them soon.

TWENTY-THREE

Not much later Francine received a call from Charlotte. "Jud's here," she said. "He'd like you to come over too."

That was fast. Jonathan isn't even back from seeing Larry's lawyer. "Is he mad at us?"

"What do you think?"

"I'll be right there."

If Jud had been angry when he arrived at Charlotte's, he'd mellowed by the time Francine got there. Charlotte had made a pot of tea, and the two of them were enjoying a cup in the dining room. Jud was dressed more like a beat cop, in uniform with his gun obvious. A manila pocket folder sat next to him on the round table. It was stuffed with papers.

Jud stood when she entered. He smiled and gave her a hug, just like he had when he'd hung out with her sons. Although she was fond of Jud, the change in attitude made her suspicious.

"Sit," Charlotte said, half invitation and half order. "Can I get you some tea? It's English Breakfast." Tea was always a safe alternative at

Charlotte's house. She might drink rotgut brandy, but she stocked a good selection of loose teas ordered from a specialty house in Boston. Without waiting for her to answer, Charlotte poured it into a fancy china cup and saucer, china that was used only when she wanted to impress.

"Jud and I have been discussing strategy for solving this crime," she said. "I think we've come to an agreement of sorts."

Jud nodded. "I can't seem to keep you ladies away from this, so what I want to do is keep you safe."

"Safe is good," said Francine. "What did you have in mind?"

"First and foremost, we have to share information." He paused to take a sip of his tea. "Isn't that right, Charlotte?"

Charlotte smiled.

Francine briefly considered that she had crossed into the *Twilight Zone*. "Meaning…?"

"Meaning he's not very happy with us searching Friederich's house without his permission," Charlotte said.

"I admit it wasn't the brightest move, especially in retrospect, with the press showing up." She briefly considered throwing Charlotte under the bus by saying it was all her idea, but she figured Jud had already guessed that. She took a softer tack. "You'd already searched the house, hadn't you? We didn't find anything."

"Ah, but you *did* find something. You took a few magazines out of the house. Channel 59 put the report on their website. Charlotte held them up to hide her face."

"As a part of our agreement, I returned them to Jud," Charlotte said.

He tapped the manila folder to indicate he had them.

Francine was quite certain now she'd entered the *Twilight Zone*. This was a Charlotte from an alternate universe. Unless … Jud didn't know about the iPod, and she was hiding it from him.

"Was there anything significant in the magazines?"

"No smoking guns, if that's what you mean. We'd already glanced through them, especially the one at the top of the closet, but Charlotte and I have talked about the ones in the bathroom with the turned-down pages. Her reasoning is making us take a second look."

"I think the marked pages may reveal some clues to why Friederich had the other one at the top of the closet," Charlotte said. "It may relate to the crime."

"Is Emily Barringer going to get in trouble?"

Jud put down his teacup. "Technically, she didn't do anything wrong. The house is listed for sale, and it wasn't a crime scene. We would have preferred it not be shown for a while, but there's nothing we could charge her with."

"I'd feel really bad if I'd gotten her in trouble," Charlotte told Francine.

Jud looked at the two women with seriousness. "I'm more concerned about you than Emily. As I said, I need to keep you safe. The problem is, there's been no threat against you, and I can't justify the manpower to give you a police escort everywhere you go. So I want you to court the press."

Francine winced. "Do we have to?"

Jud, who had taken another sip of his tea, almost snorted it out. "I thought you loved the publicity."

"Certain members of the Bridge Club do." Francine threw a glance at Charlotte. "I'm not one of them."

"Don't look at me. I'm not the one who's been asked to be on *The View*."

Francine's eyes blazed. "I have no intention of doing that show."

Jud put up a hand to stop the bickering. "I need for you to pretend you enjoy the press. Just until we have the killer in custody. After that, you can do as you like."

Francine considered his request. She wanted to say yes, but if it went on for too long she might really end up on *The View*. "Are you close to an arrest? You sound like you might be."

"We have a lot of circumstantial evidence at this point, but we think we're close to having a case."

Circumstantial evidence likely pointed to one person.

"You're not close enough to having a case if you think it's Larry Jeffords," Charlotte said.

"Why are you so certain it's not him? Francine isn't."

"I'm not?"

"You were at the County Government Center yesterday looking into his property."

"How did you know that? And anyway, we're out to prove Larry is being framed. I was trying to find out if anyone had accessed information about the building. He didn't have that property listed, but someone who knows a lot about Larry worked his way around the security cameras and then placed the body in his shed."

"We knew where you'd been because an anonymous source called it in, and I checked it out. Everyone knows who you are. You can't skulk around doing detective work. Nor do we want you to."

Jud was getting Francine's dander up. "I've known Larry for a long time," she said. "He's not a killer."

He rested his forearms on the table. "Really? Just how well do you think you know Larry?"

"Pretty darn well," Charlotte said. "We've known him and Alice since they moved in thirty years ago."

Jud looked at his watch. "If you have a half hour, I'll show you that you don't know him like you think you do."

Francine checked her cell phone. Nothing from Jonathan, but she'd forgotten to leave a note, and now she was worried what he would think if he heard about their escapade from someone else. "Let me make a phone call to Jonathan so he knows where I am," she said.

She made her way into the hall.

Jonathan turned out to be in the truck on the way home from the lawyer's office. He hadn't heard about the Channel 59 incident, which surprised her. "Don't believe anything you might hear," she told him. "I'll fill you in when I get home. It'll be a half hour or so. Jud's taking us somewhere to prove we really don't know Larry."

"Where?"

"I don't know yet."

He sounded nervous. "Just remember, everything isn't what it looks like." He hung up.

Francine wondered if they both didn't have a lot to talk about later.

Back in the dining area, she volunteered to drive and Charlotte accepted. After locking up the house, they walked out with Jud. He pointed to two new cars parked out front.

"There's your paparazzi, ladies," he said, beaming. "Wave to them and make nice. They are your friends right now."

Francine grumbled but did as she was asked. Charlotte did, too, but with more enthusiasm.

They got into the Prius and Jud got in his police car, and the parade drove over to Friederich's garage on Adams Street.

After they arrived, the press immediately set up and began taking pictures. Jud cautioned them to stay back. He gathered the women by the shop door, using them as a shield to block the reporters from being able to see what he was doing.

He unlocked the dead bolt on the door and then went to work on the numeric keypad. His fingers flew over the numbers with practiced certainty and there was a click. He opened the door. "Let's go in," he said, leaving the press outside.

The look of delight on Charlotte's face reminded Francine that this was her first look at Friederich's garage. She stepped off the tiles in the entryway and admired the shiny garage floor. "Look how clean it is!"

"If we have time, I'll take you through the rest of the shop," Jud said. "But not now. Now I want you to see this."

He flipped a wall switch and the lights went on. Then, bending down to the first tile by the door, he removed it, flipped a lever, and a nine-tile section of the entryway slid back to reveal a staircase leading down.

The women drew in sharp breaths when the staircase appeared.

"Larry installed this?" Charlotte asked.

Jud started down the staircase. "*Had* it installed. Shortly after he bought the building, apparently. Larry was famous for the low-stakes poker tournaments he had here."

He said the last line pointedly, making Francine realize where he was going. "So more than a few people knew about this."

He nodded.

Perhaps that's what Jonathan meant when he said not everything was what it looked like.

Jud arrived at the bottom of the stairs and looked back up. "Watch your head, Francine. Charlotte, you may not want to come down. There's no handrail, and I don't want you to fall."

"Jud, if you told me I had to jump down there onto a trampoline, do a somersault, and land on a skateboard, I'd still do it. As it is, all I need is Francine's hand. I'll be careful!"

The two women took the staircase one step at a time. Francine breathed a sigh of relief when they stood at the bottom.

The first thing she noticed was a faint smell of cigar smoke and stale beer. Jud flipped a light switch and the remainder of the basement lit up. The room was not, in the current vernacular, a man-cave. It was more like an unfinished, bare-bones poker room, with a poker table in the center and a florescent light above it. Two couches in disrepair were in a corner of the room, a small table between them.

A man was lying on one of the couches, curled up, facing the back. The women gasped when they saw him. Jud drew his gun, which scared them even more. The man looked like he could be asleep, but Francine didn't think so. With all the commotion they'd made, they would have awakened a hibernating bear.

Jud motioned them back. He cautiously approached the couch.

"How did he get here?" Charlotte whispered to Francine. "Haven't they had this place closed up?"

"I have a bad feeling about this."

"Hey, buddy," Jud said. No response.

"Buddy…"

He jostled the man's shoulder. Still no response. He felt for a pulse at the man's neck. Without a word to the women he reholstered his gun, pulled out a walkie-talkie, and called 911.

TWENTY-FOUR

"When was the last time you were here, Jud?" Francine asked while they waited for emergency vehicles to arrive.

He continued to study the body and tried to keep Charlotte at bay. "Yesterday."

"And the body wasn't here then."

"Definitely not."

"Then how the hell did he get down here?" Charlotte asked. She was pressed up against the wall, out of Jud's reach, trying to get a better look at the face that was buried in the couch cushions.

"I don't know!" Jud sounded very irritated.

"You know who I think that is?" she said.

"No, but I imagine you're going to tell me anyway."

"I don't know who it is," Francine said, trying to be kind. "You can tell me."

"It's Jeff Kramer."

"The reporter you were trying to get hold of?"

She nodded. "Now we know why he's been gone for a few days. Do you know him, Jud?"

"We know all the local reporters. He normally does sports, but he covers other beats from time to time. Why were you trying to get hold of him?"

"Trying to figure out why Jake Maehler said Friederich had sabotaged his car." Charlotte inched forward as much as she could without getting Jud any angrier. "There's no blood," she said. "I bet he was bloodchoked just like Friederich."

"We're going to let the coroner decide the cause of death. I'm not going to speculate at this point."

"You know I'm right. Maybe we've got a serial killer on our hands. The blood choke could be his signature killing method."

Jud turned and planted his hands on his hips. "You better hope this is not a serial killing. None of us wants that kind of scourge in Brownsburg."

The vehemence with which he spoke made Charlotte recoil. "You're right, Jud. I'm sorry I said it."

"On the other hand, it does bother me to find two deaths, days apart, by what's probably the same method."

Francine tried to move forward, only to be stopped by Jud's forearm. "Sorry. I just wanted a closer look at his clothes. Don't they seem damp to you?"

Charlotte craned her neck for a better view. "You're right. I had totally missed that." The disappointment in her voice was profound. "Why do you think they're damp?"

And that was when it hit Francine. She'd been doing too much of the investigating, too much of the thinking. She'd meant to protect Charlotte, but instead she was depriving her friend of the chance to solve this crime and once and for all, checking off her #1 Sixty List item. If this was going to work, Charlotte had to be empowered to solve this crime. Spinning out before her was a way everything worked out, where Charlotte solved the murder, Joy had her moment in the sun, and, for reasons she couldn't define, she just knew that the others would get something they needed too.

And it all started with eight little words. "I don't know, Charlotte. What do you think?"

Charlotte stared off into space, eyes intense, but didn't answer.

"You read all those murder mysteries," Francine pressed. "Surely something in one of those would explain the dampness."

Charlotte pointed toward the body. She was so excited her finger was shaking. "Yes," she said. "It's been frozen. Or refrigerated. It's in the process of coming to room temperature, and the clothes are damp because of it. And that would mean Jeff Kramer's been dead for a while. Maybe he was even killed at the same time as Friederich."

Jud nodded his head ever so slightly. Francine caught the movement and prodded him. "What do you think, Jud?"

"She could be right. But we won't know until the coroner tells us. I'm sorry I brought you down here. You didn't need to be exposed to this."

"But we did need it," Charlotte said, "for Larry's sake."

"I guess I've proved my point. You don't know Larry as well as you thought."

"Oh, for heaven's sake!" Francine said. "You can't possibly suspect Larry of killing this reporter too. How stupid would it be for a killer to leave one body in his pool shed and then drop a second body in the basement of one of his leased buildings after he's under suspicion of killing the first."

"She's right, Jud. You'd be dealing with an idiotic murderer, and you know Larry's no idiot."

"I didn't say he was. Nor did I say the same person did both killings. It could be a copycat murder." He crossed his arms and stared at the body, thinking. "But, somehow, I think they are related."

He pulled out his cell phone and began to take photos of the couches and the body.

Charlotte moved away from the wall. She motioned Francine over. "You know what's going to happen when the police get here, don't you?" she said softly.

"The same thing that happened at Alice's house when we found Friederich?"

"Exactly. Except there aren't any rooms per se, so they might whisk us off to police headquarters."

"Great."

"So if we're going to investigate anything, we need to do it now before any more police get here."

Francine knew Charlotte was right. Watching Jud taking photos with his smartphone had made her think about doing the same with hers. She began snapping pictures of the room while trying to hide it from the detective.

The floor was bare concrete. Larry's one concession to civility was a big Oriental rug that the poker table sat on. The rug looked well-used, like it had been bought secondhand. Cigar stubs lay in ashtrays on the table, the source of what Francine had smelled earlier. She imagined the men sitting around the table placing their bets. She walked to the table and took photos of it. "So Jonathan smokes cigars? But he never smelled like smoke."

Charlotte followed. "Maybe he wasn't involved. Even if he didn't smoke, it would have been on his clothes."

Francine shook her head. "Based on something he said, I'm guessing he's been down here."

Charlotte reached to pick up one of the ashtrays.

Jud spoke before she laid a finger on it. "Please don't touch that."

She jerked her hand back. "I'm just thinking that there aren't that many ashtrays down here. And I'm wondering if Friederich smoked."

Francine thought back to when they'd been through his house. "His place didn't smell like smoke. I'm curious, though, if Friederich knew about this basement. Do you know anything about that, Jud?"

He didn't respond.

"You can't possibly suspect us of killing either of these two," Charlotte said. "So share information with us. You said you wanted our help in figuring this out."

He nodded. "Okay, but you didn't hear this from me. Larry says it wasn't long before Friederich figured out there was a basement, and he asked how to get down there. Larry wouldn't tell him, but they did come to an arrangement. Friederich was advised when they were playing poker, but it was a private game. He could either *not* use the garage that night or work with any noise they made. Larry claims he never showed Friederich how to get in the basement, and they only had poker games once a month."

Francine nudged Charlotte. "Bet you anything it was the same nights we played bridge."

"Was the basement here when Larry bought the building?" Charlotte asked Jud. "And did Larry say why he built the staircase?"

"As far back as we've been able to track, the original building had almost this full basement. The owner before Larry finished it out. Larry says he got rid of the outside entrance and had the secret staircase built for no other reason other than he loves secret stuff like he used to read about in old Hardy Boys mysteries."

Francine looked up at the ceiling and slowly rotated in all directions. "I'm guessing there are no surveillance cameras down here, or the feed would have been recorded on the computer upstairs."

Jud confirmed it. "We have no way of knowing who's been down here."

"If Friederich knew about the basement, maybe he figured out how to get down here," Charlotte said. "With no cameras, he might have used it for God knows what. Maybe something that got him killed."

"That's a lot of speculation," Jud said.

"I wonder what's in that refrigerator," Francine said, pointing out an old unit on the opposite side of the room. It was the type with a freezer compartment on top. "Or maybe what *was* in it."

"Jeff Kramer is too big to fit in it," Charlotte said. "At least, I'm pretty sure." She picked up a bar towel she found on one of the chairs. She crossed the room, continuing to ruminate. "He would take up all the room, though. So if we open it up and there's nothing in it…" She reached for the handle, holding the towel in her hand to keep from leaving fingerprints.

"Don't touch it," Jud warned.

"Why can't she open it?" Francine asked. "She's not leaving fingerprints. And it's probably just full of beer, unless that's where the killer stored the body."

"Yesterday that's all that was in it. Beer," he said.

Charlotte waved the towel at him. "So let's see if that's still true."

He thought a moment. "Let me do it." He held out his hand and Charlotte gave him the towel. He opened the door.

Light spilled out. The three of them peered in.

"Beer," Charlotte said, sounding disappointed.

Just then the emergency personnel arrived. They clomped down the stairs. Jud returned the towel to Charlotte and went to meet them. An EMT checked the body. With Jud distracted, Francine and Charlotte hurriedly examined the contents of the refrigerator. The beer bottles were lined up mostly in rows. The brands were ones their friends drank.

She closed the door and looked back at the poker table.

"Where are the empties?" she asked.

Francine pointed to an orange bin in a dark corner of the room. "They're in the recycle container. Why?"

"What I'm thinking is this," Charlotte said. "Why are the cigar ashes still there, but the bottles cleared away? Seems odd."

"The short answer would be, they're men. But it's a smart observation."

The two women strolled over to the recycle bin, trying not to attract attention. They leaned over it, not touching anything.

They stayed that way for a moment. Charlotte said in a soft voice, "Know anyone who drinks Molson?"

Francine had an 'aha' moment. "I see what you mean. There's only one Molson. No other imported beers. And there weren't any in the refrigerator, either."

"Exactly, Watson. And I can't think of anyone in our circle of friends who drinks Molson."

"I suppose it's possible the poker group could include some men we don't socialize with," Francine mused. "But it's puzzling there is only one Molson."

"Maybe whoever brought the dead body brought the beer with him."

The police and some additional emergency responders pounded down the stairs. Jud spoke to the police and then came over to the recycle bin. "We're all going down to headquarters for questioning. Me too. What are you looking at?"

"The Molson in there," Francine said. "But you won't find a Molson in the refrigerator, and we don't know anyone who drinks that particular brand."

"Yes," Charlotte said. "Could it be that whoever brought the body down here between when you left yesterday and when you returned today had a Molson with him?"

He looked skeptical. "They were responsible enough to recycle it, but not realize they were leaving evidence behind? Not likely."

"You were the one asking earlier if this was a stupid criminal."

"I'll note it. But now we need to get going."

Charlotte looked like she had more to say but was biting her tongue because of Jud and their police escort. As they reached the stairs, Francine insisted on helping her. They went up as they'd come down, one step at a time, together. Halfway up the stairs, Francine murmured, "Something's bothering you."

Charlotte checked to be sure they couldn't be overheard. "Do you remember the publicity photos we saw on Jake Maehler's website?"

"Sure."

"There was one of him by a pool, reclining on a beach towel in a beach chair."

"I vaguely remember it."

"There was a table next to the chair, and there was a beer on it. The beer had a blue label like Molson's. I want to check it. It doesn't mean anything by itself because I'm sure other people drink Molson. But I like the coincidence."

Francine hesitated. "I don't think we should say anything to Jud until we're sure."

"Agreed. But don't be discouraged, Francine. Solving this mystery is not going to be easy, but we can do it."

TWENTY-FIVE

IT WAS WELL PAST dinnertime before they left the police station. Francine thought the questioning had gone well. No one really suspected her or Charlotte of killing anyone, of course, but the police felt the women were somehow connected to the murderer, and they needed desperately to figure out what that connection was. After getting all the information they could, the police let them go.

Jud took them back to Friederich's garage where Francine had left her car. He made a big production of warning the press, now numbering four cars, to *stop* following the ladies around.

"I thought you wanted them to follow us," Charlotte said.

"I do. I'm making you irresistible by chasing them away. Just don't do any interviews, okay?"

After Francine dropped Charlotte off and returned to her house, she noticed the gaggle of press had reassembled outside her house. She pulled the car into the garage and again lowered the door before any reporters could assail the breach.

Inside Jonathan was there to give her a hug. But she pulled away. "You knew about Larry's secret basement. You played poker there."

"It was never my idea to keep it from you women."

"But you went along with it. And you kept it secret for a long time."

"It's not like we had high-stakes poker games. It was our version of your Bridge Club. We even had it on the same nights."

"But why not tell us?"

"It was Larry's idea, and we all just went along with it. He loved having secrets, and the staircase into the basement was a doozy."

"Having secrets is coming back to haunt him."

"While I agree with you it was wrong, don't pretend the Bridge Club hasn't been guilty of keeping secrets. I believe you told us you were having a slumber party, not going skinny-dipping."

"The slumber party part was true. Or was going to be, until Friederich's body fell out of the pool shed."

"You know what I mean."

She sighed. "More little secrets."

"We're all guilty." He tried to hug her and this time she let him. "Are you okay? Tell me what happened."

She told him about the events of the afternoon, the discovery of Kramer's body, and the interrogation at the police station.

"You found *another* body?"

"Jud found it at the same time. We didn't go looking for it. Don't start!"

"You *have* been through a lot."

She put her head on his chest. "I don't want to sound cold, but the sight of Jeff Kramer's dead body didn't bother me nearly as much as Friederich's did. I'm afraid I'm becoming immune."

"How did Kramer look?"

"Like he was sleeping, except his face was white. Just like Friederich, there was no blood to indicate how he died. Charlotte thinks it was another blood choke."

"What do you think?"

"I think someone needs to wrap this up quickly," she said, thinking of Charlotte. "Did you learn anything at the lawyer's?"

"Not much. I think Larry wants to tell me more information than the lawyer wants me to know. All I can figure is there was some kind of clause in the grandparents' will that made Larry do what he did. Not that we know what Larry did, other than spend the money."

"Alice told me she's considering throwing him out of the house in the hopes it will make him talk."

"The sooner he tells her what's going on, the sooner it'll be off his conscience."

Francine's stomach grumbled. "Are you hungry?"

"Famished. I haven't had dinner. I kept hoping you'd be home soon. Want to go out?"

She shook her head. "The press."

"I'll get take out. Mexican? Chinese? Pizza?"

"Chinese sounds good."

Jonathan left and Francine poured herself a glass of white wine. It wouldn't go well with the Chinese food but she'd be done with it before Jonathan got back. She started a light jazz playlist on the stereo and sat back in the recliner. Her cell phone rang.

It was Joy. "Good news. Marcy was able to cancel *The View*. They decided if you didn't want them, they didn't want you. But I don't think Marcy's taking your no very well. I think she's got something else in the works. In the meantime, the Food Network is warming up to the idea of using Mary Ruth."

"That should make her happy."

"I don't know if she knows yet. And I saw the news report about you and Charlotte and Jud finding another body."

"Already?" But then, the reporters had been right outside Larry's building and likely saw the medics pull the body out of the house. "I haven't seen it. I just got home."

"You can probably find it on one of the stations' websites. Or catch it at eleven. You might be the lead off story at eleven."

"I might use the DVR. But I think I'll just go to bed early and read about it in tomorrow's paper."

"Do you know who the dead person was?"

Francine decided it was best to toe the police's party line and not speculate. "I can't say."

"Do you think the same person killed him who killed Friederich?"

"I think it's likely. But I don't think it's Larry."

"I should hope not. Have you talked to Alice this afternoon?"

Francine didn't want to recount the trip she and Jonathan had made to Alice and Larry's house. "I've been kind of busy this afternoon…"

"Of course. I'll give her a call. I just wanted you to know about *The View*, so you wouldn't worry."

Oh, I wasn't worried, Francine wanted to say, *I was never going to do it*. Instead, she said, "I'm glad you're getting what you want, Joy.

But it may not be what the rest of us want. I'll see you tomorrow for the luncheon."

They hung up. Francine leaned back and tried to make sense of what was going on. Friederich had been killed, likely Saturday night. The killer had used a choke hold that kept the blood from reaching his brain. He then stored Friederich's body in Alice and Larry's pool shed. Why? In all likelihood, because it was close. The women had their skinny-dipping party the next night. Mary Ruth sniffed out the odor and traced it to the pool shed where they found the body.

They now knew Friederich had stopped paying Larry rent money. Larry had threatened to throw Friederich out, but never did. Why? Did he have a big heart or did Friederich have something Larry wanted? Could he have coveted the assets of the race car business? Friederich may have been working on some kind of technology for midget cars that could be valuable. It would seem so, since Jake Maehler had come back to Brownsburg in hopes Friederich could return him to his winning ways.

But how did the death of Jeff Kramer fit in? The same day Friederich was killed, Larry secretly returned from Las Vegas to meet someone whose name he wouldn't reveal, to tell him/her private information. Alice had become suspicious of Larry before he left and hired a detective to follow him, but Larry's sudden return surprised the detective and he was unable to catch the same flight. So the detective recruited Kramer as a last-minute replacement to follow Larry. But Kramer disappeared, only to be found dead three days later on a couch in the basement of the very building Friederich was renting from Larry. Kramer's time of death was unknown too. It's possible he was kept in cold storage until he was dumped on Larry's couch. He may have been killed in the same manner as Friederich. It may even have been around the same time as Friederich.

If Larry wasn't guilty—and he would have to be inordinately stupid to have planted evidence against himself—then who was guilty? Was it Jake Maehler, worried that Friederich *had* sabotaged his car in an earlier race? Although they had publicly made up, was Jake still concerned enough to just kill Friederich and take the technology for himself? Would Jake have done that to his former mentor? If he thought Friederich wasn't being loyal to him and was using his skills to help another driver, maybe. Kramer had authored articles about the Maehler/Friederich row. Perhaps Kramer had figured it out, knew for certain Jake had been betrayed, and that forced Jake's hand. Jake needed to kill Kramer in addition to Friederich to keep it all quiet.

But how did Larry's return from Las Vegas fit into that scenario? Kramer was alive to take the call to follow Larry, but no one knew what happened to him after that until he showed up dead. Jake didn't have an alibi for the time of Friederich's death, and neither did Larry. Maybe when the coroner decided the time of Kramer's death, either Larry or Jake would have an alibi for that and it would eliminate one of them as a suspect. Not that Francine seriously considered Larry a suspect. So was it Jake, the only name left, or was it an unknown? It was still possible the two deaths weren't connected, but no one, including Jud, thought it was likely.

Francine's cell phone rang again. *Charlotte.* She thought about sending it to voicemail because she wasn't finished ruminating. But the vision she'd had earlier flashed back again. Charlotte was her best friend. She needed to figure this out. Truth be told, Francine believed that Charlotte's free-thinking ways would allow her to leap to the conclusion before any of the other women would get there, including her. Plus, there was still that other item: the Bridge Club members and their Sixty Lists. Despite the horror of two deaths, some kind of magic was at play here she couldn't define. Even Alice, whose life was being affected most negatively by what was going on, seemed to be finding a strength no one knew she had. Francine couldn't say why, but she felt that if Charlotte could figure out who was guilty, they all might come through this ordeal with rare gifts no one could have imagined just days ago when everyone was afraid to go skinny-dipping and Friederich's body dropped out of the pool shed.

Francine answered the cell.

"That took long enough," Charlotte said. "Do I even want to know what you and Jonathan were doing? I've read mysteries where murder incites conjugal passion and people do all kinds of crazy—"

She didn't need her to finish the thought. "Jonathan has gone to get Chinese takeout. I was … busy. What do you need?"

"Your help. I'm sitting here looking at the pages of the magazines I got out of Friederich's bathroom. You know, the ones with the corners turned down? I know there must be a pattern, but I don't see it yet."

"But when we were at your house with Jud, you said you gave those magazines back to him."

"Please, Francine, I wouldn't be a decent sleuth if I hadn't already used my computer printer to copy those pages when I got home, just in case. The current issue I had to track down because it had too many pages I needed to copy, but fortunately they had it at the Barnes & Noble in Plainfield."

"You devil, Charlotte."

"So, can you come over?"

Francine thought a moment. She looked at the time. But more than that, she thought about her vision. "Why don't you let your mind work on that overnight, and we can talk in the morning? By the time Jonathan and I finish eating, all I'll want to do is go to bed. I'll call you."

"Okay." Charlotte said good night and hung up.

She heard Jonathan pull the truck into the garage. She got up from the recliner and met him in the kitchen.

He put the bag on the counter. "General Tso's chicken and beef with broccoli. I got fried rice. What are you smiling about?"

"I don't know. I feel bad about Jeff Kramer, Friederich Guttmann, and Alice and Larry, but I have this irrational feeling that everything's going to be all right."

"That's one of the things I love about you. Even in the midst of chaos, you refuse to give up hope." He kissed her on the lips. "Let's eat. If I knew how to use chopsticks better, some of this might not have made it home. As it is, there's a deficit of fortune cookies."

Francine looked in the bag and found one cookie still wrapped. Where there might have been others, she found crumpled cellophane and crumbs. Then she spotted a fortune at the bottom of the bag. She pulled it out. "Keep your friends close and your enemies closer."

Jonathan put serving spoons in the takeout containers. "I guess if you knew who your enemies were, that would be sound advice."

"With all that's happened, I can't help but feel they're already closer than we know." And for just a moment, Francine's bright vision of hope flickered.

TWENTY-SIX

After breakfast the next morning, Francine was a little surprised and even worried that she hadn't heard from Charlotte. When she got out of the shower and had dressed and there was still no call, Francine called her.

She could hear the grogginess in Charlotte's voice. "Hello? Francine? What time is it? Never mind, let me find my glasses. I slept here in the recliner."

Francine told her it was nine o'clock. "Everyone's going to be here in an hour to help get the place ready for the luncheon, and I thought if we were going to have time to talk ahead of that..."

"Yes. It's all coming back to me. I have this stuff spread out all over the floor in the library. You have to come over. I don't want to move it."

"Have you figured anything out?"

"Yes, but I want to show it to you to make sure you agree. You're the sensible one, you know."

"So I keep being told. You're sure you can't just bring all that stuff over here?"

"Nope."

"Let me talk to Jonathan and I'll be over."

Jonathan wasn't convinced it was a good idea. "I have to run into the office for a meeting. It's supposed to be a quick one, but you never know. Are you sure you'll be back in time to get ready for the luncheon? You said they'd be here at ten. That's only an hour away, and Mary Ruth might be early."

Francine debated her options. "I'll give Darla a key and ask her to let Mary Ruth in, in case I'm not back in time. I know she's coming to the luncheon, and maybe it'll dissuade her from taking any future actions against us."

"You can hope."

She gave him a quick kiss. "I'm sure it will be fine. I'm going to drive over to avoid the press. I'll stop at Darla's on the way."

Channel 8 and Channel 59 had news vans parked outside her house, plus there were the two dark cars that had followed her yesterday. Remembering the agreement with Jud, she waved to them as she backed out of the driveway and drove a few houses down to Darla's. She pulled into the driveway.

"What's with the entourage?" Darla asked when she answered the door.

The television crews were scrambling to set up on the sidewalk out front.

"They're my homies," Francine said.

Darla smiled and waved at them, but Francine could see the alarm in her eyes. "Is this about the warning we gave Alice and

Larry? Because it's a homeowners' association issue. You don't need to get the press involved."

Francine suddenly realized she could use this to her advantage. "Just drop the warning and there'll be no investigation. In the meantime, I have another favor to ask." She explained what she needed.

"If you take the press with you, I'll go over right away and house-sit until either you or Jonathan relieves me."

Francine gave Darla the key and left. The parade followed her over to Charlotte's, where Channel 13 had a news van parked out front.

She stopped in the driveway. The reporters were out of their vehicles before she had even shut the car off. They charged up the driveway, microphones extended. Before she could reach the walk leading to the house, they were shouting questions at her.

"Is it true you found Jeff Kramer's body?"

"In your opinion, are the two murders related?"

"You saw the body. Was the method the same as Guttmann's?"

"Who do you think is behind the killings?"

"Do you think there will be more?"

"Is the killer finished yet? Are you worried?"

Francine waved them all quiet. "I have no comment on the death of Jeff Kramer, other than to say I'm sorry for his family. He was a good reporter. Am I worried, personally? I won't rest easily until the killer is found, as I'm sure you can understand. I'm confident the Brownsburg Police are doing everything they can to solve this crime."

She turned and headed quickly for Charlotte's front door. She could see it had been slightly opened. The press trailed behind asking more questions. Her pace got faster and faster.

Charlotte yanked the door open and let her rush in, then slammed it in the faces behind her. She threw the dead bolt on the door. "I thought you handled that well."

"Thanks. I tried to channel my inner Joy. Has Channel 13 been here all morning?"

"I noticed they were here after you woke me up." She motioned her down the hall into the library.

Francine was overwhelmed by the mess. It was even worse than usual. Papers littered the floor. Some were copies and some were magazine pages. There appeared to be a method to the way they were laid out, but what that organization was, she wasn't sure. Two easels with white boards on them had been set up, and Charlotte had written notes in three colors on them. Yellow sticky notes punctuated the writing on the white boards.

"What does all this mean?" Francine asked.

"I made a log of every event photographed in the magazines, plus every person who was mentioned in every caption. There's a pattern. Jake was at every event where Sara Baggesen raced. Let me go over the evidence to make sure you concur."

"I don't think we have time. Were there any photos of the two of them together?"

"No, but it could just mean they were being careful."

Francine was not convinced. "Did Jake race as well?"

"At some of them, but not in the midgets. He was in the Silver Crown series."

The two of them took their familiar seats, Charlotte in the apricot recliner, Francine in the rocking chair, after moving papers to the floor.

"I don't know, Charlotte. It hardly seems conclusive."

"Friederich must've believed they were a couple. Why would he have gone to all the trouble to mark those pages?"

"Are you suggesting that Jake, who's twenty-three, is having an affair with a child of sixteen?"

"Do you know a sixteen-year-old who thinks of herself as a child? It's only us old fogies who know they're still children. They don't. Just keep an open mind, okay? It's a possibility. It's also possible she may be stalking *him*. Maybe she signed up to race places where she knew he would be."

Francine's eyes got wide. "I didn't think of that. Maybe she has Darla's compulsive personality." With not much time before she needed to get back, she picked up the papers nearest her, focusing on the photos of Jake. At one of the races, he was besieged by young woman fans. As Charlotte had said, Sara wasn't among the gaggle of women. But Francine thought she spotted a familiar face in the background. "Charlotte, isn't that Larry?" She thrust the page at her.

Charlotte pulled a magnifying glass from a drawer in the coffee table. She took a full minute to examine the photograph. "This copy isn't that good. I can see why you would think it might be Larry because of the goatee. We should ask Jud to let us see the original."

"If we did that, we'd have to explain why we wanted it, and if we were right it would be one more reason for them to suspect Larry. It would be better if we could borrow a copy from someone else. I wonder if the Brownsburg Library carries it."

"They might. Of course, Larry and Alice are fans of Jake's. In some ways it's not a surprise to find Larry there."

Francine checked the caption. "The race was in Florida. I don't remember them making a trip to Florida anytime recently, even in the last year."

"Larry made a golfing trip somewhere south in the spring, didn't he?"

"He did. Jonathan couldn't go because it was tax season. I don't think anyone else went with him. But it wasn't to Florida, not that I recall."

"We can check with Alice, although I'm starting to suspect he may not be truthful all the time with her."

Francine had to agree. "You don't know the half of it."

"So tell me what you know about them."

She first swore Charlotte to secrecy. Then she told her about Larry's apology to Alice and Jonathan about the large amount of money his grandparents had left him, how he'd moved it into an offshore account, and that most of it was gone. She also told Charlotte that Alice had Larry followed to Las Vegas, that she knew he'd come back earlier, and how Jeff Kramer fit into the picture as the man recruited to follow Larry when he arrived home.

Charlotte's mouth dropped open. Then she closed it. Then it opened again. Francine thought she looked like a guppy.

"And Jud doesn't know?" Charlotte stammered.

Francine shrugged. "It's Alice and Larry's responsibility to tell the police, not me."

"You have a point." Charlotte sat in the chair, still stunned. "What did Larry do with all that money?"

"He says he'll tell Alice when he meets with this mystery person and tells them whatever it is he's going to tell them."

"Did he say when he would meet with the person?"

"No, and he didn't give a time frame for making that decision, either."

The mantel clock on the fireplace in the library chimed, and Francine looked at it. "We need to get going."

Charlotte put the magnifying glass back in the drawer and pulled out Friederich's black iPod Touch. "Before we leave, tell me how to turn this thing on."

Francine took it from her friend. "I still can't believe you stole his iPod." She held down the top button but nothing happened. "It's dead. It probably needs a charge. Mine loses a charge if I don't use it for awhile. Help me remember and I'll give you my charger when we get back."

They agreed it would work best for them to drive separately, since Francine would be taking Mary Ruth to the gym immediately following the luncheon—if all went well. There was only one black press car outside now. As the reporter got out to question Francine, she waved him off and hurried to her car. He followed her and Charlotte.

Francine was dismayed to see the press was now outside her house, almost as if they knew about the luncheon. She pulled into the garage, edging past the *Mary Ruth's Catering* van. Charlotte pulled up and parked behind Francine's car. She walked as quickly as she could, wielding her cane. Francine lowered the garage door.

"I hope they don't scare the neighbors away from the luncheon," she told Charlotte.

"Are you kidding? This will make the neighbors even more excited. I bet we'll get more than we planned for. Remember, the press is our friend."

"I keep forgetting."

They entered the mudroom that led from the garage into the house. Jonathan met them there with a concerned look on his face.

"What is it?" Francine asked. He just shook his head and opened the door to the great room.

Francine took it all in. During the short period of time she'd left to meet Charlotte, the entire room had been transformed. She held on to the door frame wall with one hand. "What happened here?" she asked.

"I was afraid you didn't know about it. Darla told me the decorators came with Joy and that other woman, Marcy. They had this done in no time."

"Where's Darla?"

"She went home to change into 'something more appropriate.'"

Francine could only imagine what that meant.

She assessed what the decorators had done. The room consisted of two large spaces joined together through an arched opening. Over the arch now hung replicas of the flags used in IndyCar racing. In the larger of the two spaces were two long tables that seated ten people each. In the smaller area, artfully displayed, were way too many black, white, and checkered accent pieces. Plus, a tall display case Francine had never seen before served as the room's centerpiece. It was filled with hot rod, NASCAR, and midget car memorabilia.

"By the time I got home it was too late," Jonathan said. "At least it will give everyone something to look at."

Charlotte put her arm around Francine's waist. "It'll be okay, really."

"You think this looks okay?"

"I didn't say that. It's how I imagine death would look if someone crashed into the Speedway museum at high speed. Only with more color. What I mean is, we'll make Marcy take it all down as soon as the luncheon is over."

A crash sounded from the kitchen. "And this isn't the worst of it," Jonathan said over the outburst of voices that followed the crash. He rolled his eyes in that direction. "You need to see what's going on in there."

Francine crossed the great room and entered the kitchen, followed closely by Charlotte. Joy was shouldering a large, studio-like video camera by the door. Mary Ruth, clad in a bright pink *Mary Ruth's Catering* apron, was behind the center island with a basket in front of her. Next to Mary Ruth, in front of an identical basket, was a short young Hispanic man. His black apron, spotted with grease, said *El Burrito Loco*. Marcy stood in front of them going over instructions, in English for Mary Ruth and in Spanish for the other guy.

Francine strode up to Marcy. "What's going on here?"

"Food Network has an opening in two weeks on *Chopped*. One of their scheduled chefs backed out. They've asked for an audition tape from Mary Ruth. I thought, what better way to show what Mary Ruth can do than actually stage a competition?"

"Who's he?" Francine pointed to the young guy in black apron. "Is he really a chef?"

"It's the best I could do in a hurry. He's from that Mexican restaurant on Northfield Drive, down from the Kohl's. His name is Jose. That's all I've dared ask at this point."

Francine looked from Mary Ruth to Jose. Everyone looked young to her, but Jose looked barely old enough to drive, let alone be a chef. "*Hola,*" she told him. "*Quantos años tiene?*"

He smiled and rattled off a bunch of things in Spanish. He leered at Francine.

She put her hands on her hips and looked at Marcy. "He says he's twenty-five. I don't think that's possible. I didn't catch the rest of it, though. What did he say?"

Marcy turned red. "Ummm. He saw the *Good Morning America* clip of you in the wet dress, and he ... never mind. We don't have time for this. If we're going to get this recorded before the luncheon, we need to move."

Francine was speechless.

"I can't film with you in the way, Francine," Joy said.

She spun around. The large camera lens Joy was looking through was pointed directly at her. "When did you learn to operate one of those?" she asked.

Marcy waved her hand for everyone to be quiet. "Okay, open your baskets and see what your secret ingredients are."

The two chefs opened their baskets. Both pulled out a mango, chili paste, and huge tentacle of some kind.

Francine could scarcely believe it fit in the basket. "That looks like squid!"

"It is," Mary Ruth said, pulling a butcher knife out of her knife bag. "I haven't worked with fresh squid since chef's school, but I know what I'm going to make." She slapped the tentacle on Francine's best cutting board and began chopping it into pieces. The sight of it almost made Francine sick. She couldn't look to see what Jose was doing with his.

Marcy frowned at them to be quiet. "I think I can mute that outburst when I edit the tape," she whispered, "but you need to control yourselves." She pointed at Joy. "Keep rolling tape." Marcy took a deep breath. "For whatever other ingredients you need, you can use anything you find in Francine's pantry or refrigerator." Jose ran to the refrigerator and pulled out a bottle of beer. He opened it and took a drink, burped, then ran the beer back to his station.

Francine's breath came in short gasps.

Charlotte dragged her out of the kitchen. "I think it's better if we just let them do it. I've watched this show a lot. They only have twenty minutes for the appetizer round. Mary Ruth'll still have plenty of time to finish up anything for the luncheon. Let's get the house in shape."

"I don't understand why Marcy is doing this. We didn't even invite her, did we? What does she think she's going to do here, film the luncheon?"

"She may want a crowd reaction to Mary Ruth's new appetizer. It's not how they do it on *Chopped*; that would be more like *Cupcake Wars*. But it might help with the audition."

Jonathan pointed to a sheet of paper on top of a medium-sized buffet table that had been placed where the great room took an elbow bend into the open dining area. "Mary Ruth's instructions are there," he said. "Maybe I'd better help." He picked up the paper. "The smaller table in the dining room is for desserts. The table in the middle is for the buffet stations. Francine, why don't you work on the buffet? Here's the menu. They want our dining room table expanded all the way out to seat another ten, so I'll get the leaves and do that. Charlotte, why don't you start wrapping the eating utensils in the napkins?"

Francine started to breath easier. Jonathan was her rock. He would help her get through this.

Charlotte professed to needing help with the utensil-wrapping operation, so Francine took some time to get her organized. All the while the sounds of clattering and chaos arose from the kitchen, but she tried to ignore it, telling herself it would be okay.

When Charlotte was finally at work, Francine read over the list and studied the diagram for how to place the serving trays. She needed a station for the sesame chicken wraps, another for the pulled pork mini-sandwiches with a plate for buns ahead of the meat. Mary Ruth planned for three types of barbeque sauce so she needed to leave room for that. Then came the apricot-and-black-walnut chicken salad, served cold, and a vegetable tray with Mary Ruth's signature spicy southwestern dip. The dessert table would have chocolate fudge pecan brownies and an angel food cake drizzled with a cranberry/orange zest icing. The thought of that wonderful food made Francine's mouth water, and she momentarily forgot about the cooking challenge. Then she realized she would have to go into the kitchen to ask Mary Ruth about the warming trays.

At least, she rationalized, it wouldn't take long.

Francine entered the kitchen. Mary Ruth and Jose were elbowing each other trying to get something out of the freezer at the bottom of Francine's stainless steel refrigerator. Mary Ruth emerged triumphant, waving a package of puff pastry sheets Francine didn't know she even had. Jose ran over and stood in front of the microwave, blocking Mary Ruth from getting to it.

Francine cleared her throat to get everyone's attention.

"Stop tape!" yelled Marcy. "What are you doing in here?"

"I'm here for the warming trays so I can set up the buffet table."

Mary Ruth put the puff pastry package down at her station. "They're in the van. I'll give you the keys." She bent down to get her purse.

Mary Ruth came up in time to see Jose snatch the puff pastry. She threw her keys to Francine and grabbed the other end of the package. She and Jose played tug of war momentarily, but Jose had more strength. He rattled something in Spanish, then yanked it away from her.

Mary Ruth yelled, "Hey, that's mine!" She picked up a pan and whacked Jose in the head with it.

Jose was momentarily stunned. He dropped the package on the floor. Before Mary Ruth could retrieve it, he recovered. He swore at her in Spanish and brandished his butcher knife in front of her.

She held up the frying pan in a defensive position.

"Rolling!" called Marcy.

"I don't think so!" Francine marched over to Marcy. "I will not have this kind of behavior in my house. You get him out of here."

Jose gave Francine the once over. He said something in Spanish.

She caught part of it. She narrowed her eyes. "Did he just say what I think he said?"

"Uh, umm, I don't think so," Marcy stammered.

"I may whack him in the head myself."

"Too late," said Mary Ruth. With Jose distracted, she'd gotten close and gave the frying pan a flick with her wrist. It banged him in the head in the same spot and this time he went down. The knife clattered on the floor as he hit.

"That'll teach him to steal my recipe," Mary Ruth said, standing over the unconscious victim. "He was duplicating my dish."

"I don't get it, either," Marcy said. "The beer-based batter he was making for the calamari looked good, even after he threw in some vodka and it accidently caught fire."

"There was a fire?" Francine said.

"A small one. We were able to put it out with a fire extinguisher."

Francine steadied herself against the bar.

"Did we get that on tape?" asked Marcy.

Joy looked sheepish. "I never stopped rolling."

Jose stood. He wobbled for a moment. He babbled in Spanish.

Marcy said something back to him. His eyes went glassy, and then he fell forward onto Mary Ruth. She wasn't prepared for his weight, and the two of them careened back against the refrigerator. The appliance slammed into the wall.

"Get him off of me!" Mary Ruth screamed.

Jonathan came running into the kitchen. He pried Jose off of her and eased him onto the floor.

"I think he might have a concussion," Marcy observed. "I hope you have a good insurance policy."

Francine stared at her.

She rethought the situation. "Um. Maybe I'd better get him to the emergency care clinic."

"Good idea," Jonathan said. "Let me help you load him into your car."

Jonathan put his arms under the young man's armpits and dragged him across the kitchen. Marcy went ahead and held the doors open.

"I can imagine how this is going to look to the paparazzi out front," Charlotte said.

Francine looked out the front windows. She sighed. "They're still out there. You'll need to load him in the Prius in the garage so they don't see him."

Jonathan glared at Marcy. "You're going to sit in the back seat and keep him propped up so he doesn't look unconscious."

She shrugged.

"Is it okay if I go ahead and finish off the calamari dish?" Mary Ruth asked. "I need to serve it for the appetizers or we won't have enough. I'd planned on using whatever Jose and I created. I may use his original idea for a beer batter as an alternative."

"Get it on tape," Marcy told Joy.

"This has been way more exciting than anything they do on Food Network," Charlotte said. "They need to rethink the *Iron Chef* competition. Mixed martial arts would be a dandy addition to the cooking battle in Kitchen Stadium."

TWENTY-SEVEN

AFTER JOSE HAD BEEN loaded into Francine's car and Jonathan and Marcy had driven it through the gauntlet of reporters, the tension eased but the activity picked up. They didn't have much time to get things ready for the event. Mary Ruth finished off the calamari puff pastry with mango chili sauce while Joy videotaped it, then she moved onto the beer batter version.

In the great room, Francine finished up the buffet and helped set the tables. "I've been thinking about your comment on mixed martial arts," she told Charlotte.

"On *Iron Chef*? It'd be fun to watch, wouldn't it? I'd bet on Chef Morimoto. He probably knows karate." Charlotte counted the number of places they'd set at the three tables.

"That's not what I meant. I was thinking about the way Friederich died. Who would know how to do a blood choke? It would have to be someone who was familiar with self-defense."

"Not necessarily. I thought about that after I had my talk with Jud. A blood choke is a sleeper hold. They use those all the time in pro-wrestling matches. So anyone who's a wrestling fan—and who isn't?—would be familiar with how it's done."

"Really? So familiar that they could lock a grown man expertly in a hold and keep it applied until he was dead?"

"I suppose you have a point."

"Do any of our neighbors have that kind of experience?"

Charlotte mused. "The more and more I think about it, the less and less it feels like any of our neighbors could have done it. On the other hand, who *couldn't* conceive of this plot? It's not like I'm the only one who reads thrillers. And who needs books? This would be rejected as tame for any of those forensic crime dramas on TV." She snorted. "In fact, this could have come out of a comedy like *Desperate Housewives*."

"Didn't Jake Maehler wrestle in high school?"

"But that's a lot different than pro wrestling."

Francine shut her eyes and tried to remember back to when her oldest son Craig wrestled. "I don't know that it's so different. A cradle hold is sort of like a submission hold, and it's legal. They wouldn't permit a dangerous one like a sleeper, but I wouldn't be surprised if the boys fooled around with it."

Charlotte pulled Francine close. "Speaking of submission, have you told Mary Ruth yet about the appointment with Jake's trainer, or are you still planning to spring it on her?"

"I'm going with the surprise. This better work. I don't have another idea."

"Good thing all of us are here to help. Listen, maybe you should find out from Brady if Jake knows how to slap someone in a sleeper hold."

"I'm sure that will come up in regular conversation," she said as they went back into the kitchen to see how they could help.

Jonathan and Marcy returned right before the guests started to arrive. Jose, his head bandaged like a mummy, was with them, still dazed. Jonathan parked him on a couch. Francine's eyes widened.

"Why is he still here?"

"It appears *someone* promised him he could stay for lunch if he participated in the competition."

"Be glad he's agreed to do that and not press charges," Marcy argued. "Mary Ruth may have done it, but it's your house and your frying pan. You could get pulled into civil lawsuit."

Mary Ruth came out of the kitchen. She spotted Jose propped up against a couch pillow. "Jose!" she said. Though she was clearly delighted to see him, he held the pillow out to prevent any aggressive moves. "I'm not going to hurt you," she said. "All is forgiven! The beer battered calamari you were working on turned out to be excellent. Want a taste?" She gently helped him up and encouraged him into the kitchen. His gait was slow but they got there. She called back to the rest of them. "Everyone's invited for samples. Come help yourselves."

The studio camera was gone, and Joy, gloved, was working Mary Ruth's coleslaw dressing with her hands into a mixture of shredded cabbage, red cabbage, and carrots. She turned the stainless steel bowl and continued tossing. "The calamari is to die for. You all have to try them."

"I love the brownies," Charlotte said. She picked up several.

"I'm sure the rest of the group would love the brownies, too, but I saw you finger the pile. Did you wash your hands?" Mary

Ruth dipped a beer battered calamari into the mango chili sauce and handed it to Jose.

Charlotte flashed a bottle of hand sanitizer she had in her pocket. "I did. And I'm just sugaring up for the inquisition. Once the neighbors get here, this is going to take a lot of energy."

"I don't think *inquisition* is the right word," said a male voice. The women all turned. Jud stood at the entrance to the kitchen, his arms folded. "Jonathan let me in," he said.

A grin broke out on Charlotte's chocolate-smeared face. "Jud! Anything new in the investigation?"

"Nothing I'm at liberty to reveal."

"That sounds like a challenge."

Francine took her by the arm. "We're not here to question him, dear. We're here to quietly find out what the neighbors know."

"Help yourself to samples," said Mary Ruth. "We're testing them before the guests arrive."

"Thank you, but I'll have some when you start serving. My wife reminds me I need to watch my weight."

Francine thought his comment was more polite than true, since the police uniform showed off his still athletic physique. Jud didn't swagger, but he did project a self-confidence that made people relax in his presence. Except Jose. Jose took one look at Jud and slinked out of the kitchen.

"Who's the guy with the bandaged head?" Jud asked Francine.

She sighed. "It's a long story. He won't be here that long. He's leaving after we serve lunch."

"By the way, I thought you handled the press well this morning. I saw it on the news before I got here."

The doorbell rang. When Francine went to answer it, she saw that Jose had returned to his semi-comatose position on the couch. Before she reached the door, it opened and Alice walked in. "It's just me."

"I'm glad you're here," Francine said, giving her a hug. "I was worried you'd decided not to come."

"Larry is so depressed I can't stand to be around him anymore. I knew this would be way more fun." She studied Jose sitting on the couch. "Who's he?"

"Part of the way more fun."

Alice gave her a questioning look, but Francine didn't explain herself. The women went into the kitchen.

Jonathan took over door duties so Francine could mingle. More and more neighbors came. The biggest surprise was that Darla, clad in an outfit reminiscent of a Hooters waitress, arrived with her ex-husband Vince. Jonathan shook their hands and called Francine over.

"I hope you don't mind," Darla told them. "Vince wanted to come along. He's been following the news in the papers and wanted to see all of you again."

"How nice." They shook hands with Vince. It had been a good ten or twelve years since the divorce, but age had been kind to him. He looked the same as when Darla had first thrown him over for a cast of successive boyfriends. His hairline had receded a little, but he had the same dark hair, wide smile, and bedroom eyes that had made the neighborhood women wonder what she was thinking in the first place when she divorced him.

The house filled with loud conversation. All twenty-five neighbors who'd confirmed their attendance showed as well as a few others, like Vince. Alice said she'd prefer to help with the food instead of chatting, so that left the rest to mingle.

Francine managed to question about fifteen of the neighbors, many of whom she discovered had already been questioned by Charlotte. She found herself dodging more questions about skinny-dipping than getting any information, though. She looked up and saw that Charlotte had Vince cornered and was chatting him up.

"Say what you will about Darla," Charlotte told her as they caught up with each other over calamari appetizers, "but she knows how to pick up guys. Vince is still a hottie."

Francine disagreed. "Her other boyfriends were never in the same league as Vince."

"Not true. Darla would never date someone who wasn't good-looking. Her other boyfriends may not have been as robust, but they were all distinguished. And older."

"And with money."

Charlotte laughed, then got serious. "Did you know Vince worked with Friederich at Excalibur Racing?"

"No."

"He said he only knew Friederich through work, though. He wasn't forthcoming about much else. I did ask about Sara and got around to the topic of her boyfriends. That put him off. He said she was too young to be dating anyone seriously, and then he found someone else to talk to."

"I'm not getting anywhere either. If a neighbor was involved in killing Friederich, I'm not sure who it could be. They all seem clueless."

The two split up again. Francine focused on the couple who lived behind Alice and Larry. Those who saw Charlotte coming flocked elsewhere. Francine presumed they either had already been questioned by her or warned by those who had. There were three exceptions, however—Darla Baggesen in her low-cut top and an elderly couple who knew Francine was a former nurse and always wanted to talk about their latest ailments.

So when Charlotte dragged Darla over and the elderly couple followed, Francine considered bolting but it was too late.

"You've got to hear this," Charlotte said.

The older man's head swung in toward Darla. He was practically staring into the V-neck that barely covered Darla's ample breasts.

"Hear what?" Francine asked politely.

"Darla thinks the police have it all backwards. She says they've become obsessed with what Friederich was hiding from Larry."

Darla said, "I'm just making the observation that Friederich must have known something about Larry, something Larry didn't want known. I mean, he wasn't paying rent, and Larry threatened half a year ago to throw him out. So Larry must have been afraid to push Friederich's buttons. Why?"

"Isn't that a great observation?" Charlotte asked.

Before Francine could answer, the elderly man said, "Are those things real?"

The three women looked at him. His leering at Darla's breasts left no doubt as to what he was asking about.

She gave a short laugh and jiggled her torso. "Wouldn't you like to know." She winked at him.

The man's wife yanked him toward the buffet table.

Francine shook her head at the retreating couple. "Larry said he was afraid he couldn't get another renter in this economy and hoped to work it out with Friederich."

"Really?" Darla said skeptically. "Well, I think from all the rumors going around that Larry has no problem lying, even to Alice. So if the police focused more on what Friederich had learned about Larry that kept him in that building when he wasn't paying rent, they'd improve their chances."

"Improve their chances of proving Larry is guilty of murder?" Francine's mouth tightened. "Is that what you believe?"

"He doesn't have an alibi for the night Friederich was killed. If it looks like a duck and quacks like a duck..." She stepped away.

No doubt in pursuit of someone else she can shake her tatas at, thought Francine.

"How did Darla know Friederich wasn't paying rent?" Charlotte asked.

"How does Darla know anything?"

"I suppose it could be that she attracts gossip like she attracts men. She doesn't have to work at it very hard."

Darla approached Jose on the couch. He saw her coming and stood—shakily, but he stood. He seemed very formal around her. "I don't know," Francine said, "I think she *does* work at it. Does Jose know Darla?"

"Maybe she's a frequent customer at El Burrito Loco. Or maybe she hires them to cater events. They're cheaper than Mary Ruth if all you want is Mexican."

"Do you think Darla has a valid point?"

"Who knows? She also suspects Jake Maehler."

"So do we."

"Which reminds me that we need to check his website to see if I'm right about the Molson being in that one photo."

A shrill whistle sounded at that moment. Startled, they all turned to the doors that led into the kitchen.

Joy stood in front of them on a step ladder. She held out her arms like she was getting ready to conduct an orchestra. "Sorry for the whistle, but it was hard to get your attention with all the noise. Thank you all for coming. As you know, Francine McNamara is hosting this tasting for our very good friend, Mary Ruth Burrows, who I know you will all agree if you don't already know, is a wonderful chef and should be a bigger part of the racing industry. We hope you will support her getting more of this business. Now, let's eat!"

The crowd surged toward the buffet.

"Let's use the restroom first," Francine said, pulling Charlotte out of the way. "The one upstairs."

"Upstairs?" She indicated her cane.

"I have my reasons. And we all know you use that cane when it suits your purposes more than because of your knee."

Charlotte had a twinkle in her eye, but she admitted nothing. "I'll come with you, but all I need to do is wash my hands. I went earlier when Andrew Starling farted loudly and tried to cover it up by acting like his wife had done it. She slapped him, and I nearly peed my pants trying to keep from laughing. So I headed as fast as I could to the ladies' room."

Upstairs, Francine headed for Jonathan's office.

"Ah," said Charlotte. "You have an ulterior motive."

"Precisely. You said you wanted to check Jake's website. We might as well do that while the others go through the line."

Francine called it up on the computer, located the beach photo with the beer, and then kept clicking to enlarge the area where the beer bottle was. Before they could read the label, the photo became distorted.

"Too bad the label's not turned toward us so we can see it dead-on," Charlotte said, "but I think enough is there to establish it's a Molson."

"I disagree. The photo's so muddled there's no way to be certain."

"You sound like you don't want it to be Jake Maehler. We need to find a reason someone other than Larry wanted this guy dead, remember?"

"I remember. This just seems tenuous."

"We know Jake was in the building for a reason," Charlotte insisted. "He came to get his car. The Molson bottle could establish that he knew about the hidden basement. If he knew about it, then Friederich had to have revealed it, which would mean Friederich used the basement."

"For what purpose?"

Charlotte held up a finger. "We need to ask that of Jake Maehler."

"We're a long way from getting to him. I'll be lucky to get anything out of Brady Prather when I drag Mary Ruth to the gym." She checked her watch. "Speaking of which, we need to get back."

Downstairs, Jud sat at the first table. Neighbors had crowded around him by pulling up extra chairs to be seated close to him. Clearly he was the main attraction. Jonathan and Vince were at the same table but at the opposite end. At the second table, Darla and some of the more gossipy neighbors sat with an elderly Japanese couple, fairly new to the neighborhood, who were hard of hearing. Darla was practically yelling at them in Japanese.

"Darla never misses an opportunity to show off her ability with Asian languages," Francine groused as they went through the line. Darla had spent her middle school years in Asia. Her parents had been hired by foreign companies to teach their employees English.

"I've had my fill of her," Charlotte said. "Let's join the third table, the one closest to the desserts."

They could hear Darla's voice above all the others. She talked about Sara's racing season. Francine listened in while she watched Charlotte devour the chocolate pecan brownies first. "Just how good is Sara, anyway?" she asked under her breath. "Is she a threat to Jake?"

Charlotte licked a brownie crumb off her finger. "Only if she were trying to seduce him. The girl wants to be a model, not a race car driver."

"Where did you hear that?"

"I didn't hear it. I read it, or read it between the lines, in those magazines Friederich had. *Sprinting Midgets* or something like that."

"You didn't mention it before."

Charlotte picked up a sesame chicken wrap. "Because you were hurrying me when I was trying to tell you what I'd figured out. She's far more interested in being Cheryl Tiegs than Danica Patrick. She was wearing a t-shirt that had some sponsor's name on it, and the caption implied she was pursuing a contract." She took a bite. "This is good, but I'd rather have another piece of that angel food cake. Do I have time?"

Francine looked at her watch and almost panicked. "We've got to move this thing along. Jud hasn't talked about the neighborhood watch yet, and then we need these people out of here so we can get Mary Ruth to the gym."

"Don't have a coronary, I'll take care of it." She struggled to her feet and waved at Joy. When Joy looked over, she pointed to her watch and said, much too loudly, "We need to get this moving."

Francine rested her hand on her forehead and averted her eyes.

Joy hastily got back on the step ladder. "I know you're all enjoying the food. Could we have a round of applause for Mary Ruth?"

Francine applauded loudly, grateful to have the attention shifted elsewhere. Charlotte gave an appreciative, "Woo-hoo!"

"While you're finishing your dessert, Detective Brent Judson of the Brownsburg Police Department is here to talk to us about forming a neighborhood crime watch program. Let's all give him our attention."

Jud was poised, handsome, and smiled so much Francine thought he should run for office. She was relieved when the group agreed to have a follow-up meeting. The last thing she needed was more discussion. He passed out a pamphlet describing successful neighborhood watch programs and urged them to come prepared next time to discuss practical ideas on implementing a program.

Even then, it took forever for people to leave. They lingered and gossiped about Alice and Larry, especially when Alice returned to the kitchen with an armful of trash.

But finally they were gone. Francine clutched Charlotte. "It's two fifteen. I've got to get Mary Ruth to the gym! She's going to resist a lot. But she can't say no! We may not get another chance like this."

"Not to worry. We'll all just tell her she's going and drag her out of here. It's too important. You can explain on the way."

Charlotte gathered up Joy and Alice, and the four of them ambushed Mary Ruth in the great room. As predicted, she was horrified at the prospect of going to a gym.

"Nooooo! I'm not going to do that." She backed away from them like they were dentists coming at her with a needle.

"Believe me, if there was any other way to question him without it seeming obvious, I wouldn't ask," Francine said.

"There's *got* to be another way."

Charlotte got in Mary Ruth's face. "C'mon, what's the worst that could happen? I bet I've been in a gym at least a hundred times with all the physical therapy I've had. It's not so bad."

"That's different. You were in a gym with a bunch of older people who needed rehab."

"Not true. There were some young people there too."

"Young or old, they all needed rehab. You're talking about putting me in a gym with healthy, skinny people. What are they going to think of me?"

"They're going to think you're extraordinarily brave." Francine managed to swoop in behind Mary Ruth, and the four women propelled her toward the mudroom that led into the garage. "They're going to admire you for taking control of your life. And anyway, we're there to get information out of Jake's trainer, Brady Prather. He's really nice, but if you don't like him, you never have to go again."

"*After* you've gotten the information out of him," Charlotte added. "It could take several visits."

"You're not helping, Charlotte," Francine said.

"Several visits!" Mary Ruth stuck her heels into the floor, and with her weight, provided plenty of resistance.

"Yep. You'll probably need a note from your doctor too."

"She's always trying to get me to exercise. I'm doomed!"

Joy put her back into giving Mary Ruth a boost. She pushed her completely into the mudroom. "But it's a good kind of doomed."

"Joy! You're in on this, too?"

"We're all in on this, Mary Ruth. We were going to tell you earlier, but there just wasn't time."

Charlotte pointed at her watch. "Time is something we have very little of. Remember, Alice and Larry are counting on you. You've got to do it."

Mary Ruth grabbed onto the door frame. "But what will I wear?"

Joy began to pry the fingers from the woodwork. "Not to worry, dear. Francine borrowed one of Jonathan's t-shirts for you. It's in her car, along with some sweatpants from Alice. And you're wearing sneakers. You'll be fine."

She still didn't look convinced. She let go of the door and held on to Francine. "You won't leave me, will you?"

Francine gave her arm a squeeze. "Of course not. I'll be with you all the time. You just follow my lead and do whatever Brady asks as we question him. And remember, today is just an evaluation."

"Yeah," said Charlotte. "He won't ask you to 'feel the burn'. Not today."

Mary Ruth made a grab for the doorpost again. "Feel the burn!"

"Charlotte! Be quiet!" Francine said, intercepting Mary Ruth's hands before they reached the door. "Let's go," she said.

Mary Ruth held on to Francine as the women did an awkward dance pushing and pulling her into the garage and over to the car.

Mary Ruth gave one last whine as Joy reached in and buckled her seat belt, but it was the whine of a horse that had been broken. Francine climbed in the driver's seat and, with one eye watching the car clock, drove away toward the Brownsburg Fitness Factory.

TWENTY-EIGHT

"Okay, I admit he's good-looking, but if he comes at me with a tape measure, I swear I'll kick him in the balls," Mary Ruth whispered to Francine.

She sighed. "He *will* want to take measurements, I'm sure of that. But I'm also certain he won't make you feel bad. He wouldn't be a good trainer if he did."

They were upstairs in the free weight area watching Brady Prather put a young woman through the final part of a workout. She was on a slanted board, and as she reached the bottom of the sit-up position, he tossed her a small medicine ball. She caught it and tossed it back when she completed the sit-up.

"That's Sara Baggesen, isn't it?" Mary Ruth asked.

Francine squinted to see the young woman's face clearly. "I think you're right."

"She's sixteen? Ha! She's going on twenty-five. Do you remember having boobs like that when you were sixteen? I wonder if she's had a boob job. I bet you Darla would buy her a set. Of course, she ought to have them naturally if she's Darla's daughter. Although, maybe Darla's pair isn't natural, either."

Sara wore a black and lime green tank top that hugged her chest like it was two sizes too small, but it was Sara's toned arms that caught Francine's attention. She could see the girl's triceps move as she threw the ball to Brady. "Do you remember when we were young and our arms didn't wave like politicians in a parade?" she asked Mary Ruth.

"Speak for yourself. I was never that firm." Mary Ruth raised up on her tiptoes so she could whisper in Francine's ear. "And I wouldn't be caught dead with a tattoo like that."

"Like what?" Francine strained to see what Mary Ruth was talking about.

"Not on her arm. Just above her ankle. How could you not notice?"

Try as she might, Francine couldn't locate it. Mary Ruth shuffled her to where they could get a better view.

"You're gawking at her! Don't do that!" Mary Ruth hissed. "You might as well take a picture."

That gave Francine an idea. She really did want a chance to study the tattoo. It looked like a Japanese symbol of some kind. She took out her phone out of her workout capris, touched the camera app, and palmed the phone with her thumb on the button.

"What are you doing?"

"Shhh."

Sara and Brady finished the workout, and Sara strode toward the women on her way out. She acknowledged them with a nod.

That was neighborly, Francine thought, but she smiled back. She aimed the phone at Sara's calf as the girl passed and snapped off several photos. She hoped they came out, but she didn't have time to check. Brady said good-bye and shifted his attention to the two women at that moment. "Hello, Francine. I see you brought your friend." He offered his hand to Mary Ruth. "I'm Brady Prather."

Mary Ruth gave a giggle as she took it. "Hi. I'm Mary Ruth Burrows."

"It's nice to meet you."

Francine slipped the phone back in her pocket.

Another giggle. "It's nice to meet *you*."

"Why don't we sit down and talk?" He pointed to an area that had folding chairs and a big-screen television, and the three of them found chairs around a small table.

Brady leaned up on the table, his beefy forearms taking up a good portion of the space. He wore a dark blue synthetic t-shirt that conformed to his body. Mary Ruth's breathing was tense, but Francine was beginning to think it was because Brady was affecting her libido, not her nervousness.

"Tell me about your goals."

"I'm tired of being so overweight. I know I need to slim down, but it's difficult, being a caterer. I have to taste food all the time."

Brady's eyes lit up in recognition. "Mary Ruth's Catering! You're the caterer!"

"What caterer?"

"You do that flourless chocolate cake that's so good."

Mary Ruth blushed. "Well, I like to think it's pretty good."

"You're single-handedly responsible for me becoming a personal trainer."

"I am?"

"My mother got hold of your recipe and made it all the time. It was delicious. Our whole family packed on pounds."

Mary Ruth's face fell. "This isn't a happy story, is it?"

"I don't think you can blame that on Mary Ruth," Francine said, indignant. "Besides, she zealously guards her recipes. Your mother couldn't have gotten it from her."

"Look, I'm not blaming her for the weight gain. We have to take responsibility for what we eat and how we exercise. But if we hadn't all been seduced by the cake, hadn't put on all that fat, I may never have had to struggle with how I looked. That got me into sports. From there I realized I had a calling."

Mary Ruth sounded a little more hopeful. "So it's a good thing?"

He laughed. "Yeah, it's a good thing. I guess. Stand up, please."

She struggled to her feet. He circled her, frowning. Francine thought he looked like an inspector at a meat factory.

"This will take a lot of work, mostly on your part," he said. "I can design the program and be here to guide you through it, but the biggest part of this is going to be nutritional. I can't be in your kitchen making sure you eat the right things. That's something you'll have to do. The fact that you're a caterer will make it hard. Especially if you have any more weapons in your arsenal like that cake."

Now it was Francine's turn to laugh. "Oh, she does."

"What do you put in that thing to make it so addictive? Crack?"

Mary Ruth stepped back, aghast. "I only use natural ingredients. Real food!"

"I'm not saying it's crack. People's bodies react differently to all kinds of foods. My family's genes just seem to have a thing for your cake." He pointed to a scale in a corner of the gym. "Let's get your weight."

"Do I have to?"

"If I'm going to help you, we need to know your starting point." He took her by the arm and piloted her over there. "It won't hurt you, you know."

She tittered nervously. "I'm afraid I might hurt it."

"It's held a lot more weight than you have."

She stepped on the scale and Brady adjusted it. He wrote the weight down but didn't say anything.

"You can step off the scale now." He pulled a tape measure from his pocket. "Hold your arms out straight, please."

She hesitated.

"I can assure you, you can't hurt the tape measure either."

"In this case, I'm afraid it will hurt me."

"If you just follow the plan we're going to make out, both with exercise and especially the nutrition, you'll see these inches start coming down immediately."

As he worked on taking Mary Ruth's measurements, Francine said, "That was Sara Baggesen ahead of us, wasn't it?"

He nodded.

"She doesn't look like she has any food addictions."

"Sara is very dedicated. She sticks to the plan."

"How much of that is her mom, do you think?"

"What do you mean?"

Mary Ruth understood what Francine was doing. "We all know Darla. She's the definition of a helicopter parent."

"It's not my place to say." He started to measure Mary Ruth's neck. She held still as he slipped the tape measure around her throat.

Francine kept talking. "We think Darla wouldn't let Sara stop racing, even if she wanted to do something else, like modeling for example. What do you think?"

Brady wrote down some measurements. He made a noise that sounded noncommittal. "I wouldn't say that," he said, picking up the tape measure again, "but I do think she wants Sara to be a race car driver as much or more than Sara does."

"I can hardly believe she's only sixteen. She looks so mature."

"She works hard." Brady interlocked his fingers and put his hands behind his head. "Put your hands behind your head, like this, please." As Mary Ruth copied his movement, he measured her biceps.

Francine watched him record the figure. "Sara's good looking, don't you think? She could be a model *and* a race car driver, like Danica Patrick. Don't you think?"

"Probably."

Mary Ruth started to put her arms down.

"Please hold that position for a moment more."

"Sorry."

He started to measure her around her bust. Mary Ruth's posture stiffened.

"Just relax."

"Easy for you to say."

"I just have a few more measurements to take."

Francine was alarmed Brady could be done so soon. She hadn't even shifted the topic to Jake Maehler yet. "You train a lot of race car drivers, don't you?"

"You can put your arms down now." He bent down to measure her calves. "I train a few."

"Well, I know you train Jake Maehler."

"He's another great client."

"He's had a lot of press lately, hasn't he, with Friederich Guttmann's death and their professional relationship being rocky after the last race?"

He gave her a sideways glance. "Unnecessary press. Jake was upset. He said some things he shouldn't have. I'd like to kill the reporter who keeps bringing it up."

"I'm sure you're right he was just upset," Francine said, noting that Brady had used the word *kill*. "Although there's quite a bit of speculation why Jake reacted so strongly. You have any idea why he accused Friederich of sabotage?"

Brady gave Francine a suspicious look.

"We're just interested because we found the body," Mary Ruth said.

He straightened up. "Okay, how serious are you about this program? Are you here just to ask questions about Jake and Sara or do you want to lose weight?"

The two women looked at each other, horrified. Mary Ruth faced Brady squarely. "Both. If you can really help me lose weight, I'm in."

"If you're in, I can definitely help you lose weight. I can't help you with your questions, though. You'll have to ask Jake."

"How do you propose we do that?" Francine asked.

"I'll ask him to talk to you."

She squelched a laugh. "It's that easy?"

He folded his arms over his chest. "I know about you and your friend Charlotte. My mom talks about you. I think it would be easier on Jake if he just made time to answer your questions."

If Charlotte had been there, she would have had some witty retort. Francine, however, was left speechless.

TWENTY-NINE

BETWEEN STRESSFUL MEETINGS, FIRST with Brady Prather and the upcoming one with Jake Maehler, Francine drove Mary Ruth back to her house to gather up her equipment and her car. Two media trucks were sitting outside again. Francine waved to them as she parked in the garage and closed the door behind her, relieved she had caught them off-guard. When they got inside, the place was spotless. Everything had been cleaned and Mary Ruth's van had been repacked. A note from Marcy was taped to the refrigerator with Mary Ruth's name on it. Francine pulled it off and handed it to her.

She unfolded it and started to read. "Oh, my Lord, listen to this!"

"What?"

"She's editing the audition tape, but that's not the best part. I have a catering job for tomorrow! This is so last minute! Fox Sports has decided with all the mystery surrounding Friederich's death and Jake's being in the race, they're sending a crew in tomorrow to cover SpeedFest. Marcy talked them into letting me cater it. It's not very big, but it's with a national network! This could be the break I've needed. Marcy is like a fairy godmother."

Francine wondered if she was the only one of their group who didn't agree. Maybe Alice. But she was happy for Mary Ruth. "Does Marcy have an in at Fox?"

"Either that or she doesn't take no for an answer."

"I bet it's the latter."

Mary Ruth read farther down. "It says Joy is going to be part of the Fox crew. They're going to audition her by having her do some interviews!"

"I thought she was auditioning with ABC. Or was it CBS? This is crazy." Francine shook her head. How they could go from obscurity to having networks fighting over getting them on television was ridiculous. She knew it was how the Internet worked—YouTube videos could go viral and make instant stars out of anybody—but she hadn't wanted it to happen to her, and she worried about how it would affect her friends. If anything, she was now more determined to solve the mystery of Friederich's death—with Charlotte's lead—in hopes things would return to normal.

"I can't just stand here!" Mary Ruth said. "I need to get going. I need to see what food I've got and if I can beg my supplier into delivering things today. Maybe I'll have to run to Gordon Food Service."

Francine walked her to the van, yelling at the reporters to get off her lawn. They did, but still they taped the two of them as she said good-bye to Mary Ruth. It made Francine mutter under her breath.

Mary Ruth laughed. "This is all your fault, you know. If you hadn't hoodwinked me into meeting Brady Prather, I'd be home already prepping for tomorrow's event and you'd be in the house with the window shades drawn."

"You're not mad about Brady, are you? I know it caught you off-guard, but if I'd told you ahead of time, would you have gone? And if you hadn't gone, would I have an appointment to talk to Jake Maehler?"

"It all works out."

———

Francine surprised Charlotte with the news that they had an interview with Jake Maehler before his training session at five o'clock. She drove, and the two women arrived at the Brownsburg Fitness Factory well ahead of time. They waited in the former church's vestibule, which served as the reception area. Alone except for the thin blond receptionist, Charlotte learned on her cane and sat in one of the molded plastic chairs. Francine paced, pausing every so often to look out the glass window in the arched doors.

"Stop it, Francine. You're making me nervous."

"Stop what?" She suddenly realized what she was doing. She sat in the chair next to Charlotte. "Sorry."

Two minutes later Jake came through the door. He was dressed in a white tank top that hugged his lean compact frame. The effect was … exploitive? Francine smiled. *No worse than Danica Patrick.* She hastily stood and introduced herself. Jake had arrived so that the women had ten minutes at most.

"I know who you are," he said. "When I did cardio in here yesterday, you and your Bridge Club were on every television in the place. And there's a reporter outside."

It made her look out the window. Had she missed it before, or had the reporter just arrived? In any event, one of the female reporters from the local paper had a camera and was taking photos of the front of the building.

"We're getting tired of them," she said.

Charlotte rose from the chair. "Speak for yourself." She shook Jake's hand and introduced herself.

"Let's get his done," Jake said. "I don't know why I should talk with you other than Brady asked me to do it."

"We appreciate your time," Francine said. "We're here because we discovered Friederich's body, and we're trying to make sense of this."

"If the police can't make sense of it, why should you?"

"Can we sit, please?" She and Charlotte used the same chairs they'd been in, and Jake scooted another of the plastic chairs so that he was across from them.

He sat and stretched out his legs. He looked like he was trying to appear unconcerned. "Fire away."

Charlotte referenced a notebook on which she'd scribbled a few questions on the way over. "You're a NASCAR driver now. Why are these midget races so important to you?"

"C'mon. You've read the papers. You know I'm not winning in the big leagues."

"Is it costing you sponsors?"

He shook his head. "I don't have a lot of them, but my sponsors are sticking with me."

"Really?" Charlotte continued. "We hear you're running out of money."

He paused as if deciding how to answer that. "What I've lost is a patron, not a sponsor. I don't know if they ran out of patience or money or what. Translated, it means I'm not getting the practice time I need."

"You don't know why he stopped supporting you?"

"I don't even know his name."

Francine was surprised. "This guy's been sponsoring you and you've never met him. That's odd. Any idea why?"

"No. He's tried to meet me twice now, but he must've changed his mind. Each time I went to the meeting place, no one was there. The last was the night Friederich died."

Charlotte's eyes lit up. "Then that's why you don't have an alibi for that night. You went alone and he didn't show up."

Jake gave his head a slight shake, which Francine interpreted it to mean that *wasn't* the reason he didn't have an alibi. But he didn't elaborate. "Without that patron," he said, "I need two things, one of which is another sponsor with deep pockets."

"And the other is victories?" Charlotte asked, pressing. "If not in NASCAR races, then in midgets?"

"You want me to confess it?" He glared at her. "Okay, I came back here to work with Friederich and win again. Get my mojo back. There. Are you happy?"

Francine decided it might be best to help with the questioning. "Let's go back and talk about your relationship with Friederich. I imagine he was a father figure to you."

"He was all that and more. He became the only family I had left after my mom and grandma died. Friederich not only taught me about auto racing, he taught me about life." He swallowed hard.

Francine wished her next question wasn't going to sound so mean, but it had to be asked. "He sounds like a loyal friend. Yet you accused him of sabotage. What evidence did you have of that?"

He stopped slouching and sat up. "Let me make one thing clear: What I said was in the heat of the moment. I didn't think it through. He and I were working together again just a few days afterward. That should prove something. Friederich understood. I expect everyone else to."

"Did Friederich have any other close relationships?" Charlotte asked. "Was he getting ready to take on another protégé, someone you displaced when you came back?"

"You ask that like you have someone in mind."

She looked to Francine for help.

"We have reason to believe he might have been taking an interest in Sara Baggesen," Francine said.

His mouth dropped open. "Why do you think that?"

"He had marked some pages in a racing magazine. She was one of the people he seemed to be tracking."

Jake leaned back in his chair. "He knew."

"Knew what?"

"Nothing."

"C'mon, Jake," Charlotte said. "We know you know something. We're going to keep pursuing this until we find out. It's like Brady told you earlier—easier to just work with us."

He considered that for a moment. "I'm not going to explain myself to you or to the police. This has nothing to do with Friederich's murder."

"How do you know that?"

He stonewalled. "Next question."

Francine wondered how many next questions they would get. She decided to take a different tack. "Tell us more about Friederich.

If he was such a good mechanic, why did you leave him when you moved up to NASCAR?"

"Two reasons. First, the owner who hired me had his own mechanics. But second, Friederich's specialty was midget cars. He was really good with them."

"How so? Was he good at developing new technology?"

"Not at *developing* technology." He squirmed a bit in the chair. "But he was brilliant at *adapting* it. He knew how to cheat legally." He paused. "Look, what I'm telling you is not a secret. Here's what's great about midget cars, and honestly, what I miss about them. There's nothing quite like them. The association has fairly tight regulations on how they can be built, so when it comes down to racing midgets, it's often a matter of who's the best driver."

"Often," Francine said. "Not always?"

"Exactly. There are ways to get around the regulations, the best of them perfectly legal, at least until the association learns what they're doing and rewrites the rules. Friederich was a master at it. You're sure you didn't know this?"

Both women shook their heads. "Can you give us an example?" Francine asked.

"Sure. Take shock absorbers. You know what those are, right?"

Francine said yes and Charlotte said no. He sighed and borrowed a sheet of paper and a pen from the receptionist. He drew a little diagram of the front end of a midget car on a napkin and placed it where they could see what he was illustrating. "The association states that you have to use a specific shock absorber. It's a good one, but not an excellent one. But what if you took out the rod that absorbs the shock and replaced it with one from a more advanced shock absorber?" He circled the spot where the rod was placed in the shock. "In a sense, you're borrowing a better technology. Is it cheating? Well, that's a gray area. You *are* using the specified shock absorber, only modifying in a way that no one is likely to see. It's all internal to the shock."

"It doesn't sound legal."

He tilted his hand up and down in a *maybe yes, maybe no* signal. "It's legal until someone finds out."

"Does it make that much of a difference?"

"In the case of the shock, it did. I gave you that example because it was discovered several years ago and the result was new regulations."

"Are there many cases like that one?"

"Oh, sure. Someone discovered they could fit larger injectors in the engine than the standard ones. That was clever. Another person relocated the fuel pump, which usually runs off the engine, into the fuel tank to keep it cooler." He shrugged. "There will always be ways to cheat the system. All it takes is ingeniousness. Friederich had it. Of course, it also takes money."

"Let's go back to the money angle," Charlotte said. "You're very good-looking … even more so with your shirt off. Isn't there money for people who can race and be a model?"

Jake relaxed for a moment and laughed. "Thanks for the compliment. But the looks and build only work if you prove you can win. Yes, I'd rather be a winner, rather be a NASCAR driver. But I'm not going to be poor the rest of my life." He jutted out his chin. "You know, I have a lot of contacts in the industry. I could get a job as a sales rep for any of them."

Francine hadn't thought about it before, but Jake had the goods to make a great sales representative. "You say now you're not desperate for a win, but you acted like you were after you lost the Night Before the 500."

"Only because we came so close, and we would have won if it hadn't been for the car."

Charlotte said, "So if this isn't about money, why was Friederich broke?"

Jake's surprise showed on his face. "Who said Friederich was broke?"

"He must've been. Our friend's husband Larry, the one being investigated by the police, was owed money by Friederich. He hadn't paid the rent on his garage in a long time."

"Maybe it didn't have anything to do with money."

That stopped the two women. "What else could it have to do with?" Francine asked.

"You asked me earlier if Friederich had any other close relationships. He had one other."

"Who?"

"I don't know," he said.

Charlotte frowned. "I don't understand."

"It was a complicated relationship. Friederich was in love with her, but he wasn't sure she was in love with him. He mostly just hinted about their relationship. All I know for sure is Friederich said he used hidden cameras to record a little insurance to make sure she wouldn't leave him."

The door to the fitness center opened. It was the woman reporter. Francine motioned Jake closer. He bent his head toward her. "Did you tell the police that?"

He whispered in her ear. "They know, and they're looking for the video. I should have told them right up front, but when they started pushing hard to make me their prime suspect, I finally told them. I needed to hand them someone else to look at."

"Because you don't have an alibi?"

He shook his head. "Because I can't reveal it."

THIRTY

Jake stopped on that note. "I've said too much. I've got a work-out to get in."

"Thanks for giving us so much of your time," Francine said, standing up when he did. "I know you're busy."

"And there's a race to win tomorrow." He gave her a wide grin.

The reporter snapped a photo.

"No interview," Jake said. He flashed his membership badge and went past the front desk into the fitness area.

The reporter pointed the camera at Francine. She put a hand in front of her face, took Charlotte by the arm, and hustled the two of them past the reporter.

Charlotte smiled big for the camera. "What do you think of Jake's answers?" she asked after they were in the car.

"I don't know. I need to think about it."

"What were the two of you whispering about?"

"I'll tell you when we get home. Right now I want to watch for any reporters following me." There were two now, and they followed her back to her house. They parked in front.

Once safely inside, Francine invited Charlotte to stay for dinner. She sent Jonathan out to get the grill going while she shaped some hamburger patties.

"Jake told me two things," she said. Charlotte was listening but went to the refrigerator and pulled out a plate of brownies left over from the luncheon. "One, he told the police about Friederich's secret video, and two, he has an alibi for the night Friederich died, he just can't reveal it."

"I'd like to know what's on that secret video."

"So would the police. He said they're looking for it."

Charlotte sat at the kitchen island and prepared to devour a brownie. "Why would Jake not be able to reveal his alibi?"

"It must be a deep dark secret."

"You know I'm not the compassionate type, Francine, but what struck me about our conversation with Jake was discovering how difficult his life still is. Here he is, growing up without a father, losing his mother and his grandmother in his teens, gaining a mentor in Friederich, blossoming under his watch, getting into NASCAR but failing, and when he returns to his roots and to Friederich, he uncovers some reason to believe even his beloved mentor has abandoned him."

Francine slapped the fourth patty on a plate to give Jonathan. She went to the sink and washed her hands. "That sounds almost like a plot summary from one of those mystery novels you love."

"If it were, it would provide the motivation for Jake to snap and kill Friederich, and then off Jeff Kramer when Kramer continues to

257

hound him for a story. But I think it's more complicated than that. Do you believe Jake has a solid alibi for that night?"

Francine dried her hands on a kitchen towel and hung it back on a towel bar. "He isn't revealing it, but why lie to us that he has one if he doesn't? Who are we?"

"Let's assume for a moment that his alibi is good. That would eliminate him from the suspect list. We've already eliminated Larry. That doesn't leave anyone else we can name."

Francine pulled a bag of broccoli slaw mix out of the refrigerator. Charlotte eyed it with suspicion. She hated vegetables. "Not to worry," Francine reassured her. "You'll like the slaw. Let's get back to Suspect X."

"I like that name. Suspect X."

"So what do we know about him?"

"We know he killed Friederich late Saturday night and dropped the body into the pool shed at Alice and Larry's house," Charlotte said. She paused to finish the brownie she'd been working on. "Suspect X knows Larry didn't have an alibi for that night because he's trying to cast suspicion on him. The same person also killed Jeff Kramer, probably the same night, who was supposedly following Larry."

"So maybe Kramer knew Suspect X killed Friederich and then the killer had to take care of Kramer to keep him from talking?"

Jonathan came in from the patio. "Suspect X?"

"This is detective work," Charlotte said. "We don't expect you to understand."

Jonathan rolled his eyes. He scooped up the plate of brownies and returned it to the refrigerator. "You'll ruin your supper, Charlotte."

"Huh."

"It's nice outside," he continued. "Let's eat on the patio. I'll clean up the table." Without waiting for confirmation, he pulled a spray cleaner bottle from under the sink, grabbed a roll of paper towel, and went back out.

Francine measured oil, sugar, and vinegar into a bowl and began to whisk it together. "I like the notion that Kramer knew who killed Friederich, which meant Suspect X had to eliminate him. But let's suppose that Kramer was following Larry when he discovered it. Wouldn't that mean that Larry also knew who killed Friederich?"

"Larry would have told the police if he knew. Surely. But that does beg the question, where did Larry go to meet this mysterious person? Let's call him Suspect Y. We don't know that, do we?"

Francine laid the whisk on the granite counter. She knew they'd met in the parking lot outside Friederich's garage, but she couldn't tell Charlotte that without letting her know she and Jonathan had met with Alice and Larry. She decided to ask a different question. "Could Suspect X and Suspect Y be the same person?"

"That would mean that Larry wanted a secret meeting with someone who would kill Friederich and then kill Kramer because he knew who killed Friederich. Sounds like Larry is meeting with the wrong kind of people."

Francine put the bowl of dressing in the refrigerator. She got out another bowl and dumped the slaw into it. "Would Larry meet with people like that?"

"If he has a secret offshore bank account and won't tell Alice where the money has gone, maybe he has connections to the mob."

"That doesn't sound like the Larry we know."

"I'm not sure the Larry we know exists."

Jonathan came in and threw away the paper towels he'd used to clean up the table on the deck. Francine handed him the plate of burgers. "Will you start these? We'll be ready soon." He washed his hands, took the plate, and went outside.

Francine added sunflower kernels and crunched-up ramen noodles to the bowl of slaw. "What do you make of Jake's story that Friederich had a lover who didn't love him back?"

"We have no way to dispute it. We don't know enough about Friederich."

"We could ask Jud about the video Friederich made of her as insurance."

Charlotte snorted. "Like he'd tell us."

"We won't know until we ask."

"You're right. I should give him a call after dinner."

Francine broke up cashews and put them on top of the sunflower kernels. "So could this mysterious lover be Suspect X, who killed him to get the secret video, if there is such a thing?"

Charlotte got a distasteful look on her face. "It couldn't be Sara Baggesen, could it? I mean, that's just disgusting. She's only sixteen. Friederich was nearly fifty."

"No," Francine said. Then she added without thinking, "Darla would have killed him."

They looked at each other for a moment. Then they shook their heads at the same time.

"There's no way," Charlotte said. "Darla keeps her under constant surveillance."

"I agree. Besides it being so creepy, there's no way Sara could have had that much time with Friederich."

"But he did have some kind of fascination with her. Or with her and Jake. What if they were having a relationship and Friederich knew of it and disapproved?"

"I offer the same defense as we used for Friederich: Darla would have killed Jake by now if that were true."

Jonathan opened the sliding glass door from the patio. "Five minutes."

She handed him a package of cheese slices. "I don't want cheese on mine, but I know you do."

"I love cheese," said Charlotte. "Two slices, one on each side of the hamburger."

"I can't grill it that way, but you can put the bottom one on your bun," Jonathan said. He took the cheese and returned to the patio.

"Speaking of Sara, she has an interesting tattoo on her ankle," Francine said. She pulled a bowl of fruit out of the refrigerator and carried it to the table. "Mary Ruth spotted it today when we saw her working out. Some sort of Chinese or Japanese symbol. I took a photo of it with my iPhone."

"Can I see it?"

"Sure." She pulled the photo up on her phone and handed it to Charlotte. "Here's what it looked like."

"I've seen something like this before. Can you get me a copy?"

She fiddled with the phone. "There. I just emailed it to you."

"What it comes down to is this," Charlotte said. "We only have two suspects if we discount Larry and Jake. We have Suspect X, the mysterious lover, and Suspect Y, the person Larry was going to meet."

"What would a detective do in those novels you read?"

"If this were a cozy, she would start a rumor."

"Like what?"

"That Jake has found the secret video that reveals Friederich had a lover, that she was the likely killer, and he's going to release it to the police after he wins the race tomorrow. He won't release it ahead of the race because he's afraid it might take attention away from his win or prevent him somehow from racing."

"I can see how that would work if there's a mysterious lover because it would make her go after the video. But how would that work on Suspect Y?"

"We start a second rumor." Charlotte went into a blank stare as if her brain needed total concentration to process possible scenarios. "Larry now has an alibi. We don't say what it is, but we add that the police have leads on who Larry was going to meet, Suspect Y, and they are tracking those leads. Suspect Y is a wanted man, because everyone else has a valid alibi."

"How will Suspect Y react upon hearing the rumor?"

"The most logical response would be to leave the area before the police track them down. We've said all along whoever killed Friederich is a neighbor. All we have to do is watch for whichever of our neighbors disappears for a while."

Francine wrinkled her forehead. "How do you propose to do those things?"

"*We* will work together to do those things. I'll spread the rumor about the secret video. You'll spread the rumor about Suspect Y."

"Who do I spread that to?"

"You're resourceful, Francine. Think about it, and I'm sure the answer will come to you."

She crossed her arms. "How are you going to spread your rumor? And what if you put Jake's life in danger by doing that?"

"You worry a lot, Francine. We're only supposing there's a mysterious lover out there and that lover killed Friederich. Even if there is such a woman, we've both seen Jake without a shirt and you yourself said he used to wrestle. I suspect he'd be pretty good at defending himself from a blood choke."

"The killer might use a different method. It seems kind of reckless."

"Look, Jake will be at the racetrack all day tomorrow. There'll be people around him constantly. Plus, they have a lot of security. And we should go to the race too. We know about the rumor and we can be on the lookout for any danger to him."

Francine walked over to the Bose iPod dock she kept in the kitchen and started up some Frank Sinatra music.

Charlotte noticed the iPod. "Don't forget, you said you'd give me the charger so I could juice up my new iPod."

"*Your* new iPod?"

"I'm telling you, Francine, Friederich won't miss it."

She sighed. "Here, take my charger. Plug this end in the bottom of the iPod and this end in a wall socket, and it'll charge up."

"Thanks. I'll return this."

"I'd rather you return the iPod to the police. Or at least to Friederich's house."

"I think Jud would throw a fit if I tried to get back in the house."

The phone rang. Francine answered.

"Good news!" Joy announced. "Marcy has arranged for all of you to get free tickets for the race tomorrow."

"Really? That's great!" Francine relayed the message to Charlotte, who was more excited than she was. "Let me guess. We have to do an interview of some kind."

Joy made a *tsk* noise. "Why do you have to be so negative all the time?" She paused. "But, as it turns out, you're right. You, Charlotte, and I will be interviewed by the track's network. Mary Ruth will be busy catering, so we probably won't get her, although I may interview her when I'm doing color for Fox Sports. I'm supposed to get the rest of you interviewed too, but you won't be nearly as difficult, since you'll be there as celebrities and won't have anything to do but look glamorous."

"I'm hardly a celebrity, and I'm never glamorous."

"You're wrong on both accounts. Have you checked Twitter lately? You're trending right now. In fact, you were number three last time I checked. Your hashtag is wetsundress. ABC's been promoting it after you rescued Mary Ruth on their show yesterday morning."

Francine was horrified. "Now I might not show up at all."

"No, no, no," said Charlotte, overhearing. "We have to show up. Remember, we need to watch Jake to see what happens with the rumor."

"What did Charlotte say? What rumor?"

"I'll fill you in tomorrow. When do we have to be there?"

"I have to be there at one, but I was wondering if you and Charlotte could meet me for an early lunch at Bob Evans. Maybe eleven?"

Charlotte responded enthusiastically to the idea.

"I guess we're in," Francine said.

"Great! See you tomorrow."

She hung up. "I wonder why Joy wants to meet us for lunch."

"You didn't ask if Marcy was coming along."

Francine had a feeling of dread. "You're right. I didn't."

"I'm not saying she'll be there, but that woman seems to pop up a lot lately. Maybe she's going to try to get us on *Jerry Springer* next."

"Now that's one show I absolutely refuse to be on."

"Me, too, but I wouldn't mind being in the audience." She began chanting. "Jer-ry, Jer-ry, Jer-ry."

Jonathan maneuvered the sliding glass door open, juggling the plate of hamburgers and the grill tongs. He watched Charlotte chant. She noticed him and stopped.

He put the plate on the table. "I don't want to know what that was all about."

Francine took the tongs from him and put them in the sink. "Trust me, you're better off not knowing."

THIRTY-ONE

FRANCINE TOOK CHARLOTTE HOME after dinner. Her plan was to drop her off at the door so as to avoid any invitations to drink brandy, but since there was a dark sedan she didn't recognize parked at the next-door neighbor's house, she decided it would be best if she went in. She should at least make sure her friend was safe before she left.

"Want a nightcap?" Charlotte toddled down the hall toward the library.

"No, thank you. It's only seven thirty, a bit early for a nightcap." She glanced into the family room, the kitchen, and each bedroom on the way down the hall.

"What are you looking for?"

"Nothing. Just making sure there's no one here."

"It's creepy to think we have to worry about that, isn't it?"

"Yes, but that's the reality."

Charlotte played with her cane. "We need to get the rumors out quickly, about the secret video and the mysterious Suspect Y."

"I never agreed to participate in this rumormongering."

"You're going to leave it all up to me?"

"Do me a favor and don't tell me how you'll do it." She reminded Charlotte what time she would pick her up for lunch the next day and said good-bye.

Francine hadn't even gotten herself buckled into the Prius when she got a phone call. "Hello?"

"Shhh! It's Mary Ruth."

"Why are you whispering?" she whispered back.

"Because I don't want Alice to hear. I need for you to come over."

"Why? What's Alice doing there?"

"Larry moved out. She gave him an ultimatum, and he moved out. She's distraught and she's slowing me down. I have to get this food ready for tomorrow!"

"I'll be right over." She called Jonathan to let him know why she'd be late, then she speed-walked over to Mary Ruth's house. Alice opened the door when Francine rang the doorbell. She wore flowered capris Francine had never seen before and hoped she wouldn't see on Alice again. A black polo with dots of cookie dough on the collar was underneath a pink *Mary Ruth's Catering* apron. Her ever-present cross pendant was missing, which Francine immediately noticed.

"I'm going to invest in Mary Ruth's business," Alice announced, slurring the words a bit.

"Really? Why is that?" Francine stepped warily into the house.

"Why not? Larry's hidden his trust fund in some sleazy offshore bank. The least I can do is use our money here in the States to help my friend expand her business."

Mary Ruth's house was a two-story Colonial design, but small. Inside it felt even smaller because of the enlarged commercial kitchen she'd had built that took over most what had been the dining room. But the house always smelled wonderful, and right now it smelled like cakes baking in the oven. Alice, however, smelled like alcohol. She held a Manhattan in one hand. Francine guessed it was not her first drink of the evening.

"Not that I don't think it's a good idea to invest in Mary Ruth's business," she said, "but don't you think you ought to talk to Larry about your investments?"

"Not anymore. I'm madder than the proverbial Mad Hatter. He still won't tell me what he did with all that money from his grandparents. The old nutcases probably had something in the trust fund provision that prevented me from getting my hands on it. They never liked me from the start."

Francine got that empty feeling again, like maybe she and Charlotte were letting their friendship with Larry color who they suspected. He did seem to have a lot of secrets. There was circumstantial evidence that Friederich was flaunting something. Was it one of Larry's secrets? Would Larry kill to keep it hidden? Or did Larry think that trying to frame himself was clever and would make him look less suspicious in the end?

"Do you know why he's afraid to tell you?"

"No, and whatever the reason is, I don't know how it can be more horrible than the mistrust it's put between us." She took a belt of the Manhattan. "Want a drink?"

"Maybe I could use a glass of wine."

"I've got your favorite Chardonnay in here," Mary Ruth called from the kitchen.

It seemed to snap Alice back to reality. "Oh, dear, I'm shirking my chopping duties."

Mary Ruth's kitchen was in commercial duty mode. Dirty dishes were stacked next to the industrial-sized dishwasher, trays of cupcakes were lined up to be frosted, and prep for several other dishes was going on at a granite-topped rectangular island. Mary Ruth stood at a mixer, alternating wet and dry ingredients into the mixing bowl. "Do you mind helping, Francine? I don't know how we're going to get all this done without being up all night."

Under Mary Ruth's direction, Alice resumed chopping vegetables for a southwestern Cobb salad. Francine put on a pink apron and began piping cream cheese frosting onto carrot cake cupcakes that had cooled.

Alice continued her nonstop patter about her difficulties. "So I just asked Larry to leave. And he did."

Francine looked up from the rows of cupcakes. "Just like that? He didn't say anything?"

"No. I mean, he showed some emotion, thank God. Cried a little. Kept saying he was sorry, and that one day he hoped I would understand, but there was something he had to do before he could tell me anything."

"No hints as to when that might be?" Francine asked, hoping for clues of some kind.

"He acted like whatever it was he was going to do, it would be done in the next couple of days. I told him he could come back when he was ready to tell me."

A couple of days, Francine thought. Jake, too, hoped to have his fortune decided in that time frame, with a big win tomorrow. Charlotte was starting rumors that might affect someone in the next couple of days. And Joy was trying to land a correspondent position with a network. That was a lot of big events in such a short period of time.

"So you came over here to get away from the loneliness?"

"The loneliness, the anger, Darla Baggesen. I tried Joy, but she's not answering her phone."

Francine thought it was weird Joy wouldn't answer Alice's phone call. Before the skinny-dipping incident and Joy's hiring of Marcy as a publicist, the two had been close friends. She hoped this whole craziness would end soon.

Mary Ruth quieted the mixer and entered the conversation. "What was Darla doing to you? Checking the pool shed for more dead bodies?"

"In a manner of speaking. I don't know how many times she's been over, asking what the latest is on how Friederich died and whether Larry's been cleared yet. I don't know why *she's* so anxious to have Larry cleared. Will the homeowners' association throw a party for us and drop the grievances for the violations she's dreamed up if he gets cleared?"

"You know what a gossip Darla is. She's probably fishing for information more than she's hoping for Larry to be innocent."

Mary Ruth's comment struck Francine. Darla had told them Jake was a hero in her daughter Sara's eyes. That could explain it. Maybe she was trolling for gossip to reassure Sara. Or could there be a different motivation? Friederich had kept track of photos of Sara. What were Sara's secrets? What did he know about Sara? Did Darla suspect that Friederich knew something, and so was checking up? Maybe damage control? Certainly Darla and Sara had a complicated mother/daughter relationship. Sara reportedly wanted to be a model more than she wanted to be a race car driver. Darla kept Sara on a short leash. Her ex-husband Vince had filed for custody. Alice had said that Sara wanted the custody change.

But maybe it had nothing to do with anything.

She piped a few more cupcakes. "Do you think Larry's being back from Vegas while we were having the skinny-dipping party had to do with the secret bank account?"

Alice had been banging on the cutting board, taking out aggression on the poor vegetables. She stopped to answer. "Maybe. If we knew what the secret bank account was all about."

Darla had made a comment during the luncheon that the police seemed to be ignoring whatever Friederich may have had on Larry. "If we assume that the killer knew Larry would be back early for a secret meeting, I wonder if he also knew about the bank account. Maybe Friederich knew about it."

"If *I* didn't know about the secret bank account, I don't know how Friederich or the killer would have known," Alice said.

Mary Ruth poured the batter she'd just created into the paper cups that lined her cupcake trays. "I still find it creepy to think that the killer might live in our neighborhood."

"It makes sense, though," Francine said, "since the killer had some inkling of what Larry was doing and had the ability to track him."

Alice put down her knife. "I just feel so blindsided. My decision to have Larry followed was a last-minute thing. Should I have noticed something sooner, done something sooner? If the killer lives in our neighborhood and noticed…" She let the thought trail off.

"Don't stop, Alice," Mary Ruth said. "We have to keep plugging away if we're going to get this done."

Alice resumed hacking the vegetables into pieces. "I'm a terrible business partner. I'm sorry."

When Mary Ruth didn't answer immediately, Francine filled the silence, hoping Alice didn't notice. "I wonder if Charlotte shouldn't refocus on her original question about why Friederich's body ended up in Alice and Larry's pool shed?"

"She did say right from the start that if we wanted to find the killer, we needed to answer that question," Mary Ruth said.

"Doesn't it feel like it was a long time ago, even though it's only been a few days?" Francine said. "A lot of what happened changed our focus. But in the end, it's still a major question that needs resolving."

A timer went off. Mary Ruth stopped it from beeping. "Francine, would you mind taking those cupcakes out of the oven? I'm just about ready to put these in."

Francine went over to the oven. Sitting next to it was a cross necklace, the one Alice never took off. The one that held the clue to her #1 Sixty List item. Just yesterday Francine had said in jest that it would require divine intervention or too much liquor for Alice to take it off. And here it was. She blocked Alice's view and turned it over. There was an inscription, Genesis 18:12–14. She memorized it and set the necklace back down.

Alice successfully finished cutting broccoli and cauliflower and moved to slicing zucchini and yellow squash. "I've been in real estate long enough to answer the pool shed question. The body went into that particular shed because of location, location, location."

Mary Ruth ran her finger around the top edge of the bowl and licked the batter off of it. "Mmm, that's good. If I do have to say so myself."

"What kind of cupcakes are you making?"

"It's a banana cream pie cupcake. I've got crushed vanilla wafers mixed in with the banana batter, and I'm going to frost them with whipped cream. It was a special request from Darla."

"Darla?" Francine asked. "What are you doing making cupcakes for Darla?"

"She got me the catering job, remember? I told her I'd also make cupcakes for Sara's racing team tomorrow."

"Wait! Is Sara in the same race as Jake?" Francine remembered that Charlotte's detective work with the magazines from Friederich's place revealed the two were at the same events but hadn't raced against each other. If they were an item, why would she suddenly race against him now? Were they in a relationship or not? Or was it more complicated than that?

"They're in the same race. I don't think it's a big secret," Alice said. "Darla's mentioned it to me at least twice since she's been visiting so often." She went over to where Mary Ruth was sampling the batter and picked up the spatula. "Can I lick this?"

"You're as bad as Charlotte. No. Francine, did you notice that I refrained from doing any more tasting than just a little bit of the batter?"

"Brady would be proud of you."

Alice snatched up the spatula and licked it anyway. "Mmm. I can't wait to taste one of those cupcakes."

Mary Ruth looked at the messy kitchen. "Tomorrow, Alice. Tonight, we finish the prep work or die trying."

Die trying, Francine thought. She hoped nothing so drastic would happen today or tomorrow.

THIRTY-TWO

THE MINUTE SHE GOT home, Francine looked up the passage from Genesis. It was the story of how the Lord told Abraham that though Sarah laughed at the idea she could have a child in her old age, nothing was too wonderful for the Lord. And he promised that she would have a son.

Francine's heart went out to Alice. Her #1 bucket list item was to have a child! To be in her seventies and living with such regret must be painful. Alice and Larry had been married late in life, too late for a child. They were probably too old to adopt by then too. Francine wasn't sure what to do with the information. She might tell Joy, since Joy was the one who'd found out that the key verse could be found on the cross. But maybe not. Maybe such a far-fetched hope would be best kept secret until Alice decided to reveal it.

Francine didn't sleep well that night.

The next day she rolled up in front of Charlotte's house at 10:45 to pick her up and take her to the Bob Evans for their meeting with Joy. Two reporters in news vans followed her from her house.

Charlotte waved at the vans before getting in. "I'm hungry. I dreamt all morning about their biscuits," she told Francine.

"It's better than what I dreamt about last night. Friederich's dead body flopping out of Alice's shed, but instead of eyes he had vanilla wafers and instead of a mouth he had a peeled banana. In place of his hair he had whipped cream."

"Sounds delicious. Did you eat a banana cream pie before you went to bed?"

Francine backed the car out of the driveway. "Kind of. After I left your house yesterday I ended up helping Mary Ruth and Alice get ready for her catering event today. She was making banana cream cupcakes."

Charlotte buckled her seat belt. "And you got to help. I never get to help. She's still sore about the time I stuck my finger in that batch of chocolate chip cookie dough and took a lick of it in front of Betty the lunatic health inspector, isn't she? Because I thought we all got over that."

"I think she would get over it if she thought you wouldn't do it again. You know she was on probation for nearly a month."

"That Betty Partlow, she really knows how to hold a grudge. All because I ran for secretary of the Hendricks County Garden Society thirty years ago and beat her, she's never forgiven me."

"You have a way of inflaming resentment."

Charlotte leaned right and looked in the passenger side mirror. "How long have the paparazzi been with you?"

"They were waiting at the curb this morning when I got up. They've been really bad this morning. They've knocked on the door, rang the doorbell, called. Jonathan tried to shoo them away but they kept asking him weird questions about Ravel's *Boléro* and wouldn't leave."

"Is that anything like a sombrero?"

Francine chuckled. "Ravel is a composer. *Boléro* is a ballet piece he's famous for. I feel like it was in the soundtrack of a movie, but I can't remember which. Maybe I'll look it up later."

"I wonder why the paparazzi are asking about it."

"Who knows? I just want this murder solved so they'll go away."

Charlotte folded her arms. "You know what's weird? Until you picked me up, I hadn't seen any of them today."

"That is weird. Ever since Marcy's managed to get us on the "D" celebrity list, she keeps finding ways to extend our fifteen minutes of fame. We need for Joy to get rid of her."

"Fat chance of that happening. And I don't see why you're complaining. You could have had *The View*. I'll be lucky if I get a cameo on *Jersey Shore*."

Francine didn't know what *Jersey Shore* was, but if Charlotte didn't want to be on it, she probably didn't want to be on it either.

Charlotte pulled Friederich's iPod Touch out of her purse. "I got this thing charged up last night, but now I need a password to get in."

"Really? I didn't know you could password protect those things."

"You got any ideas on what to try?"

"Have you thought about the police?"

"Why would he use a password like 'the police'?"

The joke was bad, but Francine laughed in spite of it. "Don't be obtuse. You know what I mean."

"I do, and you know I'm not going to take it to them. I keep telling you, they don't care about listening to Friederich's music."

"You can store other things on iPods than music."

"Like what?"

"Like videos." The moment it came out of Francine's mouth, she made the connection. From the look on Charlotte's face, she made the same connection. "What if Friederich stored the video of his secret lover on there?" Francine asked.

Charlotte stared at the iPod in her hand. "It's possible."

The paparazzi followed them into the parking lot of the Bob Evans.

"Maybe we should take this directly to the police station," Francine said, cruising for a parking spot.

"I don't know. The police have Friederich's computer. Wouldn't it be on the computer instead of his iPod? Or, at the very least, wouldn't it be on both?"

"The newer iPods have cameras. That's why I didn't think about it before. Mine doesn't. He might have recorded it directly onto the iPod instead of using a camera and then transferring it." She parked the car.

"That's not what Jake said. Jake said Friederich told him he used the hidden video cameras to make the recording."

Francine glanced up in time to see a cameraman getting out of a news van and a female reporter with a handheld mike advancing toward them. "Stick the iPod in your purse and let's get into the building, quick. Here comes the press."

Charlotte jammed the device into her purse. Francine opened her car door and said, "No comment."

Charlotte swung her door open, leaned on her cane, and slid out. She stood and waved. "I'm having eggs and biscuits, in case anyone wants to know."

The reporter babbled something about YouTube, but Francine did her best to ignore her as they pushed their way into the Bob Evans front doors. There was a crowd, which surprised her, but they got seated immediately with Joy and Marcy, who were already there, leaving the reporter and the cameraman in the lobby.

"Whew," Francine said, looking back toward the entrance to the restaurant. She spun in her chair and confronted Marcy. "This is all your fault."

"No, it's not," Joy said. "It's mine. That's why I wanted you to be here. We need to clear the air." She was wearing an RTV-6 polo shirt, slightly too large. The material bunched in front, and every few seconds she shrugged her shoulders back in an attempt to straighten it up. "I never thought it would be like this when I hired Marcy. She's done what I asked."

Marcy had her cell phone on top of the open menu and hit a few buttons. "I knew that if I focused this on Joy alone it wouldn't have the impact we needed if we were going to get her opportunities to work with the media. It had to be that all of you were worthy of attention. And for the most part, it worked. That *GMA* interview was the best. Francine, you really stood out. That water rescue couldn't have played better if we'd scripted it."

The waitress came over carrying a coffee pot, saw that Joy and Marcy's coffee mugs were empty, and filled them. "Y'all ready to order yet?"

"I think we need a few more minutes," Joy said. She left and Joy turned apologetic. "I'm only sorry you ended up being played for comedy, Charlotte."

"That certainly wasn't my intention," Marcy added. "But on the other hand, if you're willing to say the vomiting episode was caused by lactose intolerance, I may be able to get you a commercial spot for Lact-Away. It's a small company. There's not much money in it, but they're very interested."

"I don't know," Charlotte said. "I might want to hold out for something a little more … glamorous."

Marcy stopped smiling. "That might be tough. I have some bad news. Except for Francine and, to some extent, Joy, the rest of you are yesterday's news."

Charlotte thought a moment. "Is that why the reporters were gone this morning?"

"Yes. The Food Network turned Mary Ruth down, no one cares about Alice, and Fox Sports dropped their offer to audition Joy, although Mary Ruth is still catering for them. Fortunately Joy is still being considered by *GMA* as a correspondent for senior issues."

Joy sniffed. "I've been reduced to working for the track network as a roving reporter. I may even have to do my own camera work."

"But you, Francine, are still hot," Marcy continued. "I've booked you on *The Dr. Oz Show*."

Francine started to object, but Marcy waved her quiet. "It's really too late for you to say no. They've agreed to fly you out of Indianapolis on Monday for Tuesday's taping. You'll be talking about staying in shape in your seventies and keeping up your swimming skills."

"It's not too late. I just won't go."

Marcy buried her head in her hands. "Please don't do this to me. You're the only thing left I've got going. Besides Joy, of course." When she looked up, she had tears in her eyes.

Francine hated to see people cry. "I'm sure you can come up with something else. Why'd Fox Sports drop Joy?"

"You don't get it, do you? The media's fickle. You have to capitalize on what you've got when you've got it. One of the Kardashians changes gender, gets a quickie divorce, or has a baby and suddenly you're yesterday's news. Well, not you personally, Francine. You're a YouTube sensation, at least for the moment. It's why I had to sign the contract for *Dr. Oz* right away. They've already started promoting your appearance." She handed her phone to Francine.

A YouTube video was playing. Francine recognized the scene as being from the *Good Morning America* segment. Mary Ruth, with one hand on the side of the pool and the other grasping a stair rail, gulped air with a crazed look in her eyes. Everything was in slow motion. Francine rose slowly out of the water next to Mary Ruth. She shook her head, her hair flinging water droplets from side to side. She placed both hands on the stair rails and pulled herself onto a step. In slow motion she ascended the stairs, the wet sundress clinging to her body. Francine still had a good figure, and the dress showed it off. The way the video had been crafted reminded her of a movie segment, but she couldn't place it. Then she recognized the music, only because she'd heard the name earlier in the day. "That's *Boléro*!" She put it altogether. "This is a parody of Bo Derek in *10*!" Francine sat in a horrified stupor.

Charlotte snatched the phone away from her just as the announcer said, "Francine McNamara, the septuagenarian YouTube sensation who saved her friend's life. Learn how she stays in shape. Tuesday on *Dr. Oz.*"

"This is a great still picture of you at the end of the commercial. I don't think they played *Boléro* at that point in the movie, but it hardly matters. This is no parody, Francine. You look pretty good. I can see why he would want you on the show."

Francine's face reddened. "How do you…?" She realized she was shouting at Marcy and quieted her voice to a terse reprimand. "How are you able to sign a contract for me? I never hired you as my publicist."

"No, but Joy did. And my agreement with her calls for me to do whatever is necessary to fulfill certain expectations, which I can't do without promoting you. I hate to play hardball, but if you sue me, I'll drag Joy into the lawsuit, and then you'll be suing your friend. You really don't want to do that, do you? Especially when it's much easier to just go along and do the interview. They're flying me, too, so I can coach you through this."

Francine looked to Joy, whose eyes pleaded with her to agree. "It's not like it isn't a huge compliment to you," Joy said. "And remember, you'd be fulfilling your Sixty List number 10, Encourage Fitness Among Peer Age Group."

Charlotte put her arm around Francine and gave her a quick hug. "Well, she's got you there. It *is* on your list. And you could knock that one out of the park with an appearance on *Dr. Oz*."

Francine gritted her teeth. "I was going to cross it off once Mary Ruth started working out with Brady."

"See that table over there," Marcy said, stealthily indicating a family seated in the corner. "One of them has her cell phone out."

Francine glanced their way. Sure enough, the young mother was recording their interaction on her phone. "Let's turn and wave at them," she said.

They all pivoted toward the table and waved. The mother waved sheepishly and put the phone away.

Charlotte said, "Seriously, Francine, you've got to do this. How many people get a chance like this? And you know Jonathan will be supportive. He'll be proud of you."

"We're ready to order," Marcy said, summoning the waitress.

Francine knew Marcy was only trying to avoid a confrontation. "I want that video taken off the air and replaced with something more dignified."

"I'll see what I can do, but I don't know if I have that much leverage."

Marcy ordered a sandwich, Francine a salad, and Charlotte eggs, biscuits, and a side of pancakes. Joy, who hardly ever ate anything, ordered toast. The waitress put her order pad in her pocket, topped off Joy's coffee, and left.

Charlotte waved to someone across the room. "Isn't that Mary Ruth's grandson Toby over there?"

"The one trying very hard to ignore us?" Francine said.

"Toby!" Charlotte called.

"Shush." Francine hit her with a dessert trifold she picked up off the table. "Everyone's looking at us."

"They've been doing that since we got here."

Toby lumbered over with a sheepish look on his face. "Hello, Mrs. Reinhardt." He nodded at Marcy and Francine.

"Toby, your face is pale compared to that bright yellow *Security* shirt you're wearing. Who's that girl you're with over there?"

"She's a friend."

"Has your friend got a name? She's not from around here, is she? I don't recognize her."

"Her name is Ashley. We have econ class together."

"Econ, huh? Are you supplying what she's demanding?"

Toby blushed. Francine hit her again with the trifold. "You're embarrassing the boy."

She winked at Toby. "That's the whole point. Are you working security somewhere, Toby? Mary Ruth didn't say you had a job."

"I'm working security at SpeedFest this week. Ashley's dad works for the firm they hired to run security, and they were looking for big guys, so he hired me."

Toby looked like a security guard with his size and his tattoos, but Francine figured with his passive nature he probably needed an in. "Sounds like a good girlfriend to have, Toby," she said.

"We're just *friends*, Mrs. McNamara." He looked back at Ashley. "And I need to get back to her. Nice to see you all."

Charlotte was close enough to grab hold of his beefy forearm. "Hold on a minute, Toby. You said you're working security at SpeedFest?

He nodded. "It's why I have get back and finish my lunch. I've got to be there at one."

"Do you know where you're going to be located?"

"Infield, I think."

"So if we need help, we should look for you."

Toby wrinkled his nose. "Help?"

"Unsavory types like the media. You know." She tossed it off like it was something she had to deal with every day. "Say, you're good with video games and that kind of stuff, aren't you? Do you think you could find a way to reset the password on my iPod? I'm having trouble with it." She handed it to him.

Toby turned it over in his hand. "Sure. What'd you do, forget the password?"

"In a manner of speaking."

"I should be able to get around it."

"Thanks."

He returned to his table.

Francine waited until Toby was out of earshot. "What was that all about, Charlotte?"

"Oh, I just had to tease the boy. We spent that whole morning running tours together at Alice and Larry's house, and he never once mentioned a girlfriend."

"I mean involving Toby in breaking into Friederich's iPod. It's one thing to get yourself into trouble, but not the boy."

Joy was aghast. "You have Friederich's iPod?"

"Well, not anymore. Toby has it."

"You know what I mean. Where did you get it?"

"She took it out of Friederich's Corvette," Francine said.

"I acquired it when we when we broke into Friederich's house," Charlotte said defensively. "Our little adventure that made it into the news."

"The iPod didn't," said Joy. "Does Jud know you have it?"

"No. And we don't want any … Imperial entanglements." She said it like Alec Guinness in *Star Wars*.

"Well, that's the trick, isn't it?" Joy responded.

"Enough with the *Star Wars* dialogue," Francine said. "Jake told us Friederich had a mysterious lover, and supposedly Friederich made some kind of video to use as blackmail in case she planned to dump him, which he was afraid of. We think if that video really does exist, it might be on the iPod."

"And the mysterious lover might be the killer," Charlotte added.

"No way."

Francine nodded. "Way."

Joy scooted a little closer to the table. "This is kind of exciting."

The waitress returned with their food at that moment. She distributed the meals, refilled coffees, and left.

Charlotte spread out the scoop of butter on top of her pancakes. "And last night I started a rumor that Jake has a copy of the video and planned to give it to police after the race today."

"Whatever for?"

"Because we need to force the killer to do something other than frame Larry."

"How many people did you tell?"

Charlotte thought a moment. "Francine told me last night she didn't want to know how I was going to do it, and I think maybe I'll stick to that. Because I have an idea who the killer is."

"Who?" they all asked at once.

She teased them with a smile. "Let's just say that everything seems to revolve around Jake's return to the midget car races. So something will happen today. We just need to watch Jake carefully. And Sara Baggesen. Friederich seemed to be tracking her movements."

Joy frowned. "Eww. Like a stalker?"

"No, not like that. But he was flagging photos of her in a midget car magazine. There has to be a reason, and I bet it had to do with his death."

"This could so work out," Marcy said excitedly. "If the killer reveals himself and Joy is there to capture it all on tape first, she could really nab the *GMA* position."

"Joy," said Charlotte, "you're not just going to be a track reporter today, you're going to be an undercover journalist."

They stared at each other. Joy's face lit up. "Okay, Charlotte. You want to solve a mystery. I want to prove I'm a reporter. Let's do this thing."

Francine glared at Charlotte. "I want you to tell me who you think it is."

Charlotte doused her pancakes with maple syrup. "I know what you're thinking, Francine."

"I'm not sure you do."

"You're wondering if I'm making a big mistake, eating a lot of food before we go to the track. In case I get interviewed. Especially since I had breakfast food the last time and it didn't turn out so well. The good news is, this is not tofu sausage and this is not artificial syrup."

"Actually, I'm thinking that you're making a big mistake not letting me in on your suspicions."

"Then I can count on you sticking by my side?"

"Like syrup on those pancakes."

"Then we are on the same menu."

THIRTY-THREE

As THEY DROVE OVER to Lucas Oil Raceway, Francine was starting to become okay with the idea that Charlotte had a plan, even if she didn't know the details of it. She almost had to. Charlotte rode to the track with Joy so they could confer alone, sending Marcy over to ride with her. Francine was grumpy to be stuck with Marcy and hardly talked to the publicist. Marcy never stopped talking, however. She babbled on and on about Lucas Oil, like Francine had never been there, even though it was a major attraction only twenty miles from the Speedway and hosted big drag races on its drag strip and lots of Automobile Racing Club of America events on its smaller oval. When they arrived, Joy went to the press area to meet with the track network's crew, leaving Marcy with them. Marcy distributed their free tickets. The three women were admitted and then walked the bare-ground trail to the first entrance. Francine tried to think of a way to get rid of the publicist but couldn't come up with anything.

To the right of them rose a massive wall of sloped concrete that held stands. Though practice was getting ready to start, there was practically no one in the stands.

Charlotte looked at the mostly empty seats. "Is this normal? It's about one o'clock. I thought this would be like the Indy 500, where people arrive long before the race."

Francine remembered having the same thoughts when she and Jonathan went to SpeedFest several years back, before Jake had been taken into NASCAR. "No, it's like this. Practice and qualifications are getting ready to start. Before the lineup of the final race is determined, they'll have a bunch of heats, probably starting around three o'clock. By then it'll be filling up. You have to remember that the real draw isn't the midgets but the Silver Crown series race that happens after that. The stands will be full by then."

One step at a time, Charlotte led the women up to the first row of bleachers, where she laid out a large sheet of paper with a crude, hand-drawn map of Lucas Oil Raceway on it. Marcy and Francine held on to the edges to keep the wind from blowing it over on itself.

Francine knew the layout. The oval was the place where the midget car race would take place. The short sides of the oval faced north and south. Along the north and west sides of the oval, inside the track, Charlotte had drawn little rectangles that were labeled *Pits*. Inside the center of the oval extending to the east side was a large area she'd labeled *Support Vehicles*.

"This is how the track is laid out," Charlotte said. "After Francine left last night I did a little research, and then this morning I called and talked to Alice because she's a race fan and knows this place like the back of her hand. The key thing will be finding out where each racer's pit will be located. We need to pay particular attention to Jake and to Sara. If they have a relationship, we should be able to determine just what that is."

"Where's Mary Ruth stationed?" Francine asked.

"Ah, yes, our spies. Mary Ruth and Alice will be back here in the support vehicles area. They need to be close to where they'll serve their food. I've alerted them to be looking for anything suspicious. If they notice anything, they'll call us on our cell phones."

"What could they possibly see back there that's suspicious?" Marcy wanted to know.

"They might hear some gossip that could be a game changer. Right now, I'm operating on instinct. With some additional intel, I might be able to zero in on the killer."

Francine had to choke back a laugh at the word *intel*. The track announcer said something incomprehensible and the first midget car raced out onto the track.

"Wow, they're loud," Charlotte shouted.

Francine handed her some earplugs. "That's with only one car out. Wait until the heats start, when more of them are running. Then it gets really loud, and you'll need these."

"Good thing we're already losing our hearing. Otherwise, I'd be worried."

The driver decided not to complete his qualification and the track was quiet for a few minutes.

Charlotte glanced at Marcy. "We need someone stationed here at the entrance to see who comes in."

"Sorry, but you're not ditching me," Marcy said. "Don't think you're going to go off and solve this thing while I sit here twiddling my thumbs."

"We need to take advantage of the fact that there are three of us," Charlotte explained. "No one who's not part of a racing team can get into the infield without going past this spot. It would be useful to know if any of the suspects are coming our way."

Marcy eyed her. "The only suspects *are* part of a racing team."

Charlotte shook her head. "Not so. Larry, for example."

Francine expressed her surprise. "Larry? Is he going to be here? I thought we agreed he wouldn't have done it."

"Nonetheless, he can't be fully ruled out. And Joy said Alice told her he was coming."

Marcy folded her hands over her chest. "Not going to work. I'm going with you."

"Ahem," said a male voice. The women turned and found Jud standing behind them. He was dressed in his police uniform.

"Hi, Jud," said Charlotte.

"Where are your friends from the press?"

"I'm sure they're not far behind," Francine said.

"The crowd's so sparse right now, I'd have thought you'd see them." He sat in the row behind them.

Marcy sniffed. "There aren't that many of them now."

"I've heard that," Jud said. A second racer went onto the track and the noise level climbed. Jud shouted his next question. "Francine, could I see you for a moment?" He indicated a spot behind the bleachers.

Francine was mystified as to what Jud could possibly want from her, but she obliged. When Charlotte tried to follow them, Jud frowned at her until she sat back down. "What is it?" she asked when they'd gotten far enough away she was certain Charlotte couldn't hear, even if the midget car was still qualifying.

"I'm worried about you and Charlotte."

"Why?"

Jud put his hands in his pockets and got a sheepish look on his face. "I've chased the press away to make you all more appealing, but it seems to have backfired. Now, hardly anyone is following you, and with the race happening, I can't spare the manpower to keep you from getting into more trouble."

"What makes you think we're going to get into more trouble?"

"Charlotte attracts trouble, and you're here on a mission. Tell me what your plans are."

"To the best of my knowledge, our plans are to follow Jake around, and maybe Sara Baggesen. Charlotte says she thinks she knows who the killer is, but she's not letting on." Francine considered telling him about Friederich's iPod, but since Charlotte technically didn't have it anymore, she decided she wouldn't. It would only make Charlotte mad, and if she was correct that the mystery would be solved today, then the iPod might not enter into it.

For some reason, Jud seemed relieved by the information. "I don't suppose there's any harm in your doing that. Just promise me that the two of you will stick together."

Francine nodded. "But since I've answered your questions, how about if you reciprocate?"

"If it's information I can let out, I will."

"Do you seriously suspect Larry?"

"Not of murder, but there's something he's hiding."

"It may not be criminal. How about Jake? Do you suspect him? He told us he has an alibi."

"He does, but it's one person's word. We understand Jake's reason for not coming forward with the information right away. That doesn't mean he's in the clear."

Francine thought a moment. "Jake told us that Friederich's strength was 'cheating legally.' Jake took one of his cars from Friederich's garage. But what about the second car that disappeared, the unmarked one? Could he have taken that one, too? Have his cars been checked to see if they have some kind of advantage Friederich concocted?"

"We thought of that. Both his car and his backup car have been checked. Nothing unusual was detected."

"Do you mind if I ask who examined them? I mean, knowledgeable people have missed these kinds of things before."

"We had Excalibur Racing do it. They wanted to help since Friederich worked for them."

Francine remembered that Vince Baggesen worked at Excalibur. "But who at Excalibur checked it?"

"I'd have to consult my notes. One of their experts. I spoke with their acting chief mechanic, not the person who evaluated the car."

"When you get a chance, I'd appreciate knowing."

Jud gave her a hard stare. "Why?"

Francine briefly considered telling him the truth. "Charlotte will ask."

Jud was not fooled. "If I get you the name, will you tell me why?"

The noise of the midget car quieted as it pulled off the track, and shortly after the announcer gave the qualifying time. The sudden quiet distracted Francine, but she looked back at Jud to find him expecting an answer. "Sure," she said. "It probably won't make any difference, but yes, I'll tell you."

Jud's cell phone rang. He looked at the number and walked away from Francine, talking to the caller. She wondered if he would remember to get her an answer.

As Francine returned to the stands, she saw Charlotte sitting on the edge of the bleacher seat gazing in her direction. "What did he want?" she asked.

"He's worried because we aren't being followed by the paparazzi. You remember that was part of his strategy to keep us safe. He thinks we'll get ourselves in trouble."

"Well, let's not disappoint him, then. C'mon, Marcy."

Marcy and Charlotte seemed to have come to some kind of understanding because they were acting chummy. "Where are we going?"

"Into the infield. It's time to find out where Jake and Sara have their pits."

The three women used the tunnel that went under the track to get into the infield. As they were walking, they heard Joy's unmistakably chirpy voice interviewing someone over the loudspeakers. The questions and answers flowed naturally.

"Listen to that!" Marcy said enthusiastically. "She's doing great."

Francine had to agree. Charlotte seemed distracted and didn't comment. When they got out of the tunnel, they hadn't walked too far along the pits before they came across Joy.

Joy pointed to the man behind her shouldering a video camera. "Look! The track network gave me a cameraman."

Marcy pumped a fist. "Cool."

"We're heading over to Sara Baggesen's pit. She's next up to qualify."

"Where's Jake's pit?" Charlotte asked.

"Way back over there," Joy said, pointing in the opposite direction. "Not optimal for our purposes, is it, Charlotte?"

"Not at all." Charlotte was clearly unhappy.

A look passed between them. It made Francine nervous. "What purposes? What have you got planned?"

"Nothing, Francine. Just stay close."

The women followed Joy and her cameraman to Sara's pit. Along the way, Charlotte pulled out her map and Joy identified Sara's area, which was located at the north end where the racers exited into the pits, and Jake's position at the southwest corner, where the cars left the pits to get onto the track.

"I bet it's a seniority kind of thing," Joy said. "Jake's been around the block enough."

"I wonder where Mary Ruth's van is from here." Charlotte shaded her eyes, even though she was wearing sunglasses and a floppy hat.

Francine pointed away from where they stood, near Sara's pit, back toward Jake's. "I thought you saw it when we were in the bleachers. Remember where all the catering trucks were parked in the back of the infield? Mary Ruth's pink van is reasonably close to Jake's pit."

"I guess we'll have to hike all the way back there to get any free samples," Charlotte said.

Joy cupped her hand around her ear as though she were trying to listen to someone talking to her. That was when Francine noticed she was wearing an earpiece. Joy said to her cameraman,

"We've been told to stand by. Sara's getting ready to make a qualifying run."

"We're here at a good time," Charlotte said.

The noise level inside the track was even louder than when they were in the bleachers.

Sara's car raced out onto the track. When it did, Joy's cameraman dashed into the pit and set up. He motioned Joy to follow him. The other women moved closer to the pit area but stayed on the outside.

Sara completed her practice lap. When the announcer gave the speed, he said it was the fastest lap of the day. She made her first qualification lap, but it was slower. "Did it look to you like she backed off on her speed?" Francine asked. "It looked like it to me."

Charlotte nodded. "It did, and I'd say it was deliberate."

Sara's second lap completed her qualification run. It came in a little faster but still behind the quick practice lap. The announcer said Sara Baggesen had the fastest qualification time so far. Francine was suspicious.

The crowd cheered for Sara. "Sounds like she has a lot of fans here," said Marcy. She moved into the pit to get closer to where Joy and the cameraman were finishing setting up.

There were no other qualifiers at that moment, so the noise abated while Joy did her interview, which was broadcast on a couple of giant screens. Joy congratulated Sara, asked a couple of soft questions, then said, "You blistered the track with your practice lap, but then you seemed to back off on your speed. What was going on with your car?"

"It felt a little loose," she said, "and I wasn't comfortable at the corners, so I had to take a bit off the speed. But the qualification run ought to hold up. It's pretty fast."

"Well, congratulations, Sara, and I hear congratulations are also in order for you having completed your black belt in karate."

Sara looked confused. "You must've heard incorrectly. I don't have my black belt. I've been focusing more on modeling lately. In fact, I've just signed with a local agency. Can't talk about where I've auditioned, but I hope to be in a commercial soon."

Francine turned to Charlotte. "Why is it I feel you were responsible for that question?"

Charlotte looked as puzzled as Sara had been. "But that symbol you showed me, Francine. I researched it. It indicates someone highly experienced in martial arts."

"She didn't deny she took karate, she just said she wasn't that far along."

"At some point she must've wanted it then, for it to have been tattooed on her ankle."

"What were you trying to do, link her to the blood choke?"

Charlotte got a sheepish look on her face. "Sort of."

Joy wrapped up her interview. Police and security guards began filtering into the area.

Francine pointed to them. "Looks like something's happening."

"There's Toby!" Charlotte said. "I'm going to go talk to him. Maybe he knows what's going on."

She started to take off, but Francine held her by the arm. "I think we should stay together. Jud is heading to talk to Sara. Let's go find out what he knows."

"He's not going to tell us anything. And I'll be fine talking to Toby. What trouble can I get into?"

"Charlotte, if addiction to trouble had a twelve-step program, I'd have you enrolled."

"I don't want him to get away. Let me go."

"Set your cell phone to vibrate and hold it in your hand. You'll never hear it ring when it gets noisy and I may need to contact you."

Charlotte made a beeline for Toby, and Francine made one for Jud.

Jud held up a hand. "Before you ask, I can't tell you what we're doing."

"Will you let me guess? You're going to check the car because it went abnormally fast. You want to know if it has any technology Friederich might have developed."

"Cannot confirm or deny," he said.

Francine smiled. "You're good at bluffing, Jud, but I've known you for a long time."

He shook his head. "I can't say any more."

"Then answer my question from earlier. Who was it at Excalibur Racing that checked Jake's car over for you? I bet you found out it was Vince Baggesen, and now this qualification seems suspicious."

"It was Vince Baggesen. That's all I can tell you."

Francine watched as Jud went into the pits. The police were trying not to attract attention, but she thought it was clear to anyone watching that something must be wrong because the police weren't in anyone else's pit. They stopped to talk to Vince Baggesen. Francine wondered where Darla was. In fact, now that she thought about it, it was strange that Darla had not been around to watch

Sara qualify. What could Darla be doing that was more important? Maybe she should find Charlotte and head over to Jake's pit. What if Darla knew about Jake and Sara and decided to put a stop to it?

Francine looked around for Charlotte and panicked. She was nowhere to be found. Then some of the crowd around the pits parted for Toby in his bright yellow Security shirt. Francine hurried over to him. "Where's Charlotte?"

He shrugged. "I don't know. She was here a minute ago. I gave her the iPod back, and she went off toward the catering area." He pointed in that direction. "She said she was looking for my grandma."

"Were you able to get the password for the iPod?"

"No, but I was able to reset it. I told her the new password, but I'm not sure she knows how to work the device."

Francine pulled out her iPhone and called Charlotte. Fortunately she answered, almost on the first buzz. "Where are you, Charlotte?"

"I'm over by the Fox Sports tent, trying to find Mary Ruth. Francine, I think I know who killed Friederich. Sara's tattoo threw me off, but now it all makes sense."

"That's great, but do you have proof? Because I think I can get proof."

Charlotte sounded cagey. "You tell me who you think it is first."

"I'm not trying to one-up you. I think we can prove this, and then we can take it to Jud. Toby says you have the iPod."

"I do, but the answer is so much simpler."

"Charlotte, please. Just follow my directions exactly. Remember, we thought the proof was on the iPod."

"I don't know how to work it."

"I'm going to tell you."

"Well, I'll have to put the phone down to get it out. I'm juggling my purse and my cane."

"Please, just do it quickly."

"Okay, I'm holding the iPod. Now what?"

Francine told her how to turn it on.

After a bit, Charlotte said, "Okay, it's on."

"Sign in. Use the new password Toby gave you."

"Is this going to take long?"

"It might, but this is really important. Did you press it?"

Charlotte sounded distracted. "Yeah."

"Now look at the screen. You should see a bunch of little icons. Is one of them 'videos'?"

"It is."

"Tap on it."

"I'm juggling too much stuff again, Francine. Let me put my purse on the ground."

The announcer said that Jake Maehler was next up to begin his qualification run. The crowd noise picked up.

"Wait, Charlotte. Before you do that, let me tell you all the steps. You'll see a list of videos after you tap on the screen. You can move through the list by putting your finger on the screen and scrolling up. See if there's something that looks homemade, like Friederich filmed it himself."

"Okay."

Francine waited. She had gnawing feeling that somehow things were wrong, but she couldn't pinpoint what. The announcer said Jake's name again to make a qualification run, but there was no accompanying noise of his midget car. "Charlotte, I think something's happened to Jake."

But Charlotte never responded. Francine heard a female voice talking to Charlotte, one she recognized immediately. Then she heard a crunch, loud and clear through the phone. The connection went dead.

THIRTY-FOUR

FRANCINE GASPED BECAUSE IT all made sense. *I should have known right from the start,* she thought. *The reason I knew it was twelve-fifteen in the morning when Jud asked me was because Darla Baggesen yelled it at us. But it came too fast! There was no way she could have done it that fast unless she was already up, watching us.*

She hurried off to where the caterers were located, looking for the Fox Sports tent.

Before Francine found either the Fox Sports tent or Mary Ruth's trailer, she came across Jose. He had a much smaller bandage on his head and was wearing a pink "Mary Ruth's Catering" apron. She rushed to where he was wheeling a catering cart across the ground. The cart had three shelves, each containing a large aluminum-covered pan, and the unevenness of the ground was jostling them.

"Jose," she said.

He saw her and reacted with alarm as though the mere fact she was there meant bad things for him.

Francine supposed it was deserved. As gently as she could, she asked in her limited Spanish, "Can you point me to the Fox tent?"

"*Sí*," he said. He stepped back to find a clear sight line. In broken English, he said, "That is it, the blue flag. Just behind the red and yellow flag."

Francine was surprised he spoke any English at all. But she knew some immigrants who felt insecure about their language skills pretended not to know English until they had to. "*Gracias*, Jose. Should I try to cut straight across or follow the road all the way around?"

"Follow the road."

Francine squared her shoulders and began to powerwalk.

"But your friend with the cane, she is in that trailer with Sensei Baggesen."

He pointed to a large unmarked tent in front of the trailer. The trailer was large enough that it could easily haul and service a couple of midget cars.

Francine looked at Jose. "How do you know Sensei Baggesen?"

"She is a black belt in the karate class I take."

The information jolted Francine. "I didn't know Darla Baggesen had a black belt."

"Oh, *sí*. Third degree."

"When did you see them talking?"

He shrugged. "*Minutos*."

"Do you know what they were talking about?"

"Sensei helped her use her iPod."

Help her, Francine thought, alarmed. *Not likely*. If Darla had recognized the iPod as Friederich's, and if Friederich died from a blood choke as everyone thought, and if Francine was putting two and two together and getting four...

"That's their trailer, the one you were to deliver those trays to?"

"*Sí.*"

"Jose, you can head on back to Mary Ruth's. I'll handle the food from here."

Francine took her iPhone out, set it to record, and put it back in her pocket. She knocked on the trailer door. When no one answered, she did it again, this time with more force. The door opened. Darla stood there. Before Francine could offer a ruse with the trays of food, Darla grabbed her by the arm and hauled her in. The door slammed shut behind them.

———

With a swift move, Darla slipped one arm between Francine's arm and body. She gripped Francine's upper arm with the other hand and used the hand on the inside to flip Francine's wrist over. She applied pressure to it.

The move had been so quick and the pain so sudden that Francine could only gasp.

The door had opened into the center of the trailer. To the right, at the front corner, were tools like Francine had seen in Friederich's workshop. Some were organized in cabinets with no doors and others were attached to a large pegboard. Closer to her was an unmarked midget car, which Francine theorized had been taken from Friederich's shop. A rolling tool chest was next to the car.

The inside of the trailer was deadly quiet compared to the noise of the qualification run outside.

Tied to a chair in the rear left corner was Charlotte, who acknowledged Francine with frightened eyes. She had a gag around her mouth, but it didn't look securely tied. She was working on it with her teeth like she could chew through it.

Charlotte must've put up a good fight, she thought. What was likely a sitting area with a small table and two chairs had been thrown into disarray, the table dumped and the chairs in pieces. *She knows how to wield that cane.*

"Where's Friederich's iPod?" Francine asked. "I know you took it off Charlotte."

"It's in her pocket," Charlotte answered over the loose gag.

"What did Friederich have on you, Darla? We know the iPod has some kind of blackmail video on it."

"You messed this all up for me and you don't even know what's on it?" Darla hissed.

"It has to connect you to Friederich in a way you don't want anyone to know."

Charlotte worked her tongue around the gag. "It's a sex tape, Francine. That's the only thing that makes sense."

Francine nodded. "Like a prostitute, only for technology, not money."

Darla snarled at her. "I was keeping Friederich focused on making Sara's car a contender."

Francine tried to keep Darla talking until she could think of same way to save them. "Then why did you kill him?" she asked.

Darla applied more pressure to the hand hold she had on Francine, making Francine yelp.

"It wasn't intentional," Darla said. "He betrayed me and I snapped. He told me he was going to help Jake using what he'd developed for Sara—what I paid for in more ways than one." Darla laughed and

Francine could hear the bitterness in it. "We're over at my house and he waits until we're getting ready to make love to tell me this. So I choked him out. Tried not to leave any obvious marks, but I knew once they did an autopsy it would all come out. The question was how to distract the police and pin it on Larry. Your Bridge Club couldn't have been more helpful providing a distraction."

"What did you know about Larry?"

"Not much. Friederich had something on Larry, but he wouldn't tell me what it was. He assured me it was big, though, so I helped him figure out a way to use it to sop up money for Sara's midget car."

"Sara backed off her qualification run for a reason," Francine said. "The police know she was leaving room for Jake, that she's in love with him. Before I left, the police were in the pits examining her car and talking to Vince."

"You're lying."

"No, and whatever happened to Jake, they'll know you were behind it too." It was a risk to keep making Darla mad, but Francine didn't have a choice. "The police'll be looking for you. That I know."

Darla dropped the wrist hold she had on Francine and wrapped her forearm around her neck from behind. Francine dipped her head quickly to block the arm from reaching her neck, but Darla laughed and yanked Francine's hair to pull back her head. Francine kicked Darla in the shins and then remembered her self-defense class. She bit down hard on Darla's forearm.

Darla gave a short scream. Francine quickly twisted away under Darla's arm, tripping her as she escaped. Darla went down but threw a foot out and nicked Francine in the knee, taking her to the ground too.

Francine crawled the short distance to Charlotte and loosened the ties on her hands. Just as Charlotte stood up, Darla was on them both. She kicked Francine in the stomach and pushed Charlotte back into the chair.

Charlotte's right hand fell back into her cane. She lifted it and jabbed at Darla, but Darla caught it in midair. Francine was on the floor in pain from the kick, but she wasn't going to let Darla get the better of this situation. She put her hand out, gripped Darla's ankle and pulled. Darla momentarily lost her balance.

Charlotte struggled to her feet and attempted to regain control of the cane. But Darla recovered her balance and ripped the cane from Charlotte's hand, gripping it in her two. She slipped it over Charlotte's head and pulled hard. The cane yanked Charlotte back into Darla's body. The cane came up against Charlotte's throat and Darla had control.

"Can't breathe," Charlotte choked out.

"One move, Francine, and I'll kill Charlotte. And once she's done, I'll beat you to death with this cane."

"iPod," Charlotte squeaked. "Evidence."

"Thanks for the reminder, Charlotte. I do need to get rid of that."

"Not what I meant. Gone. Not in your pocket."

Darla's eyes opened wide in surprise as though she realized the iPod could have come out in the melee. She let go of the cane with one hand to pat the pocket where she'd put the iPod.

As Darla's grip loosened, Charlotte reared back with her good leg and kicked Darla square in the knee with as much power as she could muster.

The maneuver worked. Darla grabbed her knee in pain. Charlotte snatched her cane out of Darla's hands and doubled back toward Francine. Francine wasn't sure that was the direction Charlotte should be going.

Once again, the younger woman recovered quickly. Darla gave a yell Francine thought sounded Japanese. Francine watched in horror as Darla leaped at Charlotte.

THIRTY-FIVE

Francine shoved Charlotte out of Darla's path. As she did, she snatched the cane and aimed it at the oncoming sensei. It connected with a force that knocked the cane out of Francine's hands, but it also momentarily stunned Darla.

Darla landed on her knees in front of the chair Charlotte had been tied to. She gripped the chair legs and jerked her head in Francine's direction. Francine could see the shock in Darla's eyes. Apparently she had expected this to be a lot easier than it was proving. Francine tried to yank the chair out of her hands to hit her with it, but the younger woman was stronger. Francine felt herself losing the tug of war and waited for Darla to tug again. She moved with it this time and used the momentum to shove the chair into her and knock her over. Darla pushed the chair to the side and rolled to a standing position. She kicked at Francine, who had already backed out of range.

Francine knew she couldn't keep this up. She turned toward the door. Then she noticed Charlotte, hobbling in obvious pain, already ahead of her. Charlotte would reach the door in a moment.

Darla crossed the distance in two leaps and knocked her hand away from the knob with a chop to the wrist. Charlotte yelled in pain and sank to the floor. Darla attempted to grab her from behind, but Charlotte threw an elbow into Darla's knee in the same place she'd whacked her before. Gasping, the sensei gripped Charlotte's shoulders. Charlotte did her best to hit the bruised knee a third time.

Francine could see it was only a matter of time before Charlotte would be taken captive. She knew she needed another weapon and needed it quickly. She glanced around the trailer and spotted the tools hanging from the pegboard. A crowbar could do a lot of damage to Darla's knee, but the rolling tool chest stood between her and it. Francine made a run for it.

Darla seemed to sense that Francine was looking for a weapon. She let go of Charlotte and dashed to make a cutoff, but she glanced back to make sure the door remained closed.

With Darla distracted, Francine went for the rolling tool chest instead, thinking she could push it in Darla's way. She reached the chest and gave it a shove. No movement. She pushed again, this time with everything she had. Still nothing. The effort unbalanced her. She fell to the floor.

Her hand landed near a plastic barrel. In it were ten or so cylindrical rods of varying lengths. *Like long ball bearings*, she thought. She looked up. Darla was going for the crowbar, but hadn't reached it yet. There was still time.

She upended the barrel, pointing it toward her nemesis. The rods spread out and covered the floor, rolling.

Darla stepped on them. Her feet started to skid. Her arms flailed. She attempted to regain her balance but banged into the tool chest. She tried to grab on to it. Her feet slipped out from under her again and again, but she remained upright. Francine began to wonder if Darla would ever fall.

The rods won. Darla's legs couldn't move fast enough. She crashed to her knees and gasped in pain.

The door to the trailer opened. Francine prayed it was help coming. "Careful! Watch the rods!" she shouted.

"Okay," the voice shouted back. Francine recognized it as Toby's. The stream of radius rods rolled out the door and onto the ground. Toby stepped in carefully, avoiding the few that remained. Jonathan was with Toby.

On the other side of the room, Darla let loose a string of profanities fly, not all of them in English.

Before Darla could regain her composure, Toby ran over, flipped her on her stomach, and sat on her back. He pulled her chin back in a chin lock.

"Nice crab hold," Charlotte said. "Where did you learn that?"

"World Wrestling Entertainment. I play it on my Xbox."

"Be careful," Francine said. "She's a black belt."

Jonathan hurried to check on Francine. "Jud will be here any minute. He got the truth out of Vince Baggesen about the car. Fortunately Toby remembered about the Baggesen's second trailer and where it was. But in the meantime," he pulled a gun from behind his back under his shirt, "I suggest you don't try anything, Darla. I know you're a killer and I won't hesitate to use this."

Francine gaped at the gun. She had no idea Jonathan even knew how to shoot, let alone owned a gun. *Another of his little secrets,* she thought. But much as she hated guns, she was not upset to see him holding one right now.

Jud and Larry arrived together. Larry shoved his way to the spot where Toby had Darla's head tilted upright. He knelt down and got in her face. "I will sue you for every last thing you have," he said, practically spitting at her. "You tried to sabotage my son's car."

Francine could hardly believe what she heard. "Your son?"

Jonathan nodded. "It's true. It's time you all knew. Jake Maehler is Larry's son."

THIRTY-SIX

"So I told Darla about the video, not realizing she was the killer, and that set everything into motion?"

Francine hoped Charlotte felt squeamish asking the question. Though everything had turned out all right, she'd put a lot of people in danger. Charlotte seemed to contemplate that as the two of them and Jonathan sat in hard chairs across the desk from Jud at the Brownsburg Police Department headquarters. Having been through the formal questioning period about everything that had happened in the trailer, he seemed willing to share information, especially since the culprit in the murder of Friederich Guttmann had been caught.

"We had warned you to keep us informed and not get into it yourselves," Jud told them. He swiveled to face Charlotte. "You, especially, should have turned in the iPod. It turned out to be the key piece of evidence. Had you done that, none of this would have occurred."

"I know I shouldn't have taken it, but on the other hand, I had no idea you could store video on it. Who knew?"

"I did," Francine admitted, "but not until that moment in the Bob Evans parking lot did I realize what you might be sitting on, and even then we couldn't be sure until Toby reset the password. Jud, if we had to do it all over again, we would have called you the minute we were in possession of the iPod."

"She's speaking for herself," Charlotte said. "I would still have made sure before I told you."

"What was the video of?" Francine asked.

"There are a number of things on it. One of them was what you suspected. Darla and Frederick making love. We're still putting things together, but here's what we think. The relationship was a complete secret. Darla saw Friederich as being beneath her standards, and she was afraid someone would clue him in that she was using him. Friederich was inexperienced enough with women to see Darla as a godsend. But Friederich wasn't stupid, and once he realized she would dump him as soon as he finished outfitting Sara's car, he borrowed Larry's idea of hidden cameras. He had a couple of places rigged, one of them in the basement. He'd figured out how to get down there. After he had a couple of segments filmed, he told her what he would do if she left him. I don't know if she had considered killing him up to that point, but it was in her mind after that. When she snapped, she knew she needed to find the video."

"What I want to know," Jonathan said, "is why Darla thought Larry would be a serious murder suspect?"

"She'd seen the secret staircase. Friederich had even shown her how he was getting around Larry's surveillance cameras with a rogue remote. Since she knew about Larry's love of secret passages and snooping, she figured she could keep us busy checking him out. She lucked into his lying to Alice about being in Las Vegas when he wasn't."

"So that night when Friederich died, Larry had been trying to meet with Jake to tell him that he was his son?"

"He had arranged for it to take place outside Friederich's workshop because he knew Jake was familiar with it. Except Sara had slipped out that night to meet secretly with Jake, so he brought her along. Jake only knew that the person who had called him claimed to be the sponsor who had been footing his bill, nothing about parentage. When Larry spotted Sara, he recognized her and didn't reveal himself. After Jake left, he waited a couple of hours, hoping Jake might be curious and return without her. Eventually he gave up and went back to the hotel."

"What did Jeff Kramer see that got him killed?"

"After killing Friederich, Darla came to get the car Friederich had been working on for Sara. She spotted Larry outside the building and had to wait for him to leave. During that time Kramer saw her and wondered what she was up to. He saw her take the car and confronted her about it. He then became a liability she needed to get rid of."

Francine leaned forward. "How much did Vince know? Darla must have persuaded him to cooperate."

"Vince only cooperated because he didn't want Sara to turn into another Darla. He had learned that Jake and Sara were having a tryst, and he was angry. Darla convinced him that if they could just get Sara on a winning track, Jake would break up with her because she was a threat. Vince was struggling with how to be a good father. He said Sara's having sex with Jake made him feel like he had failed her."

"Sixteen is so young," said Francine.

"But here's the thing," Jud said. "Jake really is in love with her. He's standing by her through all this. I don't know if Darla or Vince can stop it, but the two of them are serious about being together."

"Joy has already done the interview with them for ABC News," Charlotte said. "I think she's a lock for the *Good Morning America* position."

Francine asked, "How did Friederich know Larry had been funding Jake's rise in NASCAR?"

"We're piecing that together too. Here's what we know. Larry's great-grandparents left him a lot of money, but thanks to a codicil, he could only access it on behalf of an offspring. He'd had a brief affair with a woman after he married Alice. He didn't know until later it had produced a son. Alice was too old to have children, so he began a secret campaign to finance his only child, Jake, who was then into midget cars. Larry worked with a lawyer to unlock the trust fund and funnel it to an offshore account. Then the lawyer approached Friederich to 'anonymously' fund Jake. That's how it all that started."

Jonathan said, "Larry finally admitted everything to me on the way over to the track. There had been quite a bit of money in the account, but it was running low. He figured by that time Jake was established well enough he should be able to make it. But he couldn't. Without more money, Jake couldn't buy track time and he struggled. It's why Jake focused on exploiting his looks. He needed sponsors, and he needed attention to keep him going."

Jud continued that thread. "By this time, Friederich had figured out who was behind the anonymous money going to Jake and deduced that Larry was Jake's father. So when Darla seduced Friederich and got him to help Sara, Darla knew just enough to 'encourage' Friederich to stop paying rent and put more money into Sara's car."

"And Larry couldn't make much of a fuss because he wanted to keep Alice from learning about the long-ago affair?" Charlotte asked.

Jud shrugged. "Larry and Alice had accumulated a lot of money through their real estate business. If Alice divorced him because of the affair, it would cost him."

"Why did Friederich abandon helping Sara for Jake?"

"Partly, it had to do with his discovery of the Sara and Jake affair. Sara was the one who'd pursued Jake, much like Darla had pursued Friederich. By the time Jake returned to the midget races looking to regain the magic, Friederich had realized Darla would likely leave him once she had the technology to 'cheat legally.' So he told her he needed to help Jake. And Darla snapped."

Francine shifted in her chair. "Could Vince and Darla use the legal system against Jake, considering Sara is only sixteen?"

"Sixteen is age of consent in Indiana, and Sara was that age when she hooked up with Jake. So no, likely they can't."

"Surely Vince suspected that Darla had killed Friederich," Francine said.

"Not at first. He says he suspected something wasn't right when she brought him the unmarked car. But even as Friederich's murder became more and more of a news story, he claims he still didn't believe his ex-wife would kill somebody."

"I don't think he knew her very well," Charlotte said.

"Or he was afraid of Darla and doesn't want to admit it."

Charlotte nodded. "She's always been a scary person. I suspected she had a closet full of whips and chains. Didn't I say that, Francine?"

"You've said that about the pope." She addressed Jud. "You could have at least told us what was going on."

"We weren't certain what was going on. It had us stumped. The only thing we knew for certain was Larry Jeffords was being framed, and if we played along, the killer would relax a bit. We also knew that if you and Charlotte continued investigating—and we were certain you wouldn't stop, despite our best efforts—you'd either figure it out or get yourselves in trouble. Who knew it would be both? At the track we planned to have our force watching all of you. Joy's cameraman was even one of our officers. But when it was clear Sara had Friederich's technology and we were investigating her after the qualification run, and the two of you split up, we couldn't manage it. Thankfully you managed to stay safe."

"Alive, maybe, but not safe," Charlotte said. "I've got so many bumps and bruises I'm popping pain pills like they came from the fountain of youth."

"It's a good thing Toby knew about the Baggesens' second trailer," Francine said.

Jud nodded. "But it looks like you were doing pretty well for yourselves."

"The best part," Francine interjected, "is that Charlotte solved this mystery even before you police."

Charlotte's face sagged. "Not true. Only when Darla discovered the video and grabbed me did I know it was her for certain. No, this is a lot like the *last* mystery. I was close, but not quite there."

Francine reached over and gave her friend a huge hug. "No, you figured it out and you beat Darla at her own game. In detective novels, complete understanding often comes after the sleuth has solved the mystery. You did it, Charlotte, and I'm here to make sure this time you check it off your Sixty List."

Jud stood up. "I won't disagree with Francine's assessment. You are to be congratulated on having solved the murder of Friederich Guttmann. Really, we couldn't have done it without you." He gave her a crooked smile. "Though we would have liked to have tried."

THIRTY-SEVEN

FRANCINE FLOATED IN THE deep end of Alice's pool. Like the time two months previous, it was after midnight, it was dark, and Alice had citronella candles lit everywhere. Larry was gone. He wasn't living in the house anymore, part of a trial separation, but Francine thought it wouldn't last. She was predicting a reconciliation, and soon.

Charlotte, clad in a white bathrobe, hobbled over to the edge of the pool near where Francine was treading water. "I just checked the pool shed. No bodies." She sounded disappointed.

Francine laughed. "I'm glad, even if you're not. I don't need another mystery to solve, and frankly, neither do you."

Charlotte looked around. "If there's any mystery, it's how long it's going to take Alice to forgive Larry and take him back. I think she will eventually."

"So do I. She's getting used to the idea that Jake is Larry's son, and I think she actually likes it. You know her secret number-one bucket list item? Joy and I figured it out, and we've confirmed it with Alice. Alice wants desperately to be a mother. She's becoming convinced that maybe having Jake as a stepson is God's answer to her prayers. But don't say anything to her."

Charlotte looked around. "Speaking of Alice, where is she?"

"She's inside with Joy and Mary Ruth." Francine floated to edge of the pool. She was naked in the water. "You should come in, Charlotte. We all agreed that this time we'd go skinny-dipping. Alice even hired a pool boy to make sure the water chemicals had been added."

"In a minute," Charlotte said.

Francine decided not to push. She knew Charlotte would get in. The September night was warm, much like the July night when they'd first tried the skinny-dipping adventure. The mood was different this time, though. Much more upbeat. The water felt good, and she splashed her shoulders with it.

Joy and Alice came out of the house.

"Could we have your attention, please?" Joy called. Her tone was somewhere between her announcer voice and a whisper.

"You're not making a video out of this, are you?" Charlotte said. "I mean, I'm happy you're a big-shot correspondent for ABC, but I don't want to be on *Good Morning America* ever again."

"You don't see a camera, do you? I'm only here to present to you the new Mary Ruth Burrows."

With that, the French doors to the house opened and the remaining member of the Summer Ridge Bridge Club appeared. She was naked, and she was smiling.

"Oh, my!" Francine said. "How much have you lost?"

"Forty pounds exactly," said Mary Ruth, delighted. She twirled around so her weight loss could be seen.

They all applauded her. Francine took particular pleasure in her happy face, since she was the one who'd hooked up Mary Ruth with Brady Prather, the trainer.

"I don't know if I'll ever get skinny," said Mary Ruth, "but I don't need it to be happy. I look good and I feel better than I have in years. I used to think that if my catering business boomed like it has, that I wouldn't have the energy for it. But not now."

"I'm getting in the water," said Joy, peeling off her robe. "This time I'm checking skinny-dipping off my list."

"Look at how much progress we've all made, Francine," Charlotte said. "You said what happened two months ago was a disaster. It was anything *but* that. Mary Ruth lost weight, Alice gained a stepchild, and you appeared on the *Dr. Oz Show* and encouraged senior citizens to get fit. Joy not only got on the front page of the *Indianapolis Star*, she now regularly reports for *GMA*. And she finally skinny-dipped for the first time."

"And you solved a mystery, Charlotte. Don't forget about that."

"Oh, I haven't forgotten, Francine. In fact, in light of all this success, I think what we need are *more* mysteries, not fewer."

Francine's eyes got wide. "Don't even joke about that, Charlotte."

But from the look in Charlotte's eyes, Francine suspected Charlotte was doing anything but joking.

THE END

ABOUT THE AUTHORS

Elizabeth Perona is the father/daughter writing team of Tony Perona and Liz Dombrosky. Tony is the author of the Nick Bertetto mystery series, the standalone thriller *The Final Mayan Prophecy* (with Paul Skorich), and co-editor and contributor to the anthologies *Racing Can Be Murder* and *Hoosier Hoops and Hijinks*. Tony is a member of Mystery Writers of America and has served the organization as a member of the Board of Directors and as Treasurer. He is also a member of Sisters in Crime.

Liz Dombrosky graduated from Ball State University in the Honors College with a degree in teaching. She is currently a stay-at-home mom. *Murder on the Bucket List* is her first novel.

WWW.MIDNIGHTINKBOOKS.COM

From the gritty streets of New York City to sacred tombs in the Middle East, it's always midnight somewhere. Join us online at any hour for fresh new voices in mystery fiction.

At midnightinkbooks.com you'll also find our author blog, new and upcoming books, events, book club questions, excerpts, mystery resources, and more.

MIDNIGHT INK ORDERING INFORMATION

Order Online:
- Visit our website www.midnightinkbooks.com, select your books, and order them on our secure server.

Order by Phone:
- Call toll-free within the U.S. and Canada at 1-888-NITE-INK (1-888-648-3465)
- We accept VISA, MasterCard, and American Express

Order by Mail:
Send the full price of your order (MN residents add 6.875% sales tax) in U.S. funds, plus postage & handling to:

Midnight Ink
2143 Wooddale Drive
Woodbury, MN 55125-2989

Postage & Handling:

Standard (U.S. & Canada). If your order is:
$25.00 and under, add $4.00
$25.01 and over, FREE STANDARD SHIPPING

AK, HI, PR: $16.00 for one book plus $2.00 for each additional book.

International Orders (airmail only):
$16.00 for one book plus $3.00 for each additional book

Orders are processed within 12 business days. Please allow for normal shipping time.
Postage and handling rates subject to change.